Take a New York Jewish gumshoe adept at one-liners and a wheelchair-bound Roman Catholic Bishop who's a frustrated cop and a genius to boot. What do you get? The best detective duo since Nero Wolfe and Archie Goodwin!

THE CHARTREUSE CLUE

"SHARP, SMOOTH . . . A LIVELY ADVENTURE." —*Chicago Tribune*

"WONDERFUL . . . Bishop Regan is the most intriguing fictional churchman since Chesterton's Father Brown." —Robert Goldsborough

"A WELL-PLOTTED WHODUNIT . . . Readers surely will anticipate the sequel." —*Chicago Sun-Times*

"ABOUNDS IN ACTION AND SURPRISES." —*Associated Press*

"WELL-CRAFTED, KNOWLEDGEABLY HANDLED." *Mystery News*

"A GOOD DETECTIVE READ!" —*Dallas Morning News*

"A SLICK, ACTION-FILLED ADVENTURE." —*Library Journal*

THE CHARTREUSE CLUE

William F. Love

AN ONYX BOOK

ONYX
Published by the Penguin Group
Penguin Books USA Inc., 375 Hudson Street,
New York, New York 10014, U.S.A.
Penguin Books Ltd, 27 Wrights Lane,
London W8 5TZ, England
Penguin Books Australia Ltd, Ringwood,
Victoria, Australia
Penguin Books Canada Ltd, 2801 John Street,
Markham, Ontario, Canada L3R 1B4
Penguin Books (N.Z.) Ltd, 182-190 Wairau Road,
Auckland 10, New Zealand

Penguin Books Ltd, Registered Offices:
Harmondsworth, Middlesex, England

Published by Onyx, an imprint of New American Library,
a division of Penguin Books USA Inc. This is an authorized reprint
of a hardcover edition published by Donald I. Fine, Inc. The hardcover
edition was published in Canada by General Publishing Company Limited.

First Onyx Printing, August, 1991
10 9 8 7 6 5 4 3 2 1

PRINTED IN THE UNITED STATES OF AMERICA

PUBLISHER'S NOTE
This novel is a work of fiction. Names, characters, places, and incidents either are the product of the author's imagination or are used fictitiously, and any resemblance to actual events, locales, organizations or persons, living or dead, is entirely coincidental and beyond the intent of either the author or publisher.

To all who helped and encouraged, especially Joyce and Richard

Monday, August 22

I

I just happened to be looking at my watch so I can tell you it was 11:01 A.M. when the whole thing began. I was sitting in my office, feet on desk, fingering the two Yankee Stadium box seat tickets and reflecting on what a perfect day it was, weatherwise, to be taking Sally Castle to the game, when my reflections got interrupted, not once but twice. First, the sound of the elevator door in the kitchen, along with the distinctive whir of the Bishop's wheelchair. Punctual, as always.

The second interruption was the chiming of the doorbell. Which was when the whole thing began.

At the time, I was just annoyed. I didn't need an uninvited visitor just half an hour before I was leaving to pick up Sally.

I could just make out the visitor through the glass of the front door as I came from my office into the hall. A panhandler, I guessed, drawn by the small but not invisible brass plate outside, reading

ROMAN CATHOLIC ARCHDIOCESE
OF NEW YORK
Bishop's Residence

We get about three knights of the road a week. They're easily disposed of. Three short blocks south to the soup kitchen, if it's food; two long blocks east and two short ones north to the St. Vincent de Paul Society if it's almost anything else.

But if it's money, "Begone Satan." We don't do money.

As I headed for the door, ready to give the guy our version of the bum's rush, I did a double take. This was no bum, this was a friend—a friend of mine and, more to the point, of the Bishop's.

Father William Fuller was a monk of the Order of St. Benedict, St. Jerome's Abbey, Chicago.

But I hardly recognized him in his current get-up. He looked as if he was dressed for an afternoon at the golf course. And this was no golf course. This was the hallowed residence and office of the Most Reverend Francis X. Regan, D.D., S.T.D., Auxiliary Bishop of the Roman Catholic Archdiocese of New York. It's unheard of—well, damn near—for any priest, friend or no friend, to show up other than in correct, formal, clerical garb.

But despite my failure to recognize the man at first glance, it was always a pleasure to admit Willie to the Bishop's house. In my role as Bishop Regan's Special Assistant, I admit lots of priests through that door. Most of them, I can take or leave. Willie was different. Besides being good for five bucks on a golf bet, he had the knack of not taking himself too seriously.

But something was wrong. Willie's mildly humorous expression had deserted him. This wasn't the Father Willie I'd come to know and like over the past six months.

As an experienced private eye and former cop, I felt obliged to take note.

The name "Father William Fuller, O.S.B." had first crossed the Bishop's desk two years previously. The monk had applied for living quarters in the Archdiocese when his Abbot in Chicago assigned him to work on a Ph.D. at Fordham. Priests from other parts of the country aren't required to go through the Archdiocese when they come to New York on temporary assignment. But, if they do, all requests for places to stay get referred automatically to Bishop Regan, as Archdiocesan Director of Personnel. Practically speaking, that means I handle them.

We wound up finding a place for him at St. Bede's in the Bronx, not a bad match-up. It's manned by Benedictine monks, and it's within walking distance of Fordham—if you care to walk in that neighborhood, which I don't. (I got all the hazard pay I ever want during the six years I was in the N.Y.P.D.)

A year and a half later I finally met Willie face to face. Our meeting was precipitated by a letter he wrote the Bishop. I still have it.

> Most Rev. Francis X. Regan
> Archdiocese of New York
> 890 W. 37th Street
> New York, NY 10016
>
> Your Excellency:
>
> I am taking the liberty of writing you because I have something you might enjoy. Fordham has recently come into possession of a medieval manuscript (a bequest from a

family in Philadelphia) which I believe, on the basis of both internal and external evidence, to be a fragment of an eleventh century Latin version of the Bible. It is particularly interesting because it appears to have been translated from an original Greek manuscript in the tradition of the Codex Sinaiticus, rather than being simply another copy of the Vulgate. Though only ten leaves (proto-Isaiah, from middle of chapter ten through chapter thirteen), it is obviously of considerable historical and scholarly importance.

Being aware of your strong interest in the field of sacred scripture, I thought you might enjoy seeing a copy. I now have a very faithful reproduction, which I would be more than happy to give you.

It would be a great privilege to meet you. I have been a fan of yours since seminary days, when I came across your monograph, "The Beatty Papyri: Light on the Johannine Apostolic Community." I deeply regretted the news of your accident six years ago. However, your courage in dealing with your handicap and your return to the scholarly life with the publication of *Job: An Existentialist Prayer?* has been an inspiration to me.

In any case, please let me know if you would like to see the reproduction, and I will make arrangements.

Sincerely,
(Rev.) William C. Fuller, O.S.B.
St. Bede's Catholic Church
2001 Crotona Parkway
Bronx, NY 10457

When I first read that letter, while routinely going through the Bishop's mail, I wondered how my employer would react. Not well, I guessed. The Bishop considers "Your Excellency"—well, let me quote him—"redolent of the worst excesses of medieval sycophancy." Also, Regan doesn't appreciate being called "handicapped." (And in my opinion, "accident" is hardly the word to describe the severing of a spinal cord by a slug from a mugger's thirty-eight.) And praising the Bishop's "courage" gives him a pain in the you-know-where.

So I foresaw that letter making a quick, one-way trip to the round file.

Wrong again, David, me boy. Bishop Regan reacted to news about the manuscript the way Davey Johnson would jump at news that Dwight Gooden's clone was joining the Mets next week. The next thing I knew, I had orders to get the priest on the phone and invite him to dinner.

Naturally, Willie accepted the invitation. The upshot was a regular intellectual orgy, the studious duo poring over that manuscript.

Thereafter, Willie the Benedictine became a once-a-month regular at our dinner table. He was a great favorite of Sister Ernestine Regnery, O.S.F., the Bishop's cook and housekeeper.

I couldn't blame Ernie for taking a shine to Father Willie. After all, her range of daily contacts is severely limited. She's got her choice between the Bishop, who's in a foul mood about eighty per cent of the time, and me.

A Hobson's choice, if ever there was one.

I'm a nice enough guy. Reasonably good-looking. (A great catch for some lucky girl. Just ask my mother.) Trouble is, from Sister's perspective, I'm not even a Christian, much less a Catholic. And just about as far as you can imagine from being a monk.

So the Bishop's making the Chicago monk a regular at the mansion suited Sister just fine. And it suited me fine that Willie was a golfer. We soon struck up a conversation about our favorite sport. Eventually, Willie accepted my invitation to join the Delancey Street Irregulars, a select brotherhood of one-dozen high-handicap golfers. Every Saturday morning from Memorial Day to Labor Day, the first eight Irregulars who pay their twenty-two bucks get to utilize two permanent tee times at a public course over in Jersey.

I like to think that all of us in the Irregulars are fairly good at what we do for a living: which is everything from public accounting (Ike Schwartz) to lawyering (Dave Baker) to being a newspaper reporter (Chet Rozanski). As to the quality of golf we play, let me just say that Willie, who's about a thirty handicapper, fit right in with the rest of us.

The "Delancey Street" in the Club's name comes from the neighborhood where the three co-founders—Bernie Feinstein, Ike Schwartz and I—grew up. We started it fifteen years ago when we were in our teens, and it's expanded over the years. During that time we've proved our broadmindedness by accepting any gentiles who apply, as long as they pay their lost bets promptly and don't hole too many twenty-foot putts.

Willie was our first Catholic priest, but he was welcomed by one and all, and he quickly proved he could lose with the best of us. He paid his bets promptly and often picked up the bar tab. As he could well afford.

Because Willie's mom was loaded. A widow for several years, Marguerite Fuller was well-known in Chicago charitable circles. And one of her pet charities, it seemed, was Willie. As a consequence, he always had plenty of walking-around money on him. Not, as I understood it, strictly in accordance with the vows he took as a monk. But, then, Willie was never one to let a little thing like vows interfere with his chosen life-style.

I got the flavor of that life-style quite by accident, one evening in late June at Carnegie Hall.

Dave Goldman at Carnegie Hall?

Embarrassing, of course. But, you see, one of Sally Castle's few faults is her unshakable conviction that she is someday going to make a highbrow out of me. Maybe that delusion is a by-product of her psychiatric training. I don't know. Whatever, she misses no opportunity to drag me along to violin concerts.

So there I was at Carnegie. It was intermission, and I was in the lobby mixing with the ultra chic, Sally having departed for the ladies room. I was idly casting a semi-lustful eye at a tall, curvaceous brunette, when I suddenly realized who her date was. Handsome, nattily attired in a dark suit and Sulka tie (no Roman collar anywhere in sight!), it was my golfing buddy, Father Fuller.

I'd have offered pretty good odds that the brunette was not his mom. In fact, I strongly suspected this was a bad time to say Howyadoin' to Father Willie. As soon as Sally came back, we moved on and Willie never saw me.

Next time we played golf, a couple of Saturdays later, I picked a moment when no one else was around to casually mention I'd seen him at Carnegie Hall. Though I uttered not a word about the lady, he blushed and immediately changed the subject. Of course, I let the matter drop. But my image of Father Willie's priestliness was distinctly changed.

As I said, the episode shed new light on the guy. It looked like my priest friend was capable of getting along comfortably in a much faster social set than I'd imagined. Priest, scholar, golfer—and now, bon vivant? I never mentioned it to the Bishop, my feeling being it was none of his beeswax.

II

But to get back to that gorgeous Monday in August, Willie looked like hell.

Having seen his liquor intake on a few nineteenth holes, I was ready to guess he'd had a drop or two of the sauce. Probably, the night before.

But this was more than a simple hangover. A greenish pallor underlay the alcoholic ruddiness, resulting in a mottled complexion that was less than appealing. The day-old beard didn't help much. After years in law enforcement, I can usually sense when people are in a jam. Eyeballing my friend, Father William, I sensed a *major* jam.

Shaking hands, I tried a bit of cheer. "Hey ho, Willie! Great day for a golf game. Listen, I'd love to acquire some more of your Benedictine money, but I've got to—" I shut up. My transmissions weren't getting through.

"Hullo, Dave," he mumbled. "Sorry to show up uninvited, but I've got to see the Bishop. Do you think . . . ?"

His voice trailed off. "Come in, Willie," I said a bit more gently. "The Bishop just came down from the chapel. He's about prayed out. I'm sure he'd love to see you."

Actually, the last was a pretty big whopper. The truth was, Bishop Francis Xavier Regan was in the midst of one of his periodic depressions. When he's like that, the only part of a visit he truly enjoys is the part that goes "Bye-bye."

According to what Ernie has told me, these depressions started six years ago, when he took that slug in the spine. Of course, I didn't know him back then. But Ernie knew him plenty well for several years before.

Regardless of when they started, the Bishop's depressions can be fierce. The current one was a lulu. All appointments, meetings, consultations—ducked, canceled or postponed. I happened to know he was stuck on page one hundred thirty-seven of his current literary effort (working title: *The Suffering of the Godly: David, Jeremiah, Micah and Paul*). That's where he'd stopped dead, eight days before, when the current funk started. (I check his word processor every morning while he's up praying in the third-floor chapel.)

As far as his regular work for the Archdiocese, forget it. The "Archdiocesan Director of Personnel" was currently building a stack of unanswered mail high enough to smother him if he sneezed.

During these depressions, the Bishop never scrimped on his time in the chapel. Six to eleven every morning, come hell or high water—though what he prayed about during a funk, God only knew.

He still spent from three to six each afternoon in front of his computer, theoretically writing his book. The rest of the time, he'd read. Constantly. In a funk, he'd go through ten or fifteen books a week, easy.

So I knew that, given an option, there wasn't a snowball's chance in hell he'd see the priest, and that's why I told Willie a little white lie.

After all, one of my unwritten duties is to rouse the Bishop when he gets like this. I had a feeling Fuller's trouble might just be big enough to blast Bishop Regan right out of his funk. I'd seen it happen before.

Of course there was always the risk that he'd fire me, but it wouldn't be the first time, and I always get rehired. I have excellent job security: no one else will put up with him.

Like it or not, Regan does need help from time to time, and having someone with a bit of size and muscle doesn't hurt. He's developed powerful hands, arms and shoulders, thanks to his physical workouts. (He puts in half an hour every morning at five, before he bathes and heads up to his private chapel.) But there are some tasks around the place that neither he nor Ernie can handle. Getting him down the front steps of the mansion is one that comes immediately to mind.

But I wouldn't want to leave you with the impression that my job involves nothing but muscle. That's the least of it. More importantly, he needs someone to drive him places, take dictation, do his typing, file things, fix things around the mansion, keep out unwanted guests and visitors (sometimes), let in unwanted guests and visitors (when appropriate), screen calls, and jolly him out of his depressions.

So the longest I've ever been fired is thirty-six hours. I'll admit, I always apologize but that's just to let him save face.

* * *

Putting my hand companionably around Father Willie's shoulders, I boldly led him down the hall into Regan's big office at the end.

As I anticipated, the Bishop had made no dent in the day's correspondence. It was leaning precariously against the other seven stacks gathering dust there. Instead, he was engrossed in his latest book—*A Bright, Shining Lie,* which he had started the night before. To read he had wheeled over near the rear windows of the office.

The Bishop's reading glasses were perched on his aristocratic nose. The wide, high brow with its lines of pain and the firm jaw were limned by the bright sunlight that flooded in over his right shoulder. As always, he was dressed in his flowing, purple cassock. From the silver chain around his shoulders was hung the silver pectoral cross that had been sent to him by the Pope after the shooting. A purple beanie capped the full head of silver-white hair. ("Beanie" is my word for it. The Bishop insists on calling it a zucchetto, which I guess is technically correct. My mother thinks it a yarmulke, a belief which, the Bishop told her once, is historically well-founded.)

Hearing Willie and me come in, the Bishop looked up from the book, removed his reading glasses and peered at us through the gloom. His expression showed a mixture of emotions—irritation at being disturbed, curiosity about who I'd brought, and a vague, unfocused petulance.

"What is it, David?" he demanded irritably.

"Me," I said breezily, "with your buddy, William the Chicago monkling." Applying pressure with my arm around his shoulders, I guided the suddenly reluctant Fuller to the center of the fifteen-foot square Karastan carpet.

"He has a problem, Bishop, that I think he'd like you to listen to. Hey!" I interjected, "Don't scowl at me! Just look at the guy! Then tell me he doesn't need help."

With a snort of annoyance, Regan put on his reading glasses and took up his book again. But I wasn't going to allow it.

"Look. Give the man fifteen minutes of your damn precious time. It won't kill you! Maybe he'll even be grateful enough to find you another manuscript."

If looks could kill, I'd have been instant dead meat. But when the Bishop focused on Fuller, his face actually began to soften. Just as I'd expected—well, hoped.

"Yes. All right, sit down, Father. Leave us, Mr. Goldman. I'll have words with you later."

"Yeah. When I get back from the game this evening. It'll probably be late."

The Bishop's glare intensified, if that was possible. I was taking a chance. A big one.

The risk was that he might not let me use his Cadillac. He and I have an arrangement: he owns, I drive. Joe Rivers of Joe Rivers Cadillac presents the Bishop with a new Cadillac every two years. The current one—a very smooth-driving Seville—was four months old.

One of the perks of my job is that I may selectively use his car for personal errands—like running out to Yankee Stadium with my girlfriend, the shrink.

Trouble is, the Bishop is quite capable of coming up with sudden reasons why his current Seville is unavailable for my urgent personal use. Our arrangement is that his requirements take priority over mine. And he's the sole arbiter of what that means. Of course I could always quit and re-up the next day. I've pulled that one before. But if I quit, no wheels.

Fortunately, the Bishop wasn't going to get petty in front of Father Willie. He just ignored me as he invited the priest to be seated.

I took one last look at poor Willie and returned to my office through the connecting door, closing it behind me.

What was eating my golf buddy, anyhow?

III

It was 11:06. In nineteen minutes I'd be hiking west half a block to Fred's Garage on Eleventh Avenue where the Cadillac would be gassed up and waiting, per my instructions to Fred the previous Friday.

So, with nineteen minutes to spare, I sat at my desk, pondering how someone could spend four or five hours in prayer, as the Bishop had just done, and still be so foul-tempered.

Item: just Saturday he'd insisted I retype a two-page letter to a pastor in White Plains because of one omitted comma. A comma, furthermore, I showed him authority for omitting—*Stark on Grammar*. We're talking petty, here.

By the way, if you're wondering why, with a word processor in the house, I retype *anything*, the explanation is simple. He won't let me use the computer, and I wouldn't use it if he did. He only uses it to write his books, a process in which I play no part whatsoever.

I do have autographed copies of the three books he's written since the shooting, but have no idea what's in them. I'm not much of a reader, and, above all, not of books with titles like *The Place of the Gospel of Peter in the Synoptic Tradition,* his latest. Rumor has it his I.Q. has tested out at 220, which sounds about right. Trouble is, it takes an I.Q. approaching his to understand what he's written. I'm not exactly sure what my I.Q. is, but I'd accept three digits, if offered.

As for the Bishop's faith, I did ask him once how he reconciled his devotion to God with his sometimes lousy disposition. He smiled his little smile and said, "Just consider, David, what I'd be like, if I didn't spend those five hours with the Lord, every day!"

"Well, why not double it then—make it ten?" I offered.

"I doubt that even God could tolerate that much of my company," he had sighed.

And on occasion I reflected on what it might have been to have known him before the shooting.

I'd met the Bishop, in fact, about ten minutes after the shooting happened. I was two blocks away in an unmarked car when the call came over the radio, and I got there in time to administer mouth-to-mouth. Presumably that's what saved his life. Of course, even with the best doctors in the city, he hadn't reclaimed the use of his legs. Repairing a severed spinal cord is still beyond the magic of medical science.

Curiously, the slug that radically changed his life also wound up changing mine.

Three months later, in the process of catching the "perpetrator," my big mouth managed to get me in serious trouble with the D.A.'s office. My boss, Inspector Kessler of Homicide, recommended my dismissal from the force. Apparently I'd been a tad too frank telling an Assistant D.A. what I thought of him when his office decided to drop the case for "lack of sufficient evidence." Three months after that abrupt termination of employ, I was invited to the Bishop's mansion for lunch and some gratitude. When I left I had a new and unexpected kind of job.

At that point in our lives, both the Bishop and I were in trouble. Me, because I was attempting to make it on my own as a private investigator. The Bishop, because he had just lost his second "Special Assistant to the Bishop," the job title he had dreamed up to describe what I now do.

The first two people who'd tried to be special assistants—both priests—had each quit within six weeks. (I've met both of them since, and they're nice, affable fellows—which may tell you something about Regan's winning personality.)

In the course of my introductory lunch, the Bishop and I hammered out a mutual solution to our problems. That was six years ago, and we've both been getting along fairly well ever since.

The deal goes like this. I devote up to thirty hours a week doing whatever jobs the Bishop cares to assign. The rest of my time belongs to me. Of the hundred and thirty-eight leftover hours, I do as much detective work as I can handle—limited only by my need for sleep, recreation, and nourishment. I'll admit the salary paid by the Bishop is dangerously close to minimum wage, but fees from my investigative work keep the wolf from the door. Usually.

Other benefits include free meals—courtesy of Ernie—and free housing in the mansion. I have the second-floor bedroom, front, right across from the

Bishop's. To give you an idea of his democratic spirit, the two bedrooms are exactly the same size. Each has its own bathroom, though his is outfitted with steel bars so he can get around.

Because of the unusual nature of the relationship, I maintain a separate "office" away from the mansion for my investigative work. That's an "office," in the same sense that banks have "branches" in the Cayman Islands. In other words, a front and a mail drop.

So, if you look up "Goldman, David" in the Yellow Pages under "Investigators, Private," you'll find me at 1739 Broadway. Well, I've been to 1739 Broadway, Suite 1280, a few times, and know what it looks like. There's a small brass plate outside the door, reading "David Goldman, Investigations," under the larger one that says "DAVIS L. BAKER, ATTORNEY-AT-LAW." But don't bother looking for my personal office. There isn't any.

Dave's another guy I brought into the Delancey Street Irregulars.

I first met him on the witness stand when I was still on the Force. I was testifying against some perpetrator he was defending. As to our current business arrangement, Dave's secretary and paralegal, Cheryl Grossman, handles all my mail and calls me if there's anything urgent. That happened once when the I.R.S. thought I was another "David Goldman" and wanted to seize my car. Normally, Cheryl just forwards the mail to Thirty-seventh Street, where I'm to be found all the time I'm not (*a*) on a date, (*b*) at a baseball game, (*c*) playing golf, (*d*) investigating something for a client, or (*e*) some combination of the above.

For all these services, Dave charges no rent. If I need Cheryl for something, I pay her on a piecework basis. Of course Dave gets to represent me as my attorney on those all-too-frequent occasions when I run afoul of my former colleagues.

The overall arrangement—with both Baker and the Bishop—has worked out remarkably well. Regan enjoys kibitzing about my cases. Some of his suggestions have even proved helpful.

When I launched this arrangement with Regan, my Jewish mother was convinced this goyisher Bishop had in mind turning her son into a Christian. A couple of visits to the mansion showed her the wrong-headedness of that. Displaying unusual charm, the Bishop convinced Mom that his influence on my soul could only make me a better Jew. In fact, I've come to regret ever introducing them. I can't tell you how sick I've gotten of hearing, "Davey, you listen to Bishop Frank!"

Worse yet, Mom also met Ernie. That meeting has resulted in a combined deadly force of two determined women with only one purpose in life: finding me a good Jewish girl. I keep telling them they're wasting their damn time, but they don't quit.

My feet were on my desk when the squeak of the wheelchair warned me my nineteen minutes of freedom were about to end. The connecting door opened, and in rolled Bishop Regan. I pulled my feet off the desk and swiveled to face him. Executing a superb and graceful turn, the Bishop nudged the door closed behind him.

I checked my watch: 11:24. Time to head for the garage. Impeccably bad timing. But one look at the Bishop's face told me there was probably no Seville in my immediate future, much less a baseball game.

I'd never seen his expression more somber. Interestingly, though, his eyes were alight with excitement and something else I couldn't quite identify. Whatever was happening, it had kicked the depression, at least for the time being.

As he spun his chair to face me, I realized that the something else in his eyes was anger. When he spoke, his voice was grim.

"David, we've got a serious problem here. Father William needs your expertise."

I admit a chill ran up my spine. Regan never referred to "expertise," except in regard to my detective work. What had Willie gotten himself into?

"Problem?"

"Through his own imprudence—and downright stupidity, frankly—Father now finds himself in a situation which could well result in his imprisonment."

I felt the blood leave my face for points south. "No wonder Willie's looking like death warmed over. What's the rap?"

Regan wrinkled his nose. "You know I abhor your station-house slang." His expression got grimmer as he went on. "It seems Father William has been 'keeping company' with a young woman. He hasn't given me any details. I don't really require them. His problem is worse than even his level of stupidity merits." He swallowed.

"What's going on, Bishop?"

He scowled and took a deep breath.

"I'm just now trying to sort it out. Father William is in a state of panic. He tells me he awakened an hour ago in his young lady's apartment to find her dead. He's convinced she was murdered."

IV

Some years ago, when I was a kid—in maybe the first game I ever saw at Yankee Stadium—I witnessed a magnificent collision at home plate. The world champion Orioles were up, and Frank Robinson tried to score from second on a sharp single to right. Thurman Munson blocked the plate. The throw arrived at the same moment that Robinson barrelled into Munson headfirst. Munson's mask flew left, the ball right, and Munson went flat on his keester.

I felt the same way Munson must have. I shook my head and tried to close my mouth. The Bishop, perhaps heartened to see me silent, took the opportunity to fill me in.

"I have spoken briefly—and harshly—with Father William. Of course I will speak with him at greater length at a more appropriate time." He took another breath. "You can imagine how I feel to have someone who has dined at my table behave in this manner, here in the Archdiocese. Two thousand priests here, trying to be examples of Christ, and he does this. He should be flayed alive!"

Taking a breath, Bishop Regan resumed a little

more calmly, "My inclination is to say a prayer for the deceased young woman, send Father William packing, report the matter to the police and let the law take its rightful course. But would that be the prudent course of action? The publicity would be horrendous. Undoubtedly, every priest of this Archdiocese would be besmirched by the publicity." He glared at me. "All because of this man's idiotic lack of judgment!"

With another deep sigh, he looked up at the ceiling and slapped the arms of the wheelchair with his hands.

"However, now is not the time for such recriminations. We need to protect the good name of the two thousand priests of this Archdiocese, if that is still possible. Father William must somehow be shielded." The Bishop was choosing his words carefully. "So, David, I would like you to help him. But I need it clearly understood that your assistance to him does not imply approval on my part. At best, his was seriously imprudent behavior. At worst, it was a flagrant violation of priestly and religious vows. My name is not to be connected with this case. Is that understood?"

"Understood." (Though I didn't understand; not really.) "What are we shooting for, here, Bishop?"

He frowned. "Find the murderer, of course, and keep Father William's name out of the whole affair."

" 'Out of it,' hmm? What you mean is, 'No publicity.' " I shook my head. "Forget it, Bishop. Can't be done."

"Oh, it 'can't be done'?" His eyes narrowed. "You came up with that rather quickly, didn't you, David?"

"Quick, yes. But that doesn't mean I haven't

thought it through. Let me explain a couple of things, Bishop." I hated to burst his bubble, especially when the excitement had raised him out of what he sometimes calls "the slough of despond." Even more, I hated not being able to help Willie out. But facts are facts.

"Let's assume the lady was murdered. Let's also assume Willie didn't do it—a big assumption, by the way. I'd judge that Willie had a snootful last night. I like him, I like him a lot, Bishop. But if there was a murder, he's the prime suspect, and it would behoove us to be damn sure that he really *didn't* do it."

The Bishop opened his mouth, but I raised a hand. "Just let me finish. Let's go ahead and assume he's as innocent as little Eva. In that case, I could imagine a scenario where I might be willing to try to keep him out of it. But how am I going to do that?"

I didn't wait for an answer. "Who do you think the cops are going to be looking for? They'll figure out that *someone* spent the night there. Then they'll find out who it was. Even if Willie didn't do it, once the cops know he slept in that apartment, they're going to make him the number-one suspect. They'll tear this island apart looking for him.

"So let's say he goes back up to the Bronx and lies low. How long would it take Inspector Kessler and the boys to find him? Anywhere from fifteen minutes to twenty-four hours, I'd say—depending on Willie's luck. Maybe two days, tops, if he was very discreet in his dating patterns."

The Bishop looked at me mournfully. I knew that look. It was the same one I gave my daddy the day he put Blackie—my cocker spaniel—to sleep.

"O.K., look," I conceded. "I'll do this: I'll go with Willie down to Headquarters. A couple of those guys still owe me a favor or two. I'll tell them to play down the story. Plus, I'll vouch for Willie's character. I'll tell them he's a buddy of yours and—"

The Bishop's look didn't change. I wasn't even convincing myself. Once he turned himself in, Willie was grist for the mill of every journalist in town. I could already see the headline: "Priest Suspected in Love-Nest Murder!!!"

"All right, all right!" I surrendered. "I can't stand to see a grown man cry. I'll see what I can do. I'll *see,* that's all. Is that understood? But I'm warning you, the first clue I have that he *might* have done it, I'm going to start looking for other kinds of work. And I still think I'm crazy."

The Bishop was serene. "Thank you, David. Let's go tell him."

As I grabbed my notebook, the Bishop swung his chair around and wheeled swiftly back into his office. I followed, kissing good-bye to thirty-six bucks, the price of the two box seats at Yankee Stadium. Better luck next time. I dreaded the call to Sally, who was going to be one unhappy shrink.

Fuller, sitting in the black velvet chair with his head in his hands, looked miserable. I pulled a chair up next to him as the Bishop rolled around to the other side. Willie looked up, wet-eyed and woebegone.

The Bishop broke the silence. "Father William. David understands the problem, and has agreed to help."

"Hold it, Bishop," I interrupted. I caught the priest's eye. "I'll try to help, Willie, but I need to understand the problem. First of all, have you called the police—or anyone else?"

"God, no." He seemed genuinely shocked. "I haven't done anything but come here."

"O.K., Willie," I said crisply. "The cops don't know anything yet—we hope. I'd like to get into that apartment before the police do. Tell me what happened when you woke up this morning."

Fuller rubbed his hand over the top of his head. The gesture didn't change his hairstyle. It was already a mess. "I only stayed there because we got back late. Barb suggested I sleep on the couch instead of driving back to the Bronx. I never did that before, but I'd had a lot to drink. She fixed the couch, then went to bed in her room. I fell asleep right away.

"Next thing I knew, the phone rang. It was broad daylight, maybe nine-thirty. Yeah, definitely nine-thirty. I looked at my watch. I don't know how long the phone rang. At first I couldn't figure out where I was. When I did, I figured Barb would get it. I thought she had a phone in her bedroom. Anyway, I finally answered, but there was no one on the line. I must have fallen right back to sleep."

"Not to interrupt," I interrupted, "but I need a few details. Who's this 'Barb' and where does she live?"

"Barbara McClain. The corner of Seventy-sixth and Amsterdam—501 West Seventy-sixth. Apartment 3C."

I was jotting facts in my notebook, but I was thinking about box seats, wondering whether Sally could pick them up and whether she could still use them.

"That phone rang again at ten-thirty," mused

Willie. "Must have rung eight or ten times. I finally answered. Nothing, again." He frowned. "Whoever it was just hung up."

Willie was looking into space.

"Go on," said the Bishop.

This part was going to be tough. I kept my eyes on the notepad.

"It was so quiet!" Willie said softly. "Not a 'good' quiet, you know? I tapped on her bedroom door. I—I think I said her name. Nothing. I went into her bedroom . . ." He swallowed, closing his eyes. "She was on her back. With a knife—"

"Where?" asked the Bishop.

Unable to speak, Willie indicated a spot in the middle of his chest. The Bishop closed his eyes.

"You came straight here?" I asked.

He nodded.

I thought of something else. "Stupid question, Willie, excuse me for asking, but how sure are you that she was dead?"

"I touched her arm." He shuddered. "Her skin—her skin was cold."

I nodded. "All right." I shifted the line of questioning. "This Barbara. How many people knew about the two of you?"

"No one."

I shook my head. "O.K. Let me rephrase the question, Willie. How many mutual acquaintances—yours and hers—will identify you to the police as a friend of hers?"

"No one," Fuller repeated. "No one knew who I was."

I scowled at him. "Come on, Willie! I mean, excuse me, Father, but *surely* you see that's impossible. Maybe you didn't hang out with her friends, but she must have told *someone.*"

"A number of her friends know me, sure, but under a false, er, name," Fuller stammered, reddening. "Whenever I was with Barb, my name was, uh, 'Charles Ryder.' She never knew me by any other name. Neither did her friends." Willie looked at me, at the Bishop, back at me.

"See, no one has the slightest notion of my identity. That's why I wondered if it wouldn't be possible to keep my name out of it. Don't you think there's a chance?"

V

I frowned at the priest for several seconds. This was a new development. It required some thought. Unfortunately, thought was precisely what I had no time for. It was 11:35, and I needed to make that phone call to Sally.

The Bishop jumped in. "Do you mean to tell me," he exploded, "that you've been running around this city, using a false name?" There was a harsh rasp to his voice.

"Please, Bishop!" I intervened, "keep in mind what you're trying to accomplish, and thank your lucky stars! I still don't know if we can pull it off, but it sure gives us a lot better chance."

The Bishop glared at me, but didn't reply.

I frowned and looked at my watch. 11:37. "Trouble is, we've got ourselves a serious *time* problem. I'll try, O.K.? Which means, among other things, I've got to get to that apartment before the police do. Meaning, I need to leave about five minutes ago."

I thought hard for a moment. "Willie, just one question. Have you got any idea who *might* have done it, or how they got in?"

Fuller glanced sideways at the Bishop. He opened his mouth, closed it, and shook his head. Then he gave me a wordless "no." The Bishop's explosion had left him shaken. I didn't blame him. I've been the target of a few of those outbursts myself, and they're no fun.

I got the priest's eye and tried to sound less terrifying than my boss. "O.K., Willie, I'll take your case for twenty-four hours—tentatively. No fee. But if I catch you in one, puny little lie, I'm calling the cops and telling them everything. If you don't want me on that basis, fine: I'll forget you ever came here."

Fuller looked me straight in the eye. "I swear to you, Dave, I've told you just what happened. I'll do anything I can to help you find the murderer."

"O.K." I got up and offered a hand, which he shook. "You've got a deal, Willie. I'm going up there. I need the key to her apartment. I assume you have one."

Willie said, "No, I don't," but put his hand in his pocket and brought out a palmful of coins and keys. Raking through them, he pulled an unattached key out of the jumble. A Tinker, by the look of it.

Muttering, "Where'd *that* come from?" Willie handed me the key. I examined it. "3C" was engraved on the side. Willie shrugged. He seemed genuinely puzzled.

"Oh, as long as you have your keys out, mind if I use your car to get up there?" I tried to sound offhand.

Willie looked a bit surprised. No wonder. But under the circumstances, how could he say no? He handed over a small black keycase. "It's a black Lincoln, just around the corner, Thirty-sixth and Tenth, this side."

"Thanks. I assume Father can stay here," I said to Regan. "I need to be able to call him if I have questions."

Regan looked cornered, but at least he recognized necessity. "Very well, I suppose he can lunch with me."

As I left, I sincerely hoped Regan would be able to contain his ire with the priest.

I walked over to Tenth Avenue and looked for a cab headed uptown. I had no intention of taking Fuller's car, regardless of what I'd told him. (I only wanted the keys to see if he had anything incriminating in it. I planned to check it when I got back from Seventy-sixth Street.) One of the principles I live by is "Don't Drive Other People's Cars." (The Bishop's is the exception that proves the rule.)

But principles must sometimes yield to practical considerations. There were no taxis on Tenth Avenue. Given the overwhelming need to get to Seventy-sixth, I took a calculated risk; I located the Lincoln where Fuller had said it was. Noting its condition, I shook my head. The priest obviously paid no attention to his auto. It was dusty all over. Dried mud was caked on the rear fender, and the back seat was strewn with papers and articles of clothing.

But once behind the wheel, I found it handled nicely, almost as smoothly as the Seville. I wondered where Willie got it. I knew he didn't own one, and this sure didn't look like any parish car.

My reflections on the car were interrupted by a jolt of guilt. I still hadn't called Sally to tell her our baseball date was off. Big mistake. But I had no time to worry about it. My immediate worry was getting up to Seventy-sixth, and in and out of apartment 3C before the police arrived. I'd just have to offer Sally an effusive apology when time permited.

Maybe some flowers? Nope. Sally wasn't a "flowers" kind of girl.

I'd learned that exactly one day after I'd met her, eight years previously. A third-year resident in psychiatry at Bellevue, she'd been selected by Forensics as an expert witness for the prosecution in a case of wife-killing. I was the arresting officer. Sally and I hit it off right away, getting together for dinner et cetera, the first day we met. The next day, I sent her an expensive bouquet of roses to thank her for a wonderful evening. She told me to save my money in the future.

"Why not let things live, Dave? You don't need to chop down flowers for me. A few nice words will be fine."

Right. So, think of some words, Davey, to make up for the blown baseball game.

Later. At the moment, my thoughts were centered on that apartment. I'd have to look for signs of forced entry. If there were none, I preferred not to dwell on the implication—namely, that Willie was guilty, and I was risking a hell of a jail sentence if anyone saw me entering or leaving. I finally decided worrying would only give me a headache, so I quit thinking about it.

The Lincoln and I made such good time that my watch was showing just 12:07 as I made the right turn from Broadway onto Seventy-sixth. Which was precisely the moment my luck turned sour.

Two police cars and an ambulance were blocking the street ahead, at the corner of Seventy-sixth and Amsterdam. The traffic was already backed up eight or ten cars. I had no time for cursing my bad luck. I had to get the hell away from there before someone from Homicide spotted me.

Unfortunately, Dave Goldman is a known entity to the guys in Homicide, and cops don't like it when private eyes come sniffing around. My presence at the scene of a murder, prior to any public announcement, would strongly suggest that I knew something. Spotting me, Homicide would immediately cook up lots of questions for me to answer. And not tomorrow.

Here I was, on the block where a body had just been discovered. And driving the car of a client who had to stay out of sight. Being spotted would be highly undesirable, to put it mildly.

Unfortunately, my options were limited. Seventy-sixth is a one-way street, and three cars had already followed behind me. There was nothing to do but creep forward and join the lineup.

A patrolman in uniform was directing traffic through the tiny opening left by the double-parked squad cars and ambulance up at the corner. I didn't know the cop, which was good because it meant he probably didn't know me either. But, as cars crept forward and I moved up to second-in-line, my luck turned miserable. Immediately to my right, between two parked cars, was someone who knew me all too well—Inspector Kessler's right-hand man, Homicide Sergeant Mike Burke.

The expression on his face gave me no reason to think my luck was about to improve.

VI

It took me a moment to figure out how the electric windows work on a Lincoln. But finally I found the correct button, and the right-hand window slid noiselessly down. The smells and sounds of the city rushed into the Lincoln's air-conditioned interior.

Burke clamped both hands on the door, leaned over, poked his head in the car, and gave me an unpleasant grin. But before he could open his yap, I seized the initiative.

"I can see by the look on your face, Sergeant, that you have cracked this case at last. That's why I came back, to come clean. See, I thought it was a perfect crime, but my conscience just won't leave me alone. So you might as well know, I killed him. Want to know why? Well, because—"

"Can it, Davey!" he interrupted. "Your gags ain't any funnier now than they ever were. I wanna know what you're doing here, bub. And don't tell me you were on your way to somewhere, 'cause this ain't the way to nowhere."

Matter of fact, the same thought had just occurred to me. Obviously I was in a jam, and I didn't see any quick, convenient way out. Meanwhile, a din of horns was coming from the lineup behind me. Lacking any good excuse, I tried for a neat, quick exit line. "Sorry, Sergeant, I guess I'm holding up traffic. Always nice talking to you."

But Burke knew damn well I wasn't at the corner of Seventy-sixth and Amsterdam for nothing. Still holding the car door in his big paws, he barked: "Park your car up ahead, Davey, right in front of that ambulance. You and I are gonna have a little talk."

Getting caught was bad enough; getting into a prolonged conversation with the sergeant was a nightmare come true. Now that I had been seen, we had a new ball game. I had placed Willie in grave peril just by driving his car. If they ran a check on the license, he was in royal trouble.

But there was a worse possibility—my getting frisked. How would I explain to a curious cop why I had the key to the murdered woman's apartment in my pocket?

This wasn't going to be easy. Burke was no dummy. In fact, he knew all my tricks, having been my immediate boss during the first two years I was in Homicide. As I gave him my wide-eyed look of sincerity, his eyes told me right away it wasn't working. Panic time—and my resources were nil.

My brain rummaged around for some lie—any lie—that could remove that skeptical look from his eyes.

"Can't park now, Sergeant," I said. "See, I've got an urgent date over on the East Side." Just then, a blinding flash of inspiration hit me right between the eyes. By pure accident and sheer dumb luck, I had just told Burke the absolute *truth*.

Giving him my most winsome smile, I pulled those precious, life-saving tickets from my shirt pocket, while inwardly thanking the household gods that watch over baseball fans everywhere.

"Look here, Mike." I tried for a new level of sincerity as I handed him the tickets. "You know me, and you know how I love baseball. Check these babies out, Mike. Box seats right behind the Yankees' dugout for the 1:15 game today. Honestly, I'm meeting a dame over at 225 East Sixty-fifth and we're heading straight for Yankee Stadium. It's such a gorgeous day I decided I'd drive through the park. You'll forgive me, but I've really got to go. I sincerely hope you get whoever did whatever it is that brought you out on such a beautiful day."

Burke glowered at the tickets. He knew I was lying, but here was proof positive that I wasn't. Grudgingly he handed the tickets back, still ignoring what had now become a cacophony of horns. But he still wasn't through.

"Mickey!" he called to another plainclothes type sitting in the nearest squad car. With a poker face, he growled, "Gimme her number, Davey. My man'll let her know you're on the way."

Thank God for forgetfulness. If I'd been thoughtful and considerate, I'd have called and told Sally our date was off. Then she would have told the cops all about the lousy rat that canceled out on her.

I gave the sergeant Sally's number, and Burke passed it on to Mickey. A moment later, Mickey called out, "The lady's on the line, Sarge. What do we want with her?"

"Ask her what her plans are for this afternoon, Mickey, if she don't mind our askin'."

After a pause, the answer came. "Says she's goin'

to the ball game with a guy. Somebody named 'Goldman.' Says he's fifteen minutes late."

I immediately started the engine. "Have him tell her I'll get there as quick as I can, Sergeant. And please tell her it's *your* fault I'm late."

"You'll clown at your own funeral, Davey," he growled disgustedly, lifting his mitts off the car. "I'm reportin' this to the Inspector."

As I pulled away, taking my first deep breath, I looked in the rear view mirror. Burke was jotting down the Lincoln's license number. Relief turned to horror. Willie's goose was cooked.

Nothing wrong, I thought bitterly, with lending your car to a fellow human being; just don't lend it to some stupid jerk who'll drive it directly to the scene of a murder, so any half-smart cop can take down the number.

A block east, I spotted a pay phone and pulled over. I dialed a number I never have to look up. Sister Ernestine put me through to the Bishop.

"Yes, David, what have you learned?"

"Unfortunately, it's not what I've learned, it's what's been learned about *me*. You're going to have to postpone your discussion of sacred scripture, or classical languages, or whatever you're talking about. Some cops were already at Seventy-sixth. Unfortunately, I ran smack dab into an old Homicide pal outside the apartment building."

"And?" queried the Bishop. I didn't appreciate the intonation.

"*And* I was stupid enough to drive Willie's car up here. The cop jotted down the license number. I'm afraid that I'll have to reclassify Father William from 'provisional client' to 'jailbird.' "

For several seconds we listened to each other

breathe. Finally, "No need to reproach yourself, David. This is unfortunate, but I don't see that it's necessarily fatal to your efforts to keep Father's name out of the papers."

"Not fatal? Have we got a bad connection? I've just told you the police got his license number! I can't—"

"David. As it happens, Father and I were just discussing the car. It belongs to a priest friend who is spending the summer in Israel where he will be staying for another *three weeks* . . ."

The words hung there while I paused to consider.

"O.K. Having the car's owner out of the country is a stroke of luck, that's for sure. But I've got two recommendations, all the same. First, Willie has got to get out of the mansion and stay away from both of us till this whole thing is settled. I mean *now*. This cop—his name is Burke, by the way—may have someone on the way there, even as we speak. Secondly, I'd better stick with what I told Burke, which is that I'm going to the ball game with Sally. Needless to say, I'd *prefer* to be in the trenches with you." I thought I heard a snort, but it may have been my imagination.

I continued, "When someone arrives—and it could be Burke, but it's just as likely to be Inspector Kessler—I should be with Sally at the game. I'd hate to think what'll happen if I met the police *again*, right after telling Burke I was going to Yankee Stadium. Agreed?"

The Bishop tried some contemplative breathing, which is how a guy with a 220 I.Q. lets you know he's thinking. He knew Kessler well. The two had first met when Regan was in the hospital after the shooting. Kessler had the overall responsibility for investigating that shooting. So I knew what Regan thought about the prospect of a visit from Kessler. His tone was grumpy: "Agreed."

"Next question," I went on. "Any objection to having Father William drive your car?" I felt the Bishop wince from forty blocks away. He hates to see anyone but me driving his car. After five seconds of silence, I said, "I'd better explain. I've got his car, and I'm at Seventy-sixth, west of the Park. The Cadillac, of course, is in the garage. Fuller needs to get away from Thirty-seventh and I need to get to Sally's. Logic dictates we meet somewhere near Sally's and trade autos. If you concur, tell Willie to go to the garage and wait there for my call. I'll tell him where we'll meet."

More breathing. Finally and resignedly, "I suppose so. I'll expect to see you immediately following the game." The line went dead. Hanging up is Regan's way of stopping arguments before they start. He knew damn well I usually like to hang around at Sally's for an hour or two of R and R after the ball game. So he hung up before I could say anything.

Sissy way to win an argument, if you ask me.

VII

As with everything else I did that day, I managed to botch the exchange of autos.

The first part went fine. As promised, I waited five minutes before calling Fred's Garage. Of course, I explained to Fred the importance of having amnesia about anything that happened that day. He assured me he'd already forgotten everything, up to and including his own name.

When Willie got on the phone, I told him to meet me in front of that little deli just east of Madison on Sixty-fourth. That was where I botched it.

This was my first opportunity to search the Lincoln. I had just closed the suitcase, and the trunk lid was still open, when Willie arrived. I told him I thought I'd heard a noise somewhere back there and was checking it out. He seemed to buy it. As for the suitcase, I found nothing incriminating.

We exchanged only a few words. Willie was serious and subdued. I was concentrating on the car problem I'd created. I warned him to do two things about the car. First, I told him he needed to clear all his things out and give it a thorough wash. Every hard or semi-hard interior surface had to be polished. Then I told him to garage it for the duration.

"Why?" he asked, obviously puzzled.

"Because your damn prints are all over it, Willie! And *cops* are going to be all over it within the next twenty-four hours." I thought for a moment. "There's a car wash on Ninety-sixth, just west of Broadway. For ten bucks, they'll shine it up nice. Just make damn sure you get all your junk out of it. And I mean *all.*"

Willie seemed to take me seriously, and promised he'd do it. Then he drove off.

It was 12:53 when I double-parked in front of Sally's building. Harry the doorman, no mental giant, started complaining, "You can't leave it there, Mr. Goldman. The cops—"

"It's O.K., Harry." I slipped him the car keys and a finiff I could ill afford. "In fact I just came from a little talk with the cops." That was true. "Not to worry. I'll be down with Dr. Castle before you know I'm gone." I left Harry staring disapprovingly at the Seville.

Sally wasn't happy either. "David, darling, what's going on?" Her honey blond hair was pulled back fetchingly in a pony tail and the slinky pants suit she was wearing emphasized her slender figure. All in all she looked smashing. And mad.

"You're *never* late, Davey! What's the matter? I got a call from the police. They said not to worry, you're on your way. You'll be here in five minutes. An hour later, where are you? You had me scared to *death!*"

"If you exaggerate this much with your patients, you'll make them psychotic," I told her as I gave her a hasty kiss. "Sorry to be late, but you'll notice I'm here now. I'll make it up to you. I'll buy you all the hot dogs and soda you can stand. Only, I've got to make one teensy little phone call before we go, O.K.?"

"Well, make it short. I've been ready for two hours. If I get any better offers while you're on the phone, you're out of luck, fella."

"Idle threats don't bother me," I grinned as I called the private line of another gentile member of the Delancey Street Irregulars, Chester Rozanski, head crime reporter at the Manhattan *Dispatch*.

It took a minute to convince a distrustful female that Chet would want to talk to me. Another minute passed before he came to the phone. During the wait, I considered spilling the beans to Chet, seeing he and Willie knew each other from our Saturday morning golf games. I rejected the idea for a variety of reasons—mainly, that I didn't think the Bishop would approve.

Chet sounded hurried. Come to think of it, he was always in a hurry. "Make it fast, Dave. Things are happening. If you're calling about the McClain thing, I'll take the name of the killer for the first edition."

My eyes widened, but I kept my voice indifferent. "How'd you guess? I'll give you the murderer's name tomorrow. Right now I want all you've got on it."

He didn't bother to hide his surprise. "Are you kidding? That just came in fifteen minutes ago! I don't think our guy's even on the scene, yet. You're talking about the one on West Seventy-sixth?"

"That's the one. Give."

"Au contraire, oh Great One! You give! How the hell did you get onto this so fast? The Bish get a message from the Holy Ghost?"

"Nope. I ran into a Homicide Squad roadblock on my way to Yankee Stadium. Now give!"

"You *what?* Ran into a roadblock on Seventy-sixth on your way to Yankee Stadium! It is to laugh, chum! You don't get to Yankee Stadium via Seventy-sixth!"

"Yeah, that's what Burke said. Speak to me!"

"Oh, you've talked to Burke?" When I didn't reply, Chet continued, "O.K., so you're standing mute.

"Well, really, there's not much to give," he continued blithely. "I've got my gal hunting down some background info, but she hasn't—wait, here she is. Thanks, Nance, stick close by, will you, hon'? Let's see . . ."

There was a pause, while Chet went through whatever Nance had brought him. That would be Nancy Ryan, his current gofer. "Yeah, Dave, here's something interesting, maybe. What do I get for it? Maybe a map showing how you get to Yankee Stadium via Seventy-sixth and Amsterdam?"

"Nothing today, Chet. Maybe tomorrow. I believe I asked you a question."

"O.K., tightwad. Don't forget you owe me one. Dead lady's Barbara McClain, thirty-one, school teacher. Says here she owns a bank. Or part of one. Yeah, she and her brother inherited a bank six months ago . . . February 3. That's when her father died, Robert McClain, owned a bank in the suburbs —yeah, Alsip—Alsip Traders Bank."

I was jotting rapidly in my notebook.

"Guess that's all, Davey. Looks like this Barbara McClain was never married. Survived by her brother, Robert, Junior. Described as an 'investor'? That figures. Means you're wealthy and clip coupons for a living. Guess that's it for survivors."

Which was all I could get out of him. He still wanted something in return, so I had to hang up on him. Rude, but he's used to it.

Besides, he's got enough of my money from our weekly golf games to forgive a little rudeness. Calls himself a sixteen, plays to about a nine. Sandbagger.

VIII

If you care to know about the rest of the afternoon, it was O.K. We got to our seats in the top of the second, when the Yanks were already down, one-zip. In fact, they trailed all the way until the bottom of the eighth, when they roughed up three Cleveland relievers for four big ones and won going away, seven to five. Little else happened. Sally had three hot dogs, one over her average, and I got zero spots of mustard on my shirt, two under mine.

To be perfectly frank, I couldn't get real interested in the whole affair. Sally, expert psychiatrist that she is, picked up on my distractedness, but didn't press.

At least until I returned her to Harry the doorman. "Darling, David," she murmured as we kissed good-bye in the car, "if you come back this evening and take me dancing, I might forgive you for making me miss two innings. I also might be able to take your mind off whatever it is that's got you so worried."

She wheedled and wheedled, and of course got her way. As usual.

"Well, all right," I finally grumped. "I'll pick you up at 10:30. And don't be late!"

I was back at the mansion by 5:47. Sister Ernestine came rushing from the kitchen as I locked the door behind me. For a woman of seventy, she moves fast, especially when she's distraught. Her white hair, usually so neatly knotted up, was falling out of its combs and pins. She was wringing her hands.

"Inspector Kessler called around four o'clock. He *insisted* on speaking to him. The Bishop refused! He told me to tell him he was gone. It was horrible, David! He knew I was lying, because he could hear him talking to me, I'm sure. He wanted to know if you were really at the baseball stadium! The Bishop overheard as he was going to the elevator. He snatched the telephone from me. And the *way* he spoke to the Inspector! He just told him to come at six o'clock and hung up. He was *very* angry!

"It was horrible, David! He instructed me not to admit him until six, and then, only if he apologizes —to me, David! Oh—and he must see you in his office, immediately. David, my heavens! What is happening?"

Now you might think that I didn't have the foggiest notion of what Ernie was talking about. All those "he"s and "him"s, with no clue as to who they refer to. But don't forget I've lived with the lady for six years. When she gets nervous, she starts tossing pronouns around like frisbees, and I've learned to go with the flow. I knew immediately it was the Inspector who had to apologize, and the Bishop who wanted to see me in his office.

I tried to settle her down with a pat on the hand. "Don't worry, Ernie. Those two are just practicing for their debate. Relax, it'll be fine."

Actually, it wasn't fine at all. Kessler was on to me. But it was encouraging that the Bishop wanted to be involved. On this one, I was ready to admit that I was in over my head. I had a feeling this case would require a certain amount of brilliance, which the Bishop could provide when he wanted to. Apparently he now wanted to.

It was highly unusual for Regan to invite me to interrupt his writing sessions. I found him, as expected, at the computer terminal in his office, his fingers flying over the keyboard. He tried to ignore my presence, but I didn't let him get away with that. After all, he had told Ernie to send me in.

"It's funny," I said in a loud voice, "how differently people react. You'd think my old boss, Sergeant Burke, would have seen enough stiffs by now that another one wouldn't bother him. But he was in a foul mood. And speaking of foul, Dave Winfield hit one in the third that must have gone four hundred feet. Two feet to the left and the game's tied. Then he pops up on the next pitch."

"David, please!" Regan muttered. He pushed himself back from the computer and gave me a level look. "Remind me, sometime, Mr. Goldman, of the reasons I put up with you."

"Don't give me that, Bishop. If I hadn't hauled in that monk this morning, you'd still be sitting here staring at that blasted screen, like you did every day last week. *That* was pathetic. And look at you now, churning out words like a man possessed. You ought to thank—"

He quieted me with an upraised hand, then rolled his wheelchair a couple of paces further from the computer. As he spun to face me, he said, "Sit down, David. I have no desire to break my neck looking up at you."

I sat.

"You want to tell me some more about Father William's car?" I asked. "Like, who owns it, and why?"

"You first," he countered. "What did you find out?"

"Nothing worthwhile. Kessler now knows, or strongly suspects, that I'm working on the McClain murder. And I'm fairly sure he's got the license number of the Lincoln." I paused. "Well, Bishop? Come on, tell me. Whose is it?"

The Bishop smiled grimly. "The owner is either a Reverend John Vessels, a Jesuit; or his father. It's Father Vessels who is currently in the Holy Land. He's expected to be there another three weeks."

"Well, whether it's his or his old man's, I sure hope the cops can't reach him," I remarked. "I think—Now what are you grinning at?"

"I don't grin, David. An occasional smirk, perhaps. I was merely noting the confusion of pronominal antecedents. You've been exposed too long to Sister Ernestine. However," he went on more briskly, "we need to get ready for the Inspector."

"Yeah, the Inspector. What's the idea of inviting him over?" (I decided to use a little reverse psychology I'd learned from Sally.) "Why is it that whenever I have a case, you always want to horn in? Like that Parkridge affair last year. You asked if I wanted some advice, and wound up getting involved hip and thigh. You know you're a frustrated cop, don't you?"

"I solved the case for you, didn't I?"

"You were damn lucky not to get in trouble with

the law," I reminded him. "But never mind that. We need to decide who's running this case, you or me. You asked me to help Father William. O.K., I'm willing to help, at least if I can be satisfied he's not guilty. But am I running it, or are you?"

"I'm merely trying to help, David."

"Yeah, 'help' is one thing, running the show's another. What's the point of having Kessler over?"

Regan nodded his head. "Your question is a good one and deserves an answer. Since you say you were able to learn nothing of value at Seventy-sixth Street, it seemed to me the only person capable of giving us a clue to Father William's guilt or innocence, is the Inspector. If you will allow me to lead the discussion . . ."

"As if I had any choice," I muttered.

"If you please, David. If I may take the lead, I hope to elicit some tiny morsel of information, some infinitesimal datum, pointing ineluctably to Father's innocence—or guilt, if guilt there be." He looked at his watch and grimaced. "Two minutes after six; the Inspector is late; but he is certainly coming. When he arrives, David, please permit Sister to let him in. I have instructed her to send him away if he doesn't apologize."

"Suppose he refuses," I countered. "What do we do then?"

He glared. "He'd better, that's all."

As we looked at each other, the doorbell chimed.

IX

Inspector Kessler's slight frame was ensconced in the black velvet chair, when I returned to Regan's office from the kitchen.

I had waited in my office while he and Sister Ernestine had talked in the vestibule. I'd been able to make out tones of voice, no words. From the agitation in her tone, you'd have thought she was apologizing to him, rather than vice versa. That's just the way she is.

Kessler is no special friend of mine—I mean, he fired me, didn't he?—but neither would he make my Enemies List if I had one. He was a damn good boss when I worked for him, and I learned a lot from him. As for his firing me, I've always known he didn't have much choice. He had been getting a lot of pressure from the D.A.'s office. That day I invited the Assistant D.A. to step outside—in front of a roomful of people—was probably not the smartest moment of my life, though it did have a pretty good feel to it at the time.

My theory is, Kessler's a frustrated accountant. A fussy little guy, very concerned about details. In fact, if he has any major failing as an Inspector, it's that he concentrates on the details and neglects the big picture. But he's a good cop. We've had our run-ins since I left the force and went on my own, but he's generally played fair, and I think he'd say the same for me.

The mug of beer Ernie had brought him was resting at his elbow, precisely placed in the center of the little cocktail napkin. His goatee and mustache were neatly trimmed, and he polished his gold-rimmed glasses with an immaculate white handkerchief. As he looked up at me, blinked nearsightedly and gave me a frosty smile, his small teeth gleamed through the mustache and beard. His eyes then left me to return to the important business at hand—getting those glasses polished to a diamond-like shine.

"Enjoy the baseball game?" he asked in a reasonably civil tone. He raised his chin and eyebrows long enough to let me know it was me, not the glasses, he was addressing.

"Oh, you've talked to Burke. Yes, thanks, it was a good game. Yankees came back with four in the bottom of the eighth and won, seven to five."

The door to the bathroom at the far end of the office opened. The Bishop wheeled quickly through the door, rolled up to Kessler, and the two shook hands. The Bishop cast a keen eye at the Inspector's beer as he released his hand.

At the Bishop's approach, Kessler had gotten to his feet. He remained standing till the Bishop rolled around his desk to his place. I reflected on the past confrontations between the two. Both, I happened to know, had been stars on their respective high school debating teams thirty-plus years before.

But a shared tendency to debate did not explain

why they always clashed. I'm convinced that most of their conflict arose from mutual envy. Kessler admired what he construed to be the peacefulness and serenity of a man of God. No doubt, he wished he could have the same sort of cloistered, sedentary life, not realizing that Regan was about as peaceful as Mount Vesuvius.

And the Bishop was a frustrated cop. You could see it in his face. And he permitted a private detective agency to be operated virtually inside his mansion. His coplike tendencies had become even plainer over the past year when he'd begun getting involved in my detective work.

Regan is undoubtedly the brightest guy I've ever met. Far brighter than Kessler, for sure. The Bishop's ability to grasp a vast array of detailed information is almost frightening.

Take the Parkridge case: wealthy society woman duped into a money-losing business by a smooth-talking promoter. She got my name somehow and asked me to help her get her money back.

I didn't see any way, even though she promised a nice fat fee if I succeeded. Talked to two lawyers and three cops and not one of them had a suggestion worth a damn.

I described the case to the boss one evening at dinner. After listening to my description of the entire situation and asking a few pertinent questions, he came up with some highly interesting suggestions.

I spent three and a half weeks on the legwork and managed to locate some dirt on the promoter. In official hands, that information could have sent him up the river for quite a stretch.

During a long session in Regan's office, we managed to persuade the swindler to cough up the quarter-million Mrs. Parkridge had "invested," plus some interest. The police later learned of that conversation, to their acute irritation. But they had to lump it.

Mrs. Parkridge had been most grateful, and so was I, when she coughed up five percent of the total recovery as my fee. The Bishop haughtily rejected my suggestion that he share in my financial good fortune.

"Your work is your profession, David. If my few suggestions can assist you, I am all the happier. But I am most emphatically *not* a detective. What do you think the Cardinal would say if it became known that I was taking fees for these kinds of activities?"

" 'What an enterprising young Bishop'?" I murmured.

"Hardly, though I appreciate the 'young.' As to 'enterprising,' keep in mind, there are non-pecuniary motives in this world."

Immediately after Parkridge had come the Lombardi case. Extremely sad. Little six-year-old Tony Lombardi had been abducted and killed. The family came to me.

That was when the Bishop nearly came to blows with Kessler. Kessler had assigned Charlie Blake to the case.

Blake and I go way back. We were rookie cops together, twelve years ago. I formed an early opinion about his character and brain power I've never felt inclined to change, despite his elevation, two years ago, to the exalted rank of Lieutenant.

Blake got nowhere with the Lombardi case. Whereas, thanks to a few, highly astute suggestions by the Bishop, I was able to locate the abductor/murderer. Distrusting Blake's abilities, I turned over my evidence directly to the D.A.'s office. The Lombardis were filled with gratitude, and gave me a nice-size check. Kessler and Blake were somewhat less pleased.

Two meetings ensued between Kessler and the Bishop, both in the Bishop's office. Eventually the dispute reached as high as the Commissioner's level, and beyond. Regan was told that I was an embarrassment. They asked what was he doing, hiring an ex-cop Jew as a Special Assistant anyway? And so on.

This I heard second-hand. The Bishop never let on. I had the later opportunity to hear the tape of a phone conversation between Bishop Regan and Police Commissioner Rawlins that took place around that time. I excerpt it here to give you the flavor of the exchange:

RAWLINS: I'm a church-going Catholic, Your Excellency, and it's just not right for that Goldman guy to be working out of your office. If you like, I can tell you exactly why he's off the force.
REGAN: I imagine you can, Mr. Rawlins. No doubt, you can also explain how he found the murderer of that little boy, while your salaried employees looked on in helpless amazement. I'm sure you have excellent reasons for keeping the inept and incompetent on your staff. Possibly you should consider hiring more Jews and atheists; your department's performance might improve markedly.

Thus, Bishop Regan and Commissioner Rawlins.

Regan's confrontations with Kessler were at least as acrimonious, though the two did sort of patch things up. The Bishop held a dinner at the mansion for just the three of us. Kessler and the Bishop discovered they had a great deal in common. Each of them was half-Irish and half-German. Not only that, the German sides of their families both came from the same town in southern Bavaria, a village near Ravensburg so tiny that their forebears must have known each other.

But at the moment, each wanted something from the other. Their cordiality would last exactly as long as each thought he had a shot at getting what he wanted.

Kessler sighed deeply. "This McClain thing is a mess. Here it is, coming up on six-thirty, and I'm late for a function my wife and I have been planning to go to for two months. Silver anniversary of two of our friends. Renewal of vows and all. I'll make the party, but I missed the church ceremony, and I hate that."

He sat back comfortably, put his fingertips together and gave Regan his sly look, the one that always put butterflies in my stomach. "Of course both of you know all about the McClain case—since Davey's already been up there to investigate the scene of the crime."

He grinned at us as he reached for his beer.

X

The Bishop looked convincingly blank as I directed my next words to him. "I should explain what the Inspector's talking about, Bishop. I was taking a roundabout way to Sally's this morning. I ran into a traffic jam on West Seventy-sixth. Turned out, the jam was caused by the police department.

"Sergeant Burke—I don't think you've met him—pulled me over to find out what I was doing. Fortunately I was able to show him my baseball tickets. He had to call Sally to be sure it was a real date. Next time, I'll remember to bring a permission slip from the teacher."

"Do that, Davey," said Kessler, unfazed by my sarcasm. "Good to hear you explain everything to the Bishop here. As if he didn't already know." He showed us his teeth, mirthlessly, through the beard. In addition to everything else, Kessler didn't approve of Sally. He'd never appreciated my dating someone who had any official involvement in police matters. Considered it "unprofessional."

"It's interesting, *Mister* Goldman," Kessler went on, narrowing his eyes at me. "You told Burke Dr.

Castle lives on East Sixty-fifth, right? So, explain to me how you get from West Thirty-Seventh to East Sixty-fifth via Seventy-sixth and Amsterdam!"

I sighed. "As I tried to tell Sergeant Burke, I was going to take a little drive through the park and miscalculated the time, so I decided to cut across on one of the side streets—was it Seventy-sixth? I really didn't notice. I was just unlucky enough to run into Burke's monster logjam."

The preceding was not an easy lie to tell. Kessler's got the meanest eyes of any animal in captivity, and they were pinning me every second. Nor did he take his eyes off me in the ensuing silence.

I gave him my sincere, wide-eyed, innocent look. Trouble was, he'd seen that look too many times before.

Finally he gave up the staring contest. "O.K., Davey. Maybe I can buy that." He took a breath. "I would like to ask you just one question, though, and maybe get a straight answer for once. Are you retained on the McClain murder?" He raised a hand quickly. "And don't tell me it's none of my business, Davey, because everything related to a murder I'm investigating is my business."

I tried to give him a steady, unwavering look. I was hoping for help from Regan, but he gave me nothing but a watchful eye and plenty of silence.

"Look, Inspector," I finally said. "I don't think that's a very fair question. I can tell you truthfully that at the moment I have no interest in the case. But what if something comes up in the future that would bring me in? I'm not going to guarantee that I'd turn it down."

I thought for a moment, then added, "It's just barely possible that I may have some information that could have a bearing. But right now I don't know anything. Could you just tell me the basic facts?"

I shut up, and tried to figure out what I'd just said. Regan raised one eyebrow quizzically. I hoped that meant I'd asked the right question, but it might have meant anything.

Kessler stared at me. " 'If something comes up in the future'? What does *that* mean?" He paused to take a final delicate sip of beer. He placed the empty stein carefully in the exact center of its napkin and frowned.

"All right, my friend, I'll give you what we've got. You can read the same thing in tomorrow's *Times* if you're not too lazy.

"A woman named Barbara McClain, thirty-one, unmarried, a school teacher, was killed last night in her apartment—that's 3C, 501 West Seventy-sixth, corner of Amsterdam." He swivelled his head to the Bishop. "If you don't know where that is, Bishop, Mr. Goldman can show you. It's apparently on the way to East Sixty-fifth." He glanced at me out of the corner of his eye to be sure I got the sarcasm. Resting his head on the back of the chair, staring at the ceiling, he went on. "Stabbed once in the chest, probably while sleeping. Knife went straight in the heart. Knife not withdrawn, death probably instantaneous. Little exterior bleeding; plenty inside.

"Weapon almost certainly from the woman's own kitchen. It's part of a set. No prints on the weapon. From what we've got so far, no sexual molestation of the victim. No sign of forced entry, so it was probably someone she knew, or someone who had a key.

"We have good reason to think her boyfriend spent the night, so he's the man we're looking for, at least for now. It appears, by the way, that he may have skipped, which will give you a clue as to his guilt or innocence. So far, we've been unable to locate him." He looked at me out of the corner of his eye. I didn't care for the glint I saw there.

"So you have no one in custody?" Regan murmured.

"Not yet, Bishop." He was still eyeing me. "We've talked to a number of people who knew her. The boyfriend was probably the last to see her alive, whether he spent the night or not." Kessler now transferred his full attention to me.

"Are we *going* to find him, Davey? You had better believe it, my friend. And when we do we'll know who might have been an accessory-after-the-fact." He looked at me, hard and mean. I hoped I was up to the challenge—at least I didn't blink. Of course, he didn't either. Call it a draw.

"Who discovered the body?" I asked in an innocent tone of voice.

Kessler snorted, then narrowed his eyes and nodded knowingly. "Funny you should ask that, Davey. We got an anonymous phone call. And there are some interesting coincidences about that call. Let me run something up the flagpole and see if you geniuses salute."

He pulled a pad from his jacket, and ticked off items as he read: "11:33—anonymous phone call. 11:42—first patrol car arrives, officers get into apartment, discover body. 11:49—second patrol car arrives. 12:01—Burke arrives." He paused, and added, triumphantly, "12:06—Goldman shows up! Anything strike you about that timetable, Davey?" Getting no satisfaction there, he turned to Regan. "How about you, Bishop? Any profound thoughts about that timetable?"

My face was getting weary of doing its impersonation of an angel, so I was happy the Bishop jumped in.

"What do you want us to say, Mr. Kessler? If you have suspicions, voice them and we'll either refute them or we won't. There is no jury sitting here. Why waste your breath asking rhetorical questions?"

I said before that Kessler's eyes were mean and black. Regan's eyes are green, and hard to read. But I've known him for six years, and I've paid attention. I now saw a glint that told me he had something. But what? My mind raced over what Kessler had just been saying, and I couldn't find a hint. But Bishop Regan, my high-powered advisor, definitely could.

"All right, let's forget rhetorical questions," Kessler snapped. "That timetable I recited says Davey arrives at the murder scene thirty-three minutes after the anonymous call comes in to the police station.

"I'll tell you frankly," he went on, "my first thought was that Davey also made the phone call to the station. 'But,' I said to myself, 'Davey wouldn't do it that way. If he had a client, he'd go up there first, check out the apartment and call us later.'

"But then I thought about it and the answer hit me just as I was walking up the steps to your front door." The Inspector smiled at us. "Whoever called us called you at the same time, Davey! We get a call, Davey gets a call; we go, he goes." Kessler paused to show me his teeth.

"I hope you follow my meaning, Davey, because the individual who called us somehow neglected to leave his name. And I have this funny feeling you may know it. If it turns out you're holding on to the name of a material witness, it won't go down well in city court. Am I making any sense, *Mister* Goldman?"

"I congratulate you, Mr. Kessler," Regan intervened calmly. "Very neat. Unfortunately, you are wrong—" Kessler opened his mouth but the Bishop continued.

"Please, Mr. Kessler, permit me to finish. You are wrong, I say, solely because you are not privy to an essential fact known only to Mr. Goldman and me—the fact that, today, from eleven o'clock until after twelve noon, no call came into this house. You may wish to obtain phone company records to establish that fact, but I, personally, give you my word of honor."

Kessler squinted at Regan for a moment before replying. "Very well. I'm certainly not going to call a Bishop a liar." He took a breath and turned to me. "Just for the record, Davey, do you back the Bishop up on that? No phone calls this morning?" He grinned apologetically at Regan. "Just in case you might have missed one, Bishop."

"I'll get a bible and swear on it," I said. "In fact, the Bishop's got seven. One's in Greek, one's in—"

"Yes, yes," Kessler interrupted snappishly, "and I'm sure he keeps one for you in doubletalk. Never mind." He took a breath and thought a bit. "O.K., well, if it wasn't a phone call, someone could have come here and . . ."

I was giving my body orders not to squirm, because it was beginning to want to. Kessler was on the verge of asking the question that could force me into a premature decision: to risk a felony by telling an out-and-out lie on a matter of substance in a murder investigation, or to turn Fuller in.

And I still didn't have a clue as to whether Fuller was guilty or innocent.

XI

Ernie saved me. She was standing in the doorway. When Regan looked up, Kessler interrupted his monologue.

"Yes, Sister Ernestine?"

"Excuse me, Bishop, but will the Inspector be having dinner with us?"

"Inspector Kessler has an engagement, Sister. I'm afraid he will be leaving shortly." As the nun departed, the Bishop continued smoothly, "It's approaching our dinner hour, Mr. Kessler, and I know you have things to do. Let me save us all some time." Regan's tone was honeyed. "I myself might have some information which could assist in your investigation. But, in order to determine its relevance, I need to ask a question. What can you tell me about the anonymous call?"

My mind was racing. Something about the anonymous phone call had tipped the Bishop about Fuller's guilt or innocence.

Kessler's eyes narrowed as he studied Regan for several seconds. He didn't know him as well as I did, but he knew him, and he smelled a rat. But Kessler's sense of smell was temporarily overpowered by his curiosity. The prospect of getting new information from the Bishop was tempting. Kessler fumbled in his side coat pocket and pulled out his pipe. Holding it by the bowl, he gestured with the stem, using it for a pointer. (I remembered him doing the same thing, back when I worked for him.)

"All right," he pointed the pipestem in the Bishop's direction. "We weren't planning on giving that out, but . . . O.K." He started fumbling through his other coat pocket, then looked back at the Bishop. "Mind if I smoke?" Regan gestured assent.

Kessler loaded up from his plastic pouch, and applied the flame from his lighter to the tobacco. "Thanks, Davey," he said absently, sucking flame into the pipe bowl as I placed an ashtray on the table next to his empty beer glass.

He exhaled a fragrant cloud and stared at the ceiling. "The call came in to the Twenty-second Precinct, at 11:33. Voice hoarse, probably disguised. He said: '501 West Seventy-sixth Street, Apartment 3C. A dead woman there. If you want to know who did it, ask Charles Ryder.' Then he hung up. The receiving officer rates it an eighty percent probability that the caller was a male adult."

"Who is 'Charles Ryder'?" muttered the Bishop, glancing at me.

"That's the boyfriend. He's the one we're looking for at the moment."

"I see. Well, have you considered—" the Bishop began.

"Excuse me, Bishop," Kessler interrupted, "but that's it, I'm not taking any more questions. Your turn. What have you got for me?"

"Nothing," the Bishop responded calmly.

There was a moment of silence while the whole

world held its breath. Regan had never been this brazen with Kessler, not even at the height of their tiff in the Lombardi affair. This was so outrageous, in fact, that Kessler didn't take him seriously at first. "Come on, Bishop, I know you've got something."

"No," Regan was adamant. "Nothing at all."

I wanted to put my hands over my ears to prepare for the coming explosion. But it never came. Oh, Kessler was steaming, all right. His beard trembled and so did the pipe in his hand. He took a puff and very slowly and ominously took the pipe from his mouth, stared at Regan through the smoke, and asked, "Are you absolutely sure you mean that?"

The Bishop didn't answer.

The Inspector got to his feet. Looming over me, he gestured with the pipe. "What about you, Davey? Any idea what the Bishop knows?"

I grinned up at him and shook my head. "Nope. Not a thing."

He held me with his eyes for a few seconds. "Well, gentlemen, I hope you know what you're doing. And, Davey me boy, I'm going to give you some good advice." His voice hardened as he bit off each word. ". . . Stay! Out! Of! This! Case!" He glanced hard at the Bishop.

"Because if I see you, or the Bishop, nosing around anywhere, or talking to any of the witnesses —if I spot either of you within a mile, I'm going to have your license, Davey. You can bet the ranch on it." He continued to pin me with his eyes. "Got that, Davey? I don't want any misunderstanding."

"Nope, no misunderstanding, Inspector. But I hope you don't intend to abrogate my constitutional right to make a living." What the hell, if the Bishop could be brazen, so could I.

"Inspector Kessler," the Bishop broke in. "I understand your disappointment, but I suggest you drop your threats. Mr. Goldman has no desire to interfere, nor do I. We will help you if we can. At the moment, I know nothing which could assist you, and I'm sure the same is true of Mr. Goldman. If we hear anything, you will be the first to know. Now, sir, if you will please excuse us. Our dinner hour is at hand."

Kessler tapped the tobacco from his pipe into the ashtray, studied the pipe bowl to see if it was clean, tapped it once more and, satisfied, returned it to his coat pocket. Turning to the Bishop, he nodded.

"Well. I wouldn't want to cut into your dinner hour. But, I should tell you, Bishop, that I believe you and Davey both have information about this murder. I've asked you for it, and you've withheld it.

"And why *aren't* you giving me the information? There's just one reason. If you give it to me, your young friend, Goldman, can't turn it into a fee. And you won't get to play unofficial cop."

He glared down at Regan. "Well, Bishop, I'm telling you, you and Davey have a problem. Because I'm going to be watching him. And the first time I see him using that information for profit, I'm coming down on him like a ton of bricks. My advice to both of you is, be *very* careful.

"Thanks for the beer."

I followed Kessler to the front door. Just because he'd lost his manners was no reason for me to lose mine. But as soon as he was gone, I hurried back to the office.

"All right, Bishop. You wouldn't tell him, but you'd better tell me. Give! Something about the anonymous phone call told you Fuller was innocent. What was it?"

XII

Regan was almost as pleased with me as he was with himself. "Very perceptive, David." I waited. He frowned at me.

"All right. Consider the implications. That call to the police was made at 11:33. At that moment, your client—and now you may indeed call him that—was sitting right there." He pointed his finger at the chair Kessler had just abandoned.

"Excuse me, Bishop, but we already knew Fuller didn't notify the police. I'll admit I'd like to know who did; but who says the murderer and the anonymous caller have to be the same person?"

"You haven't thought it through, David." Regan put his hands on the wheels of the wheelchair, spun ninety degrees to his right, and moved. He was going into his version of pacing the floor.

"The caller sought to remain anonymous. That is noteworthy. Why would a maid or janitor—why would any employee in that building who might have discovered the body—call anonymously?" He was now heading back my way, arms busily pumping.

"A person reporting a crime has only two reasons to withhold his name—to evade suspicion or to avoid involvement. So my antennae were quivering the moment I heard that the call was anonymous," he went on. "The call was made at a time Father William could not have made it. Certainly that elevates the probability of his innocence. Furthermore, the timing of the call—11:33. You'll recall, the two earlier calls were made at 9:30 and 10:30. The pattern of calls, once an hour, is interesting. If it was the killer, he probably intended to keep calling until he—or she—received no answer. Then immediately, he would notify the police.

"That was what impelled me to ask Mr. Kessler the contents of the call. Possibly, that call could confirm Father William's innocence once and for all. Which it did. That the call had been anonymous, and been made just after the half-hour, were already persuasive. The contents of the call, as described by Inspector Kessler, make it all but absolute."

I was frowning. "But how? I still don't see why the caller couldn't have been some innocent third party, who just happened to—"

"No, David. The only two people who could have known that a body was in that apartment *and* that 'Charles Ryder' was involved were Father William and the murderer. And Father William didn't make the call. So he is not the murderer. Which frees you to work on his behalf." The Bishop leaned back in his wheelchair. "But settling his innocence by no means resolves all your dilemmas. Need I expatiate?"

I thought a moment, frowning. "You're right," I said. "We can try to keep Father William out of this. But how do I go about finding out who killed his sweetie?"

The Bishop winced at my use of the word "sweetie."

"There is, of course, one way you could proceed," the Bishop said thoughtfully, after a moment's pause.

I cocked my head. "How's that?"

"If you were to find a different client in the same matter, you would have an excuse to delve into the case. The Inspector wouldn't like it, but he'd be unable to prevent you."

"Would *you* like to hire me?" I grinned. "I'd give you a bishop's discount."

"I should think so." Regan remained bemused. Obviously he didn't want to drop the case either. "Unfortunately, I have no legitimate interest in this . . . situation. But if—" He paused, looking at me, then sighed and shook his head. "I'd like to see Father William again."

"There's just one problem with that," I said.

"What?" Regan asked.

"Kessler. He's undoubtedly got men watching this house, since he's sure that you and I know something. They're probably out there already. And they're going to follow me wherever I go."

"You think Mr. Kessler is going to have us watched?"

"We'd better assume it. He's probably got a decent description of Willie from someone by now, under his other name, and he feels in his gut that we know him, despite our denial. You heard what he said. It would be a risk to let Willie come here again." We looked at each other, each of us pondering ways and means. Then the Bishop erupted.

"Wait, David!" the Bishop exclaimed, suddenly lifting a finger. He looked at me with a smile and spread his hands wide. " 'God is good to those who trust.' " He was triumphant. "Do you realize, David, tomorrow is fourth Tuesday?"

I frowned at him. "Fourth Tues—Oh! The district mass!"

"Certainly. We'll have ten or twelve priests arriving all at once, at a quarter to seven in the morning."

The district mass was something that had been going on for a couple of years. Regan had decided that, as Archdiocesan Director of Personnel, once a month—on the fourth Tuesday of the month—priests from one of the eight districts into which the Archdiocese was divided, would come to the mansion, concelebrate mass with him, then stay for breakfast and conversation. It had turned out to be a fairly good idea. The priests could voice their opinions and concerns, some of which were news to the Bishop.

As the Bishop had just remembered, and I should have, the next day was fourth Tuesday, and we were expecting nine priests from Staten Island. What if *ten* priests should show, instead of nine? Would any cop know the difference? And, would even the most alert observer recognize one 'Charles Ryder' amidst ten identically black-suited, Roman-collared clergymen? Not a chance.

Regan gestured at the phone on his desk. "Get me Monsignor Williams, David."

Within a few minutes, the Bishop had made arrangements for Willie to be picked up by the Monsignor and two other priests from Staten Island in the morning. He also informed the Monsignor that he—Regan—would be unable to join the priests for mass or breakfast.

I then called Willie and gave him instructions, along with his new pseudonym, "Father Smith." He was a little nervous about it, for which I couldn't blame him, but he agreed.

"We should have a good two hours in which to talk with Father," the Bishop said, when I hung up. "The priests don't normally leave till nearly nine o'clock." Ernie had appeared again. "Yes, Sister?" Regan looked up. "Ah, dinner? Wonderful!"

The wheelchair moved so fast, I had to jump out of the way.

Tuesday, August 23

XIII

At 6:37 the next morning, as Sister Ernestine and I admitted the four black-suited priests, including "Father Smith," I was asking myself why I'd bothered to go to bed at all, two and a fraction hours earlier. I know: you wonder how I could have been so stupid as to stay out with Sally till 3:30 when I knew perfectly well I'd have to be up in time to open the door for a bunch of priests at six-something. All I can say is, you have no concept of my psychiatrist girlfriend's persuasive powers when it comes to one more dance, or one more whatever.

So, as I'd prepared for bed, I'd considered just staying up. Only question was, "And do what?" I could have sat there pondering the McClain case and how I was going to get my buddy, Willie, off the hook. But pondering is Regan's thing, not mine. My thing is action. And without some action, I wasn't going to be able to stay awake. So I'd set the alarm for six bells and hit the pillow.

Fortunately, the car that delivered Willie—"Father Smith"—was the first to arrive. I'd already located the cops' surveillance team. There were two faces behind the windshield of the nondescript Ford Fairlane parked across the street, about forty yards to the east. A good location.

Picking out the Fairlane was easy, since it had tailed me the night before, when I left to pick up Sally. (That was a little after ten.) I'd made no effort to shake the tail, for two reasons. One, it might have suggested to Kessler I had something to hide; and two, I wanted my followers to get the notion I was an easy tail, just in case I might *need* to lose them later.

As the Staten Island contingent came in, I greeted Willie as "Father Smith." We shook hands. Then I took him by the elbow and steered him unobtrusively away from the group to the stairway and up the stairs, leaving Ernie to tend the door.

My client was in a much better frame of mind than the day before. My guess was he'd avoided demon rum for the past twenty-four hours. I hoped he might turn that into a habit.

"I do believe the tables are turned, Dave," he said, with a smile. Seeing my puzzled look, he explained, "You look worse than I do. Fun evening?"

"I don't want to talk about it," I moaned. I led Willie to the door of the Bishop's bedroom and tapped lightly.

"Come in." We obeyed. Regan had on his purple robe and pectoral cross, and his purple beanie was planked firmly in place. His wheelchair was backed up to the south window, through which was visible the gray and dreary day. Baroque music emerged from his stereo: one of the Brandenburgs, I'm fairly sure, but don't ask me which one. Between him and Sally, I'm learning, but lowbrow minds can only absorb so much.

The music and the surroundings provided an unusually soothing ambience for an interrogation. Willie didn't realize how much better he had it, answering questions here rather than at Headquarters down on Twentieth Street. I hoped he'd never have to try the other.

Anyone who walks into the Bishop's room immediately notices a contraption next to the bed, consisting of bars, pulleys and straps. This is both Regan's personal get-out-of-bed mechanism, and his exercise machine. He works with that thing a half hour every morning without fail. As a result, he's got an upper body that would be right in place in a Kung Fu movie.

"Please be seated, Father," Regan began abruptly. "We'll do better with eyes at a level. David, sit down, please. Thank you, both."

Having the client where he wanted him, he began, "Father William. Let me make my own participation clear. I am assisting Mr. Goldman in his efforts to clear you of the mess you're in.

"In reflecting overnight on your situation, I see no reason to alter the conclusion I reached yesterday. While your life is unquestionably in need of alteration, no purpose would be served by your exposure: for the Church, for you, for your family. Above all, looking at it from my own perspective, for the Archdiocese of New York.

"I have, therefore, besought Mr. Goldman to work for you at his own expense and he has agreed to do so, out of friendship for you. In this effort, I will assist. But I want to stress that, in no way are you to construe my assistance as an endorsement of the double life you have been leading. Is that clearly understood?"

Pale but unwavering, Fuller returned the Bishop's stern gaze. "Yes. Of course. I'm grateful for your willingness to help me. For the record, I agree with your assessment of my conduct."

Willie turned to me. "I appreciate what you're doing, Dave. It means more than I can tell you."

"All right then," the Bishop continued impatiently. "Just so we understand each other. David, shall we proceed?"

I nodded at the Bishop, who rested his head on one hand as he prepared to hear my interrogation. I had taken a few notes, and referred to my notebook from time to time.

"Father William. You guessed that the police would be interested in your identity and whereabouts. You were correct. Late yesterday afternoon, the Bishop and I were 'honored' "—I flashed a brief grin—"with a visit from Inspector Kessler of the Homicide Bureau. I think he came to see whether you—under the name of 'Charles Ryder'—are my client. I denied it without lying"—I grinned again—"because your name is not 'Charles Ryder.' But he's suspicious.

"I checked Thirty-seventh Street from my bedroom window this morning. Kessler's men are out there." The Bishop gave me a sharp glance and Willie got a little paler. "There's a Fairlane down the block toward Tenth, on the other side of the street, with two guys in it. I didn't recognize them, but I know what they're doing. From now on, both the Bishop and I are going to assume that we're being watched at all times."

I looked at the priest. "So far, they haven't got a clue who you are, Willie. We'e going to try to keep them in thc dark.

"Nonetheless, you're in big-time trouble. The police are dying to find you, and their burning desire is going to escalate every day that the murder goes unsolved. They've got 'Charles Ryder' picked as the murderer, and he's dropped out of sight. So just imagine what they're thinking.

"I'll bet they've got an artist working on a picture of you right now. It's called an 'identikit.' They get anyone who met you to pick some common facial features. Then they put together a composite drawing. Once the composite is done, they'll send copies around to the papers. A lot of people are going to see that portrait because this is a very high profile crime you're involved with here."

The priest was listening intently. "How accurate are those pictures, Dave?" he asked.

"All over the lot. Sometimes excellent; usually poor. We'll just hope this is on the poor side. We'll just have to live with the risk that you may be recognized. Nothing we can do about it.

"We've got other problems too. The police probably have your fingerprints from Miss McClain's apartment. We can hope it'll take them awhile to separate yours out from others. That'll prolong their search. Still, the F.B.I. has excellent fingerprint files. There's no way of knowing if yours are on file, but they probably are, nearly everyone's are. So we've got to recognize the likelihood that they'll identify yours eventually."

The priest winced. I continued. "Which brings us to the point of today's meeting. I'm committed to helping you, Willie. But, let's be clear on what the agreement is. You agree to be absolutely honest with me, and tell me everything you know about anything I ask. Understood?" Fuller nodded.

I nodded and grinned encouragingly. "Good, Willie. Speaking for myself, I'll use my best efforts to identify the murderer of Barbara McClain. To the extent it doesn't conflict with the primary goal, I'll try to keep you out of any publicity. Practically speaking, this means we've got to work like hell to solve this case as fast as we can. You can just bet, every day that goes by, the cops are getting that much closer to finding you."

Fuller nodded nervously. I gave him a long, steady look, which he met. He was in lots better shape than the day before.

"O.K., let's take it from the top. Tell us how you met Barbara McClain, and how you came to be 'Charles Ryder.' "

By the time my golfing pal Willie finished his complete dissertation, I would have a notebook full of shorthand.

XIV

"It's this way," Willie began. "I've got a friend named Jack Vessels, a Jesuit priest, about my age. That's the guy with the Lincoln who's currently in the Holy Land. I met him in Washington four years ago, when we were both at Catholic U.

"That summer, he and I started—well, we called it 'fooling around.' Pretty innocent, really. Just meeting girls, maybe taking them out to dinner or something. Innocent stuff."

He raised a hand to ward off the look he was getting from the Bishop. "Oh, we knew it was wrong, Bishop. It was against our vows. I suppose we just looked on it as a summer's fun, no harm done. We'd missed out when we were in our teens, locked up in a seminary. Neither of us was getting any younger, and it was 'what the hell?' time. Uh, sorry, Bishop."

"Just continue, please," Regan said, grimacing.

"I'm trying to be honest," Willie said almost defiantly. "I'm afraid neither one of us was getting much support from inner faith. Such as it was." He glanced at the Bishop, whose eyes had closed after the last exchange. Willie turned to me. "The Bishop and I talked a bit about my crisis of faith, yesterday." Regan nodded assent without opening his eyes.

"Well, after that summer, Jack and I stayed in touch. A year ago, by sheer chance, we were both assigned to graduate school here in New York. He got his Provincial to put him in the Ph.D. program in archeology at Columbia, and my Abbot decided to send me to Fordham for scripture. We were both delighted. Jack tried to get me a room at Campion House—that's the Jesuit House of Studies up at Columbia."

He looked at Regan, who seemed to be playing Buddha. "As you know, Bishop, they'll admit non-'Jebbies,' if they need to, to fill the place up. But Jack couldn't pull it off. Campion House was full up and he was barely able to get in, himself."

So Campion House was the Jesuit House of Studies where his buddy, Father Vessels, had been living. And that's where the Lincoln belonged. Things were falling into place.

"I got into St. Bede's, which was fine, though I'd have preferred to have been with Jack. Frankly, I don't have much in common with the priests at St. Bede's. They're Benedictines, but they're not academically inclined. Right now, for instance, all they talk about is the upcoming football season.

"Anyway, Jack had that Lincoln for his use here in New York. His old man got it for him. When we'd go out, I'd take the subway to 125th and we'd leave from there.

"We decided to use *noms de plumes* whenever we'd meet up with some girls. He'd change his name to 'Jack Lester' and I became—well, you know what I became."

"Point of curiosity, Willie," I put in. "I've had some experience with aliases. Why 'Charles Ryder'? That's nothing like 'William Fuller.' "

Fuller was blushing. "It wasn't as difficult as it may seem, Dave. Till I entered the monastery, my first name was 'Charles.' Still is, to my boyhood friends, back in Chicago. Monks entering today don't do that—change their names—but we were still doing it when I entered. 'William' was the religious name I was given when I became a monk, and it's now my legal name for all intents and purposes—driver's license, passport, and so on—but I've been 'Charles' longer. As to 'Ryder,' that was sort of a caprice: I was thinking of 'Charles Ryder' in *Brideshead Revisited.* One of my favorite characters," he added.

Regan snorted. I, on the other hand, was pleased. Willie's choice of a false name gave us a slight advantage in keeping him out of sight. The cops, once they realized "Charles Ryder" was an alias, would be alert to names with similar sounds or initials. A small thing, but we could use all the help we could get. (I made a mental note, by the way, to bring up "Brideshead Revisited" next time I wanted to get a rise out of the boss.)

Fuller continued. "Jack and I were down in the Village one evening in April, listening to a folk group in a coffeehouse. The place was jammed. There were these two gals, and we wound up together in the same booth. When Jack and I left, we had their phone numbers. We called them the next weekend, made dates, and became friends. One was Barb. The other was her girlfriend, Ann, who lives in the apartment next to Barb's. The four of us wound up going out together about every other weekend.

"Barb and Ann called us the 'mysterious duo' because we wouldn't give them our phone numbers or addresses, but it didn't seem to bother them much. Well, actually, Barb *did* ask me once if we weren't married guys on a fling. I managed to convince her we weren't. We told them we were bachelor-archaeologists, working at Columbia temporarily.

"Jack and Ann didn't get as close as Barb and I, but we all had fun. Ann is more sociable than Barb, and I think she had more friends. When Jack left for Tel Aviv in June, I continued dating Barb—just the two of us—while Ann went her own way with her own group. In fact, Jack's departure sort of gave *me* more freedom, because he left me his car. I didn't have to take the subway to 125th Street whenever I wanted wheels."

"I see," I said, glancing at Regan, who returned my look. We'd both gotten a little more from Fuller than we'd bargained for.

"O.K.," I said. "Now let's jump forward to yesterday morning. Tell me how you happened to wake up."

Fuller told us again about the two phone calls, the one at 9:30, the next at 10:30.

"So, when did you get up?"

"10:30. I wondered why Barb didn't answer her phone. I finally decided she must have gotten up early and gone somewhere. I looked around for a note, but there wasn't one. I guess I had a premonition, because—I had a real dread of looking in her bedroom."

Fuller took a deep breath. "The door wasn't all the way closed. I went in." He paused, looked up at the ceiling and continued. "She was lying on her back with that knife—" Willie clenched his hands, blinked, and went on. "I went over and sat on the bed. I put my hand against her arm. Cold! Her eyes were open. Wide. Like she was scared to death. That's the worst part, her eyes! I couldn't look at her—"

Willie closed his eyes for a moment, then lifted his head and looked at me inquiringly. I gestured for him to continue, and he did.

"Anyway, I tried to pull her eyelids down with my fingers. Her eyes wouldn't stay closed. That's when I realized there was nothing more to do. I left the bedroom, went back to the couch and tried to think.

"My first thought was, 'Who did this?' And then I realized that I'd been sleeping on the couch, while a murderer . . . killed her, looked at me, and walked out. *Why*?" Willie looked me in the eye.

"I swear to you, Dave, if it would help catch the guy who did that to Barb, I swear I'd turn myself in right away. But somehow I think it would do the opposite. Turning myself in would be playing right into his or her hands." He looked at me for agreement; I gave it to him with a nod.

"I knew I was in a lot of trouble. I must have sat there three or four minutes. Then I thought of the Bishop. I realized he was the only one I could talk to about all this. So I gathered my stuff, got out, and came straight here."

"Questions, Bishop?" I asked.

"Not just now," he murmured without opening his eyes. "Later perhaps. We'll see."

"O.K., Willie, let's try to figure what the police are finding and where you stand. Did you tidy up the place before you left?"

He frowned. "No. I just dressed, collected my things, and got out. Well"—he hesitated—"I guess I did try to rearrange the couch. Just force of habit."

"What are the chances anyone saw you coming out?"

"The first person I saw was around the corner on Amsterdam. No one saw me in the hallway."

When I asked about fingerprints, he smiled ruefully. "The first time I thought about fingerprints was right after I'd left the apartment." He frowned. "I would have gone back in, but I didn't realize I had that key—the one I gave you yesterday." He rubbed his hand over his face. "I wish I could remember where that came from. Barb only had *one,* and it was on her key ring. Why would she take it off and give it to me? I can't even remember her doing that. It's frustrating!" He shook his head. "Anyway, I wiped the doorknob—on the outside. As to leaving something behind, I don't *think* so, but it's hard to say. I was pretty hung over. My memory still isn't too good about all that happened Sunday night."

"O.K., about Sunday night. What did you and Barb do?"

"We went to her brother's apartment, on the other side of the park. He invited her for dinner, along with a couple of other friends. I guess she'd told him about me, because he said I should come along. We were there from about eight until eleven-thirty, I think."

"Did you and Miss McClain have a nightcap when you got back to her apartment?"

"No. She suggested it, but I was pretty bleary. Anyway, I figured on getting up and leaving early."

"That's good." I turned to the Bishop. "Without

a glass or cup, it'll be tough for the experts to get a usable print."

Regan nodded.

"O.K.," I said. "Now, Willie—"

"Wait a minute!" Fuller interrupted. "Wait a minute! I just remembered!"

We both looked at him.

"That key!" The priest was the most animated I'd seen him since he'd caught the Bishop mispronouncing some Greek word one night.

"That key in my pocket, Dave—the one I gave you yesterday. That was *Ann's* key! I mean, the one Ann kept for Barb, in case Barb ever locked herself out. And that's exactly what happened, Friday night: Barb lost her key ring. She was locked out!"

"When did she lose her key ring, Father?" snapped Regan, eyes fixed on Fuller.

"It was at her brother's place. We were the first ones to leave. Barb started looking for her keys in her purse as we were going down on the elevator. She looked some more when we got to the lobby. We discussed whether to go back and find them. They *had* to be up there.

"Davey, they must *still be at her brother's place!*"

I had started to pay a hell of a lot of attention, the moment Willie mentioned "keys." One of the things I'd hoped for, today, was a clue as to how the murderer had got in. This was beginning to sound very much like the how.

XV

Regan shifted in his wheelchair, seeking a good thinking position. "Father," he murmured, eyes now closed again, but a new urgency in his voice. "Why couldn't she have left those keys somewhere else?"

Fuller ran his fingers excitedly through his hair: the memories were flooding back. "No, no!" he said. "She had them out while we were *there*. You see, she had to give her brother back his key. So I know that she—"

The Bishop interrupted. "If you please, Father. What key was she giving back?"

"The key to Bob's apartment. Bob—" he paused. "That's her brother. He gave it to her when he and Missy were out of town last week. Barb took care of the apartment for them. In fact, Bob made a thing of wanting the key back. He was joking, I suppose, but to me it sounded a bit pointed. Didn't bother Barb a bit. She told me later that he was miffed because she'd always let him and Missy have a key to her place. But when she changed her lock last month, she didn't give them a new key.

"Anyway, when Bob asked for his key back,

Barb got her purse, took out her key ring, pulled off his key and gave it back to him. She put her key ring back in the purse. That's how I know she had it that night."

"How many people were at the brother's?"

"Bob and Missy. That's Barb's brother and sister-in-law. There were two others—guys involved with the bank Bob and Barb owned."

"Where was she sitting when she put her keys back in her purse?" was Regan's next question. For the next few minutes, he and I chased that purse around the brother's apartment. Fuller and Barb had been in that apartment for nearly four hours. We'd have loved to know the purse's whereabouts every second of those four hours. But didn't find out—not even close. The priest's liquor consumption Sunday night must have been economy-size. He wasn't much help. But he *was* sure that Barb had put her key ring back in her purse after giving her brother his key.

Giving up on the purse, I tried to reconstruct the scene in the lobby of the brother's apartment building. "Why didn't Barb just go back upstairs and get her keys?" I wondered aloud.

"She didn't need to. Barb and Ann kept each other's keys for emergencies like this. Ann was leaving on vacation early Monday morning—that's yesterday—and Barb wanted to tell her good-bye anyway. So she said, 'I'll just call Bob in the morning,' and we drove back to her place."

"Go on," said Regan.

The priest's frown deepened as he tried to remember. "When we got back to Barb's, I found a place to park around the corner on Amsterdam. We buzzed Ann from downstairs a couple of times, and, finally, Ann buzzed us in.

"When we got upstairs," Willie continued, eyes squinting in concentration, "Ann was waiting for us in the hall. We chatted a while. Ann was wearing pajamas and a robe. She pretended to be mad at first. She teased us about waking her up at such an ungodly hour when she had to be up at 4:30 to catch a 7:00 A.M. flight to Hawaii. Actually, she was happy to see us. She'd wanted to say good-bye.

"After Ann got the key, she stood in the hall a while longer, talking to us. Actually, she'd already written a note to Barb—she would have left the note under Barb's door with the duplicate key if Barb hadn't come home that night.

"Barb and I were feeling no pain from all we'd had to drink," Willie continued. "Ann was in a good mood too, probably looking forward to Hawaii. We were laughing. Barb and Ann were hugging. You'd have thought Ann was going away for a year, not two weeks. They were really good fr—" Fuller stopped abruptly, swallowed and rubbed his eyes. It was a minute before he was able to resume. I looked away.

"It's so terribly sad, that's all," the priest said in a firmer voice. "Anyway, Barb handed me her key and let me open her door. I must have dropped that key into my pocket after I let us in. And there it stayed till I gave it to you."

"Let me get this straight," Regan rumbled irritably. "The women had traded keys, so each would have an emergency key when needed?"

"Right," said the priest. "And now I have—or, rather, Dave does—the key to Barb's apartment that Ann did have."

"Do you know how many other keys to Miss McClain's apartment there are?" the Bishop asked.

"There aren't *any*. Just the one Ann had, and the one on Barb's key ring. You see, Barb's apartment was broken into in July, and she lost some jewelry and things. That was the third time she'd been robbed in two years, which is why she had her lock changed. The new lock came with only two keys. Barb kept one and gave one to Ann. She didn't want any more made. She made a point of seeing that Ann got the only duplicate. I guess that's what made her brother mad."

I pursued the subject for a while, but the priest stuck to his story. There were only the two keys. He made a believer out of me; I couldn't tell about Regan.

The Bishop's next question really puzzled me. "What was the final disposition of the note written by, er—what is that woman's last name?"

"Shields. Ann Shields."

"The note from Miss Shields, then. Where did you last see it?" I frowned at Regan—What did this have to do with anything? He ignored me.

"Good question." Fuller rubbed his hand over the top of his head, and closed his eyes in concentration. "Let me think . . . Ann must have *kept* it," he finally said. "I can't remember Barb having it when we got into her apartment. In fact . . . Yes! I remember. Ann crumpled it up in her hand after she finished reading it to us."

"You're certain?" Regan persisted. "You're sure Miss Shields crumpled it up?" I couldn't believe this. The Bishop was developing an obsessive streak. But genius must be given its head.

Fuller was looking up at the ceiling. "I'm sure, yes. She definitely crumpled it up."

The Bishop and I then got a thorough description of the other two guests who had been present at brother Bob's Sunday-night dinner. We also got a description of Bob and his wife. It was clear to me and, I was sure, to the Bishop, that those four people had moved into the privileged circle labelled "Major Suspects."

Robert McClain, Jr., the older brother of the victim, was a corpulent man in his mid-thirties. He had a degree from Cornell which, so far as anyone knew, had never done him any good. He called himself a "private investor," but that was a fancy title for do-nothing.

Bob had been married for three years to Melissa ("Missy") McClain, whom Fuller described as "self-important, bossy, opinionated, and smug." A working attorney, Missy made a big thing of having graduated number-one in her class at Michigan Law School. Seeing them together, Fuller got the impression that Bob and Missy were made for each other; Bob a dedicated wastrel, and Missy a compulsively dominant female. Opposites attract.

Theodore Masterson was president of the bank that had been founded by Robert McClain, Sr. The elder McClain had died six months before, leaving the bank to Bob and Barb—making Masterson, in effect, their employee. Fuller didn't know how large or profitable the bank was. His impression of Masterson was of a man in his forties, good-looking, athletic, married, apparently happily. His wife had been invited, but had sent her regrets. Apparently, she hadn't been feeling well.

The fourth guest was Norman Hastings. He was an attorney-at-law, somehow connected to the bank, though Fuller didn't know the nature of the relationship. Self-possessed, dapper, Hastings was a debonair individual in his mid-fifties. Barb had seemed reticent about him. The way Barb and Hastings had behaved around each other, Fuller thought they might have dated at one time. But he wasn't sure.

It was nearly nine o'clock before we wrapped things up. But when Regan said, "We shouldn't keep you any longer, Father—" I jumped in, because I still had one important matter to clear up.

"Excuse me, I don't want to prolong this," I said, prolonging it, "but I'd like to talk about the car. Willie, you mentioned the Lincoln was given to Father Vessels by his family. Have you any idea whose name the registration would be under?"

"Jack's dad. His dad bought the plates and pays the insurance."

I'm afraid my disappointment showed. "That's too bad. I was hoping it would turn out that Father Vessels was the owner. The cops would play hell trying to find him on some dig in Israel. Well, does Mr. Vessels know you're driving it?"

Fuller shook his head. "I see what you mean. No, I'm sure he doesn't know. When Jack left for the Holy Land in June, he told me, 'Drive carefully, William, because I don't think you're covered!' "

"Who *does* know you're driving it?"

"You're not going to believe this, Dave. No one."

I frowned. "What about the Jebbies at Campion House?"

Fuller grinned. "What you need to realize is that Jesuits are a fairly antisocial bunch. They don't take much interest in what their buddies are doing. Right, Bishop?"

Regan allowed a slight smile. "They're not known for gregariousness."

Willie nodded. "Half these eggheads don't know where Jack is, and the rest couldn't care less. Believe me, that's the way they are. It's hard for a Benedictine like me to understand."

"The police may make their own investigation," I warned. But I had to grin at the way he described the outfit on 125th.

The notion of a police investigation didn't seem to worry Willie. "I had the car washed yesterday, like you said. And I left it in Jack's parking spot. The keys are with the porter. He's an old guy, a layman. I'll bet I've talked to him a dozen times over the past year. He couldn't pick me out of a crowd of two."

I turned to Regan, who was looking ruminatively into space, and felt a tingle along my spine. I'd seen that look before; it meant he was onto something.

XVI

After a moment of silence, Regan roused himself enough to say, "Thank you for your time, Father. Perhaps you can find your own way out? I have something to discuss with Mr. Goldman."

Willie and I looked at each other, and Willie's eyebrow went up. "Don't look a gift horse in the mouth, Willie," I advised. "Go on down. You'll probably find the nine padres in the dining room. If you can't locate them, check with Ernie. By the way, as far as *they're* concerned, you and Sister don't know each other. So don't be hurt that Ernie doesn't recognize you. She's under instructions."

He got to his feet and headed for the door, still looking puzzled. "I'll call you at St. Bede's when I've got something to tell you, Willie," I said, patting him on the back. "No later than tomorrow."

As I shut the door and turned back to the Bishop, I saw his eyes were closed. His thought processes were in high gear. I sat down to wait. After maybe forty-five seconds, his eyes popped open.

"David, a woman inherits a bank and, six months later, she's murdered. The police will be—indeed, are—operating on the assumption that she was killed by her escort. Logical, from their perspective. Indeed, given the circumstances, nearly inescapably so.

"However, knowing what we know, we must seek a different motive. It seems to me, the first place to look is that bank. We agree, I take it, that the killer is one of those four people who had opportunity to take the key ring?"

I nodded. He gave no indication that he saw the nod, but he continued, "Just so. And every one of the four has a connection with that bank, and therefore a potential motive related to the bank. It would be helpful to know more about it." He looked at his watch and muttered, "Two minutes after nine." He tapped the arm of his wheelchair with a fingertip.

"Before I go to my prayers, David, let us see if I can reach someone who could help us. Tell me again the name of the bank, please?" Referring to my notebook, I supplied what he wanted.

Regan wheeled over to his nightstand, picked up the phone and, referring to a desk secretary, tapped out a number. If you're wondering why he didn't have me do it for him, he has some formula I don't understand, that determines which calls he makes and which ones I make. All I've been able to figure out is, if he likes a person a lot, he generally does it himself.

He waved for me to sit. I sat.

"Mr. Nathanson. Frank Regan, here . . ." As the Bishop listened, his smile widened.

"Ah! *Shalom,* indeed, sir! *Shalom!*" The show-off then spoke a few other words in Hebrew that I vaguely understood, thanks to three pre-teen years of Hebrew school. All the pleasantries went along with the initial greeting. "*Shalom*" means "peace and abundance," and it serves pretty well as "hello" and "good-bye." Beyond that, my Hebrew falters. I was just as happy that Regan continued in English:

"Abe, can you give me two minutes of your time? . . . Well, thank you, sir. That's kind of you to say, but two minutes will do nicely. I am, as it happens, in urgent need of your expertise."

There was a pause, and then Regan explained: "I am interested in Alsip Traders Bank. Familiar with it? That's right, Theodore Masterson is the president." Regan listened a moment, his eyes widened. "What a coincidence! Your appointment is this morning? . . . Unbelievable, Abe! What time—eleven?

"Well, Abe, the associate of whom I speak, a private investigator"—Regan glanced at me—"a Mr. David Goldman, is looking into the murder of Miss Barbara McClain. That's right—yesterday. Well, yes, it might be related to the bank." Regan tried to sound noncommittal. "Since you have to drive out to Alsip, perhaps Mr. Goldman"—he raised his eyebrows inquiringly at me—"could drive you there, and you could tell him something about the bank. Whom are you meeting there, Abe?" He nodded at me significantly as he said the next words. "Theodore Masterson and Norm Hastings? Excellent! If I may discuss it briefly with Mr. Goldman? Thank you, Abe. One moment."

Regan held the phone against his purple-robed chest and looked at me. "David! Mr. Nathanson got a call late last night from Norman Hastings, who asked him to come to the bank today. Hastings and Masterson are talking with him about selling the bank. He's willing for you to accompany him."

I felt like the guy who found out his mother-in-law drove his new Mercedes off a cliff: mixed emotions. On the one hand, I was desperate for sleep; on the other, it was a good break to be able to meet two of our four suspects immediately after learning they were suspects. The decision could only go one way.

"Abe just got himself a driver."

Regan nodded. "Abe? Mr. Goldman will—You've heard of him? . . . Ah yes, the Lombardi matter. Yes, he did receive a certain amount of publicity. He earned it. Me? No, Abe, my involvement was nugatory at best . . . Ah, you are far too kind, I assure you, Abe. But thank you . . ."

In a few words, Regan sketched the current situation, deftly omitting a few details. Then he said, "Abe, you would be doing me a big favor if you could, let us say, employ Mr. Goldman's services—at, perhaps, a fee of one dollar. He would then have the right to investigate the bank. As partial recompense for your payment, he will be happy to drive you to Alsip. You will assist him, then? . . . I appreciate this, Abe, more than I can tell you."

After a few more words, Regan handed me the phone and I made arrangements to pick up Mr. Nathanson. As I hung up, I let my head fall forward. "I really needed this," I moaned. I looked at Regan: "Where did you find this guy, anyway? I'm not complaining, understand. You just pulled a rabbit out of a hat. But, who is he?"

"Abraham Nathanson, David, is one of the top accountants specializing in the banking industry, in New York City. His firm, Nathanson and Nathanson, has probably as many bank clients as any other C.P.A. firm in the city, including the Big Six.

"I have known Mr. Nathanson for five years, and

was once able to do him a good service when one of his children was in trouble. His gratitude is such that I felt justified in calling upon him. It's our good luck that he just happened to be going to the very bank we were discussing."

He paused to think. "Significant, don't you think, that they would discuss a sale on the day after the death of one of the owners? Even before the funeral . . ."

"Yeah, maybe," I said. "But it would be nice if I knew where I fit in. I mean, what's my story for Masterson and Hastings, when they ask me what I'm doing there?"

"It's obvious. You are an investigator, David. If it will not jeopardize Mr. Nathanson's position—and you can discuss that with him in the car—I'd recommend you be just an obnoxious as I know you can be, while there. And see what happens."

"I'm not in very good shape. I don't know how obnoxious I can be."

"As much as usual, I have no doubt." Regan applied his hands to wheels, and moved. "And now I need to talk to Someone Else." He rolled past me, through the door I quickly opened for him, and down the hall to the elevator. He was heading for his sanctuary upstairs.

"Thanks a lot!" I called bitterly after him. "Hope you enjoy your prayers—while I'm dying!"

"You should have thought of that before staying out so late last night," he called back without turning around.

I wonder if all bishops have this spiteful streak.

XVII

At five minutes to ten, disgruntled and out of sorts, I pulled the Seville up to the front door of a high rise at Seventy-ninth and Third.

I wondered how the hell I was going to get through the rest of the day. My skin felt numb all over. My muscles were shaky. Anything for a client, I reflected.

But who *was* my client?

The Fairlane tailed me all the way to East Seventy-ninth. I made no effort to shake it. I didn't mind letting Kessler know where I was going. He'd certainly be puzzled, and probably unhappy, when he found out.

Nathanson's apartment building—a co-op, I assumed—was impressive: granite with a marble facade. The semicircular drive led up to the front entrance. A marble awning with canvas sides ostentatiously sheltered the inhabitants and their guests from Manhattan's wind and rain. As I pulled up, a large, black, uniformed doorman stepped briskly from the doorway to greet me. I pushed a button and the righthand window rolled down.

"Goldman for Nathanson," I announced, sounding like a basketball sub reporting in for Yeshiva U. The doorman's large, round face was expressionless. I found myself hoping my Jewish compadre had given the gentleman my name. He had.

"Mr. Nathanson's expecting you. I'll get him." He hastened inside.

In a minute, the door opened again. Through it emerged a small, wizened, bone-thin man, immaculately clad in dark pinstripes, wearing a blindingly white shirt and club tie. Capping his sparse, white hair was a yarmulke beautifully bordered with ornate stars of David. (If you're wondering why I call his a "yarmulke" and the Bishop's a "beanie," well, I may not be religious, but I'm still Jewish, and I know a yarmulke when I see one.)

Nathanson was missing a right arm; the coatsleeve was pinned up neatly. The doorman accompanied him to the car, hovering over him like an anxious mother seeing her child off to school.

"*Shalom,* Henry!" piped Nathanson in a near-falsetto tenor, as he delicately palmed a folded bill into the black man's hand.

"*Shalom,* Mr. Nathanson, and thank you," said the doorman. As Nathanson took his seat, Henry pulled the seat belt across and snapped it with a click. He gave me a level gaze and said, "You take good care of this man." I took it in the spirit it was meant—as a direct command.

As Henry closed the door, the old accountant swung around to me with a warm smile, extending his left hand. "Abe Nathanson. Shalom!"

"Shalom, Mr. Nathanson." I took the hand awkwardly with my right. "David Goldman." I put the car in "Drive" and we rolled out onto Seventy-ninth. "Thank you for letting me join you, sir. This is a very big favor you're doing us." Nathanson smiled, his eyes twinkling. Lousy as I felt, I was surprised to find I was looking forward to the next couple of hours in Abe's company.

"My pleasure, Daw-veed," he said, using the Hebrew pronunciation of my name. "And please, make it 'Abe.' " Then he asked the question my mother asks of every Jew she meets."Do you keep kosher, Daw-veed?"

I shook my head. "I'm afraid not, Abe."

"Well, who does any more? There's fewer and fewer of us. Many Sabbaths, my synagogue, we can't get a *minyan*." He paused reflectively, thinking of the glories of the past, and giving me a moment to stew in my own unfaithfulness. The *minyan* refers to the number of bar mitzvahed males— ten—which will assure the divine presence in their midst. When you fail to have a *minyan*, you can still *daven*—that's "pray"—but it's not the same. Trouble is, without the divine presence you can't respond 'Amen.'

"But, that's all right, David. All that matters is that we be faithful to the Name. What is your tribe?"

"Yisroel." I was relieved I could remember.

"And I am a Cohen." (That's "priest.") Abe then had a thought that made him grin. "You should have brought the good Bishop along. We could have chanted the Psalms of David, having a representative of all three categories of pray-ers. We've got you from the 'Children of Yisroel'; me, a 'Priest of the Lord'; and from 'Those who fear the Name,' Bishop Regan!"

" '*Ki l'olam chasdo,*' " I said, reaching way back into childhood days, to come up with a verse—or, at least part of a verse—from the *Tehillim* (the "Psalms").

Nathanson cackled delightedly. " '*Ki l'olam chasdo'!* Very good, David. 'His love is forever'! Excellent! We'll make an observant Jew of you yet!" He took a breath and whispered the words again, lovingly: " '*Ki l'olam chasdo.*' "

"I hope you don't meet my mother," I answered, with a grin. "She'd like nothing better than to make me an observant Jew!" I turned onto the approach to the George Washington Bridge.

"Ah! Your mother, she is religious, David. And your father?"

"Gone. Ten years now."

"Ah, your mother is a widow, David. As a dutiful son, you must—But I am not to meddle. Rachel" —he also pronounced "Rachel" the Hebrew way— "Rachel, my late wife, always told me I'm a meddling fool. Besides, we aren't here to discuss *Tehillim* or *minyanim* are we? As I understand it, you need to catch a murderer. Tell me, David, what you see as the connection between the murder and the bank?"

It was interesting to hear his change of tone. With the click of a switch, he had changed from the village rabbi to the astute businessman. Even the "David" had switched from a Hebrew to English pronunciation.

"All we've got is the simple fact that the woman was murdered six months after she inherited the bank. Frankly, exploring that connection is the Bishop's idea. *My* interest is in talking to the last people known to have seen the woman alive. My luck you happened to be meeting with two of those people."

"Well, David," he piped, "I take it that these

two fine gentlemen are *suspects* in the case?" He grinned at me conspiratorially. I nodded.

"All right, David, let me tell you what I know of the two gentlemen. I have never met Norm Hastings, though we have spoken on the phone a few times. Ted Masterson, on the other hand, is a friend. I haven't been able to persuade him to use our firm for their accounting needs, though he says we are 'in reserve' if they decide to use an outside auditor." Abe smiled at me. "That *may* be true, David.

"My only contacts with Mr. Hastings came late last year and early this," he continued. "All of what I'm telling you here is highly confidential, David. And, to seal your lips"—he smiled briefly as he handed me a check—"here is your retainer for the chauffeur work: one dollar. Spend it in good health, David." We smiled at each other, and I thanked him.

"I act as financial consultant for Walters and Midline," he went on, "an investment firm which owns several banks. My services to the firm have to do with analyzing their purchases, and making recommendations as to price. The firm was approached by Mr. McClain—Senior, of course—late last year, on a highly confidential basis. I checked my files"—Nathanson pulled a notepad from his inside coat pocket—"since Frank called this morning. The first discussion was on December 14." He studied the pad for a moment before continuing.

"Robert McClain telephoned George Midline on that day and described what he wanted, in general terms. He told George that he was planning to contact three other potential buyers.

"It was to be a non-public transaction. Mr. McClain stressed that this was not to be discussed with any other personnel at the Alsip bank, or any of its shareholders—especially not his son, Robert, Jr., or his son's wife. Mr. McClain emphasized that, especially. The only exceptions are the two people we are meeting with this morning: Masterson and Hastings. McClain told Midline they were the only two people associated with the bank—besides himself, of course—who knew anything about it.

"Masterson was the key to the transaction. McClain told us that Masterson"—Abe checked his notepad—"would have to be part of the deal. At least, umm, a five-year contract for personal services, with total annual compensation to be at least one hundred and fifty thousand dollars, at the start, increasing to two hundred and fifty thousand, after five years. And stock options of as-yet undetermined amounts, not to be less than five percent of the total equity of the bank. McClain said this was non-negotiable.

"As I advised Midline, this was not an onerous condition, even though the compensation was considerably more than Masterson had been getting. Though Alsip is 'closely held'—meaning it has a limited number of shareholders—it publishes the compensation of its top officers. So it is public knowledge that Masterson got just over one hundred thousand in the twelve months most recently reported. That's total compensation, including bonuses. I don't need to tell you that's low for the chief executive officer of a bank of Alsip's size, and extremely low for a C.E.O. with Masterson's performance record. Actually, with his track record, he would have been a bargain at nearly any salary McClain might have named."

I frowned. "Sounds like McClain was giving Masterson a very high incentive for favoring the buy-out."

The old man grinned at me. "Exactly what I thought, David. In any case, I had two or three phone conversations with Hastings to work out details. The last was in January. I was representing Walters and Midline; Hastings represented McClain." Abe shook his head. "Then, right in the midst of the negotiations, McClain had that horrible accident."

My ears perked up. "An accident, Abe? This is the first I've heard about it."

"Oh? I thought you knew, David. I don't have the details. I only know it was a freak skiing accident—happened at his private lodge upstate. Terribly shocking thing for the entire banking community."

I made a mental note to ask some more questions about that accident. Two violent deaths in the same family in the same year?

Abe was eyeing me quizzically. "So the bank was on the market for about two months?" I asked. "I take it the offer to sell was withdrawn, following McClain's death."

"Not formally, no, David. But all the bidding groups knew there was no point in pursuing the matter. McClain had said no one knew of it but Hastings and Masterson, and they weren't even shareholders. It was clear that the offer was dead.

"Two weeks ago, we got another call from Norman Hastings. He called Mr. Midline, who again involved me. The offer had changed a bit. Hastings apologized. With the big, downtown banks moving into acquisitions, the price had increased. The target formula was now the greater of twelve times average yearly earnings for the past three fiscal years, or two-and-a-half-times book value, such value to be determined as of September 30, this year. That's high, David."

I stopped the man right here and asked him to translate the gobbledegook into English. He was kind enough to try, and almost got me to understand. What it came down to was, the bank was showing, on its books, "Invested Capital," or "Net Worth," or whatever you call it, of about seventeen million dollars. So they were asking two-and-a-half that, or forty-two million and change, opposed to about thirty-five million the previous February.

"Of course, that's their target price, and they'll never get it, David. In fact, in normal times they'd be laughed out of town. But with the big boys getting into the game, they probably will get forty. The Midline bid will be competitive, but keep that to yourself.

"At her death, Miss McClain was a fifty percent owner. I expected the offer to sell would be withdrawn, at least temporarily. I called Hastings last night to offer my condolences, assuming the meeting we had scheduled for this morning would be canceled. But, not so. Hastings said to come ahead, he and Masterson were anxious to meet with me."

I wondered which of the four suspects was pushing the sale forward. If the motive for the killing was tied in with the bank, that would be good to know. With luck, today's meeting at the bank could lead to . . .

I was so deeply wrapped in thought, that I almost missed Alsip. By the time I saw the sign I had to look quick and cut sharply across two lanes to make the exit ramp. The two cops in the Fairlane, a quarter-mile back on the parkway, had no trouble following. I hoped they wouldn't think that was an evasive maneuver. On second thought, I hoped they would. If they thought I was that inept, it would be easier to elude them when I really needed to.

Nathanson flipped me a quick, ironic grin. "Too much murder and banking on the brain, Daw-Veed?" Since he'd returned to the Hebrew pronunciation, I assumed my tutorial in money and banking was over.

"Right," I answered, happy I hadn't frightened him with the sharp turn. "Promise me you won't tell Henry. He told me to be careful with you."

Nathanson smiled. "Oh, he means it, Daw-veed; but your secret is safe with me. Henry is among the righteous gentiles, like your Bishop Frank. Come the Messiah, they will be among those who will join the Chosen People in the world to come."

I grinned. "I don't know about Henry, but, come the Messiah, 'my' Bishop Frank will be extremely surprised. He's written whole books explaining that the Messiah has already come, and his name is Jesus."

"Machts nichts," chuckled the old man. "With such as Frank, God will be understanding."

XVIII

I began to get a better read on the importance of Abe Nathanson, when I saw the way key employees of the Alsip Bank reacted to his presence.

Theodore Masterson, President, immediately strode out of his office. Trim and athletic, he worked with shirt sleeves rolled up. A very happy grin lit his lean, handsome face.

"Abe!" he shouted. The two embraced.

Though Masterson was in his mid-forties, he could easily have passed for younger. His baritone voice had some music in it, and his cold, calculating blue eyes contrasted with a very engaging smile. When Abe teased him for not putting on his coat to greet two such important visitors, Masterson's laugh was explosive.

"You know Mr. David Goldman?" Nathanson nodded in my direction. Masterson looked at me with what could have been annoyance. Or maybe I'm just touchy when I'm missing sleep. But a moment later, his face broke into a smile and he took my hand in a firm grip.

"Come on back to my office, Abe. And, uh, Mr.

Goldman." He threw me another look—somewhere between friendly and suspicious. "Norm Hastings is with me right now. We're just reviewing where we stand." I realized he was trying to guess who the devil I *was* and where I fit into the picture. Only reasonable, I had to admit.

He escorted us past several mournful looking bankers enthroned at oversized desks, into a quieter, more secluded area with just two desks—mahogany, of course—each equipped with its own attractive secretary. Both secretaries were trying to show the boss how busy they were. Wasted effort. At the moment the boss had eyes only for Abe.

He led us into a spacious private office, where a well-dressed, middle-aged gentleman rose to greet us.

The office was what I would have imagined for a bank president, if I ever wasted time imagining useless things. Heavily panelled in dark, gloomy mahogany, it was four times the size of my office and about twice the size of the Bishop's. On three walls hung oil portraits of important looking tycoons. Having flunked Tycoons 101 in college, I didn't recognize any of them. The fourth wall held another oil—Masterson, along with wife and two young sons, all smiling graciously into the middle distance. Very attractive family, if the artist was to be believed.

Masterson performed introductions. Hastings was all friendliness and charm but he unobtrusively gave me the same guarded look that Masterson had earlier.

Dressed in dark blue serge, Hastings was ten years older than Masterson, a bit soft around the waist perhaps, but with the look of a person who could probably move when he had to. I guessed his sport was tennis. His blue eyes were warm and intelligent.

"Let's sit over here, gentlemen." Masterson gestured toward the table where Hastings had been seated when we came in. "Drink orders, gentlemen? A little hair of the dog—or boring coffee?"

A dream girl had appeared out of nowhere—a gorgeous redhead. That fact that I'd failed to notice her on the trek to the office warned me that my wits were addled from lack of sleep. I would have to pull myself together. She took the orders—coffee for me, tea for Abe, with refills on coffee for Norm and Ted—and departed as demurely as she had come.

"O.K., Abe," Masterson began, glancing at me. "What's going on here? I thought we were going to discuss our deal. Who's the mystery man? No offense, Mr. Goldman."

"Now, Ted," Abe chided complacently, sitting back in his chair, "you know I don't keep mysteries. Mr. Goldman happens to be a private investigator. I have hired him to assist me in evaluating the bank, given the unfortunate demise of Miss McClain. My condolences, gentlemen."

Masterson smiled softly. "Thank you, Abe. Yes, it was a tragedy." He seemed prepared to say more, but just then the lovely redhead returned with a tray of steaming cups. To my regret she didn't linger.

Masterson went on. "As to the sale, Abe, Bob Junior wants to proceed as expeditiously as possible. He called last night to tell me we're going forward. As planned, the board will get together up at the bank's ski lodge in Northern Springs this weekend. That's still on." Masterson flashed a friendly grin at Hastings, who was sipping coffee.

"Over yonder is our fisherman. Nice to have someone who can put food on the table for us."

Hastings raised a hand. "I'm being set up for a fall, gentlemen! Last year I caught my limit while everyone else struck out. Ted won't let me forget it. If we don't have fish to eat this weekend, I'll never hear the end of it!"

"Oh, we'll have fish, I'm sure of it," Masterson grinned. "I'm bringing along some frozen Dover sole, just to be on the safe side!"

As the chuckles subsided, Masterson picked up his coffee, blew some of the steam off it, and took a sip. Staring into the coffee, he spoke slowly, "I assume you have some questions about Barb's death. What kind of questions are you talking about?"

"Oh, I think I'll let my investigator handle that one, Ted." Nathanson glanced sharply at both men, then looked at me expectantly.

Masterson started to speak, when Hastings intervened.

"Excuse me, Ted, but I sense we're getting into the legal arena here." He turned those guileless, blue eyes on me. I was becoming the center of attention.

"You're a private investigator, Mr. Goldman?" asked Hastings. "Uh, may we assume that you are interested in the murder itself? I apologize, Abe," he said to his elder, "but the family had quite a few conversations with policemen yesterday. I think we're a bit fed up. I know I am." His voice had a bite to it, but he made it clear that the bite was not intended for the financial expert.

I glanced at Abe, who appeared to be playing a waiting game. Hastings' face was now angry.

"I can understand what you're saying, Mr. Hastings," I began, "and I apologize on behalf of my former colleagues. I was a policeman, once upon a time, but no more. As Mr. Nathanson said, I'm a private investigator. My sole assignment is to investigate Miss McClain's death, insofar as it might have some bearing on the proposed transaction."

The reactions of the two men differed. Hastings got my meaning immediately and was madder than ever. Masterson, I wasn't sure about. He was studying me closely, maybe the way a biologist studies an amoeba under a microscope.

I went on. "Some questions naturally arise when such a large transaction is marked by an unexplained, violent death. I know very little about banks, but plenty about murder. I believe that's why Mr. Nathanson has hired me to accompany him this morning."

Hastings narrowed his eyes. "The sale of this bank is a closely guarded secret, Mr. Goldman. I trust Mr. Nathanson warned you of that. Just for the record, I warn you that everything said here in this room is highly confidential. I apologize for having to say it, but some private investigators have been known to be less than ethical. With all respect." Hastings' voice held the hint of a sneer that I resented, but I resolved not to let personal considerations get in the way of the job. He continued, "What sort of questions did you have in mind, Mr. Goldman?"

I stared into my coffee as I considered the decision I had to make. Should I go with the stiletto or the sledgehammer? I decided, the hell with it, go with the sledge. I'll admit, the sneer in Hastings' voice may have influenced my decision.

"It has occurred to Mr. Nathanson and me that

the proposed sale of this bank could have been a factor in Miss McClain's death. I suppose it's also occurred to the police, which no doubt is the reason they've been talking to you." I smiled grimly at the two men.

If my purpose was to shake up the two suspects, I had succeeded. Hastings' charm deserted him, and Masterson lost his joviality. I'm sure that Abe's presence in the room was the only thing that kept me from getting tossed out on my ear.

"Well, well, well, Mr. Nathanson," Hastings said, his eyes homing in on the old man, "you've brought quite a nest of vipers into this fair bank." He turned to me and spoke through his teeth.

"What you're saying, *Mister* Gold, is that"—the look in his eyes told me the mispronunciation was deliberate—"is that one of the *family* murdered Barbara, right? And you include Ted and me in the family. I guess that's fair, isn't it? Why don't you quit beating around the bush here, *Mister* Gold?"

Abe lowered his chin into his cupped hand without taking his eyes off the lawyer. His lips were curled in a slight smile, but his eyes were cold.

I put my cup down. "It's 'Gold-*man*,' Mr. Hastings." I matched his tone. "But O.K., I'll come to the point. Yes, the family could be involved. Obviously. Also, it's more than a possibility that the business deal could have something to do with the murder. I'm just touching all the bases.

"As far as your being bothered is concerned, whoever did this to Miss McClain doesn't deserve any sympathy. And whoever *didn't* do it shouldn't object to answering a few questions."

Hastings was just opening his mouth to retort when Masterson raised a hand and cut him off. The bank president seemed anxious to pour some oil on the waters.

"Point well taken, Dave. May I call you Dave? Thanks." He smiled at me to prove how grateful he was. "Look, Norm," he said earnestly, turning to the lawyer, "this guy makes sense, whatever you and I may think about it. I know you're looking after the family's best interests—mine as well—but you're a lawyer, and sometimes lawyers are too cautious.

"Let's hear him out, and then we'll chat with Abe. This can all be resolved. Look, Norm, the more questions we answer, the sooner we'll be past this."

"I can't let you do that, Ted," Hastings responded angrily. "I'd be derelict in my duties if I did." Hastings turned back to me, his eyes flashing.

"No, *Mister* Gold . . . stein, or whatever your name is. I'm sorry, but I'm not going to permit it. If you've got questions, go ask them somewhere else, and don't come bothering the family again."

Turning to Abe, Hastings tried to recover some of his lost charm. "Mr. Nathanson, I'm sorry, but I think you've permitted this young fellow to use you. Nothing against you, but next time you come, leave the shyster gumshoe at home, O.K.?"

He stood up and spoke to Masterson. "Come on, Ted. We can finish our discussion in the board room. I have no objection to *Abe* joining us, but I cannot permit you to say anything further in the presence of this—outsider."

Masterson, torn between the lawyer and the demands of courtesy, simply glared at me. I guess I didn't look helpful, because he quickly turned away and looked up at Hastings. "Come on, Norm," he gestured, "sit down. We can work this out."

Abe took him out of his misery. Wearing a mirthless smile, he got slowly to his feet.

"I'm sorry you feel that way about my companion, sir," he piped in that flutey falsetto, pinning Hastings with his eyes. "You may be certain I'll not trouble you again. Ever." He turned on his heel and left, ignoring Masterson's outstretched hand.

Hastings muttered something which Masterson ignored. He was already in pursuit of Abe.

I grinned at Hastings as I got up. "Sorry about that, Mr. Hastings. You know how touchy *potential investors* can be. I'll see you again, and I'll have plenty of questions, you can make book on it. For now, I'm off. You can get back to mourning Miss McClain." I hoped the lawyer felt as foolish as he looked at that moment.

I followed Masterson and Nathanson, staying a deliberate twenty paces behind. Out on the sidewalk, Masterson put his arm around the old man's shoulders. Nathanson seemed to accept the gesture. They walked that way to the Seville, where they embraced again. Opening the car door for Abe, I flashed Ted a smile of good will, which he ruefully returned. I helped Abe in, and fastened his seat belt in a way I truly hoped would impress Henry favorably. As I shook hands with Masterson, I decided I liked the way he met my eyes. I wondered what the two suspects would have to say to each other after we left.

"Sorry about that, Abe," I told him as I buckled myself in. "I guess I should've been more subtle. I hope I haven't cost you a potential client. Or screwed up your purchase."

"No regrets, Daw-veed." Hebrew pronunciation. "I'm well rid of that—" He stopped for a moment, searching for a proper descriptive. Apparently, none occurred to him; he let the sentence hang unfinished.

"I've long grown accustomed to anti-Semitism, David," he continued with equanimity, as we rolled along the beautiful, tree-lined streets of Alsip. "You know, I left my right arm at Anzio. I take no special credit for that. It was unfortunate, but it was in the best of causes, and my life, both before and since, has been rich and rewarding.

"But it's sad, after an entire World War has been fought—and, we thought, won—to have to face this kind of bigotry."

Abe shook his head. "Whenever it happens, the men are just like that—goniff." He'd finally found the right word for Hastings. "Charming, friendly people, on the surface. But deep in the darkness of their soul is rottenness and evil. That man clings to his darkness, David. Even now, Ted has a good opinion of him. At most, he thinks Hastings is a little misguided.

"But *Hashem,* the Mighty One, is not fooled, and justice will prevail. Your namesake said it best, David: 'Though I hide in darkness and the night, for You, the darkness shall not be dark; and night shall be as day.' I will never speak to that man again. Or mention his name."

As calmly as Nathanson said those last few words, I could tell he meant every syllable. For Abe Nathanson, Mr. Norman Hastings was now nonexistent.

"I assume," I said, "that Walters and Midline will not be bidding for the Alsip Traders Bank."

"To the extent that I have anything to say about

it, David, absolutely not. Unless Mr. Masterson replaces that goy in handling it." He sighed, shook his head, and put the matter behind him. "And now, David"—American pronunciation—"let us complete your education in banking and finance." He grinned. "After all, you're entitled to your one dollar's worth!"

The conversation for the rest of the drive back to East Seventy-ninth Street consisted of a learned discourse on modern banking. We rolled up to the entrance of his apartment house and Henry was there to open the door. He took note of Abe's seat belt.

Henry and I exchanged wary smiles. I felt I was returning Abe Nathanson to very safe hands.

XIX

The Bishop had delayed lunch for me—though for him it was the first meal of the day. He doesn't eat breakfast—ever. I do—always. Except days like this, when time doesn't permit. Oddly, my sleepiness had vanished. Maybe it was sheer adrenaline, but, whatever it was, I felt full of energy.

Ernie had whipped up her version of a Denver omelet—which was great, especially after a rocky night. While we ate, I told the Bishop about my findings at the Alsip bank. I was surprised at his lack of curiosity about the behavior of the two suspects.

"Hastings is a bigot," I said. "I found him—"

"If you please, David. I am more interested in what you may have learned from Abe about the sale."

For the remainder of lunch, we talked about banking, especially the implications of the sale of a bank. We explored the legal and financial implications—what was the impact on a bank's investors? I was a little lost, both in my answers to his questions, and in why he was asking them in the first place.

"David," he explained, with exaggerated patience, "I called Mr. Nathanson to learn more about the implications of bank ownership. Of course, I had no idea the call would lead to direct contact with the suspects. Now we have two invaluable pieces in the puzzle we're trying to solve—a direct feel for those two men, and knowledge that negotiations to sell the bank are still underway.

"Initially, I assumed that Miss McClain's ownership of the bank may have contributed to her death. That assumption now looks even more promising. But in order to explore its implications, we need to know more about the entailments thereof, and the implications of transfer of such ownership. That was my original purpose in putting you together with Mr. Nathanson—to become an expert in banking and then instruct me. Whereas, your inadequate answers to my questions reveal that you weren't paying close attention."

I was outraged. "Come on! I don't know anything about all this stuff! You're like a teacher who expects all his students to learn equitable calculus on the first day of class!"

"There is no such thing as 'equitable calculus,' David," he muttered disgustedly.

"See?" I threw up my hands. "Have I made my point?" He knew I had him.

"Why I put up with you, David . . ." He set his coffee down and checked his watch. "No matter. If further investigation warrants, we can always phone Abe again. It's nearly one o'clock, and we have a heavy backlog of correspondence. My office, please, David."

I could have pointed out that I was falling further and further behind on my daily complement of sleep.

I might also have noted that *his* slacking created the backlog in the first place. But I held my peace. For some weird reason I now felt full of vim, vigor and vitality.

Soon I was seated on the other side of his desk, scribbling the unique brand of shorthand I'd learned twelve years ago at Queens Community College.

By 1:40 I'd taken sixteen letters and seven memos. While I typed them up, the boss attended to his stack of personnel files. By 2:45, I had all twenty-three documents and sixteen envelopes typed, on his desk, and ready for signing. The imagination boggles at how much I could accomplish with a decent night's sleep.

After placing the pages of letters, envelopes and memos in his in-box, I interrupted the good man's concentration with an "Ahem!"

He looked up over the personnel file he was studying. "Did you want something, David?"

"Yes, if I can bother you for just a sec. Any further thoughts about the trip to Alsip?"

"Not at the moment, David." He was irritated. "We've accomplished a great deal on the McClain matter in a remarkably short time. Now, if you don't mind, I have work to do. We can discuss it further at dinner."

I studied him, not without concern. Was he actually slipping into his prior funk? After all this excitement? Was it possible he wanted to put me off till dinnertime, just when I was hot to trot?

Nope, this was definitely not funk. When he goes into a funk, he doesn't work, he reads. That's absolute. This was something else. This was a snit.

Perhaps the Bishop was feeling belatedly hurt by my teasing the previous night ("Who's running this case, anyway?"). As I've suggested, he does have certain traits more characteristic of a little kid than a full-grown ecclesiastical bigwig.

So here was my boss in a snit, possibly with hurt feelings, leaving me with no program. I'd learned in the past, my guru required special handling when in one of his snits. I decided to improvise.

"Well," I sighed. "If you won't talk about the case, at least you could tell me the meaning of 'cotquean.' " (This was a word that Willie has used to describe Bob McClain.)

"Look it up, David," he muttered. "The dictionary is there to be used, not merely admired."

This wasn't the first time I'd gotten such a reply from him. My vocabulary has probably doubled in the past six years, thanks to living with a genius. At his request, I keep running to that big fat dictionary. He sends me to it whenever he wants to be left alone.

Webster's Unabridged, Second Edition, sits on a low stand in his office, on a pivot, suitable for wheelchair viewing, between the computer and the antique chess board. I looked the damn word up, though it took a while, since I wasn't sure of the spelling.

Then I returned to my chair on the right of his desk, eager for an opportunity to work my new knowledge into the nonconversation.

"It's funny, you know, Bishop," I opened. No response from Buddha. But I went on.

"I sometimes feel like doing something. My shortcoming. And I feel that urge right now. Don't you have any suggestions for how I could spend the rest of the afternoon, in some way that might benefit our monkish friend? Or the program *we've* undertaken?"

"No," he muttered, making notes on a pad as he studied the file on some priest.

"Oh, it's *that* way, is it? You're doing your thing, so, naturally, our work for Father William comes to a grinding halt. Interesting philosophy, that." Nothing from him.

"Well, Your Excellency, I've got news for you. Whatever you may think, the police are *not* taking the day off. You may *think* they're taking it easy, but you're mistaken. Three will get you ten they're up there at Seventy-sixth right now, analyzing, detecting, fingerprinting—"

"David, you're being ridiculous," he said calmly, still not looking up.

"Not at all. And down at Headquarters they're interviewing the two suspects we haven't met yet. There's Bob McClain, the cotquean. And then, there's his wife, who could also be called a 'cotquean,' if you want to use Webster's second definition. Furthermore—"

"David, David, David!" He pushed the personnel folder away from him, flipped his glasses on top of it and looked up at me. "Your impetuosity is based solely on your anxiety to atone for the automobile fiasco of yesterday. You refuse to heed my repeated admonition not to blame yourself." He looked at me, perhaps for some reaction. I didn't honor him with one.

"Very well," he sighed. "There's something you can do which might exorcise your demon. In fact, it might actually do some good." I listened with anticipation, wondering which of the four suspects he would be interested in. Serve me right if he told me to round up all four immediately for a roundtable discussion. An impossible task like that would teach me to open my big yap. But he surprised me again.

"If you absolutely need something to do, go up to Seventy-sixth Street, get into that woman's apartment by whatever means—"

"Now that *might* be a good idea, but it wouldn't take 'whatever means,' it would take a bulldozer. Or a howitzer. Look, Bishop. Either the police are still there working, or the door will be sealed. Which is too bad, because I still have the key Willie gave me. There's no way I—"

"I should have been more precise," Regan interrupted. "Not Miss *McClain's* apartment. Miss *Shields's.*"

I stared.

"I suggest," he continued, "that you recover that crumpled note Miss Shields wrote Miss McClain when she was preparing to leave the key under her door. If it contains Miss Shields's telephone number in Hawaii, my follow-up suggestion is that you call her there. She will doubtless want to return when she learns that her friend has died. If you apply your customary courtesy, she may even do you a favor. Of course, you needn't request that till later.

"I suggest you get her here, in your office, in as receptive a frame of mind as possible." He peered at me over the file. "Well? You asked for a suggestion. Now I have given you, not one, but two."

I frowned. "What favor could she do me?"

"We'll discuss that when you get her here."

"Are you suggesting that I break and enter someone's private dwelling?"

"Oh, pardon!" His eyebrows rose so high, his beanie jiggled. "I'm sorry to suggest something so repugnant to your ethical sensibilities." Sighing, the Bishop picked up his glasses.

"I'm sorry, David, nothing else occurs to me. And since your moral code won't permit you to take the action I suggest, you may have to spend the rest of the day updating the Archdiocesan personnel files. This is a project, you may recall, I have been calling to your attention for a month. In view of your apparently boundless energy, now might be an appropriate time to get started."

"Sarcasm doesn't become you at all," I mumbled. But as I headed back to my office, the updating project he mentioned made a shudder run down my spine.

So I directed my attention to a break-in, though without a lot of enthusiasm.

As the Bishop knows, though he'd deny it, a cabinet in my office has a number of interesting little gadgets, not all of which are strictly legal. From a deep bottom drawer I pulled out a big set of keys and burglar's tools.

It would have been helpful to know the kind of lock I'd be working on. I wanted to take as few tools as possible. But I didn't know, so had to make do. I made a few educated guesses, based on the ages of the buildings in that neighborhood and the key of Barb's I still had. I wound up picking out four Tinkers, three Hotchkisses and a couple of all-purpose jimmies. These I slipped, along with the key to Barb's apartment, into my pocket.

Now only one important item needed to be handled. During the trip to Alsip, the Fairlane on my tail had never wandered more than five hundred yards away. This time, I didn't want company.

So I placed a phone call to a sometimes helpful

friend, a cabby named Jimmy, and gave him certain instructions. As I left, I stopped by the kitchen to tell Ernie I'd be back for dinner—probably.

Strolling east to Tenth Avenue, I tried to see whether I was being followed by the same two who'd followed me earlier. I couldn't spot anyone. Not that I was concerned. With Jimmy's help I should be able to shake them.

I turned right on Tenth and walked south at a casual pace, staying on the west side of the Avenue. As I approached Thirtieth, a glance at my watch told me it was time.

Shifting abruptly from a saunter to a mad dash, I tore across Tenth, dodging cars, and continued east on Thirtieth, cutting across it to the downtown side as I ran.

I kept looking over my shoulder. I saw a couple of startled expressions, but not what I was expecting—another pair of pedestrians trailing rapidly in the same direction. That was disappointing. When you've arranged something this elaborate, you feel sort of foolish if it's all wasted energy.

I was halfway to Ninth, beginning to feel both winded and pretty damn silly, when here came the Fairlane behind me. It gave me a warm feeling to realize the police hadn't lost interest.

Turning right ninety degrees into an alley, I dodged garbage cans and sidled past a parked truck blocking the roadway. Glancing back, I saw the Fairlane slew around the corner into the alley, sending a couple of garbage cans flying, then screech to a halt, horn blaring, nose to nose with the parked truck.

I burst out of the alley onto the sidewalk at Twenty-ninth. There at the curb, as expected, was

Jimmy's taxi. Jimmy's cigar, as usual, was between his teeth. I jumped into the back seat. He was rolling before I had the door closed.

"Turn a few corners," I panted. "I'll give you directions when I can breathe again." Pivoting around, I watched the street behind us while Jimmy obeyed orders.

After one right and two lefts, I was satisfied that we had shaken them. I swung around. "Corner of Amsterdam and Seventy-seventh, James."

"If you're thinkin' of tryin' out fer the Olympics, Davey," Jimmy advised, around the cigar, "I gotta warn ya, they've quit awarding points fer loudness of wheezin'."

"I'll have you know," I answered loftily, "I wasn't even breathing hard until I got within range of that stogie of yours. You know, Jimmy, your cigars actually smell worse than your exhaust fumes!"

Of course, he wasn't about to let me get away with that, so we traded insults for the next forty blocks. When he made the turn from Broadway onto Seventy-sixth, I was ready to hit the floor at the first sight of a policeman. But the scene was completely peaceful. I gave 501 a long look as we passed it, keeping it in view through the rear window as Jimmy turned left on Amsterdam. Nothing unusual there.

When I got out at Seventy-seventh, I slipped him the agreed-upon sawbuck. Jimmy said, "You didn't order it, and you don't have to pay, but I thought the truck in that alley might help. The guy's a buddy of mine. I told him it might be worth a finiff. But it's up to you. Like I say, you didn't order it."

"I like initiative, Jimmy," I said, peeling off a

five and adding that to the ten. "Thanks for the thoughtfulness."

"Any time, Davey," he grinned. "Watch that wheezin.' I hear it can indicate a loss of virility."

"Beat it!" I snarled.

I took ten minutes to cover the one short block from Seventy-seventh to Seventy-sixth, just to be sure no cops were around. I spent another two minutes scanning the front entrance of 501 from across the street. Observing nothing suspicious, I walked quickly across Seventy-sixth and up the eight steps to the front entrance of 501.

XX

The key to 3C was already in my hand. Fuller had said it worked the outside door as well as the door to the apartment. Inserting and turning it in one motion, the way they teach you in detective school, I closed the door behind me without stopping to look around. Two flights later, I was on the third floor.

My nose was able to form a fair impression of the cooking that went on around there—heavily Italian and eastern European, with some preference for garlic. I decided that neither Ernie nor the Bishop would approve of the cuisine—their loss.

The building was old, but well maintained.

I wouldn't have been surprised to find someone from the N.Y.P.D. on the third floor, keeping an eye on things. But the hall was deserted. It was a dark hallway, fifty feet long, with four doors: 3A through 3D.

As expected, 3C had a police seal and a plug in the lock. A small sign read "Closed by Order of N.Y.P.D.," below which, in larger letters, were the words "NO TRESPASSING." I put my ear to the door; not a sound. Either the scientists had all they needed, or the Homicide boys were on to other assignments. I moved quickly. Twenty feet away was 3B. I tapped loudly on the door.

No response.

I examined the lock. As I'd feared, it was a Hotchkiss. In case you haven't picked many locks, let me tell you, Hotchkisses are the worst. I will also tell you, the worst job you can get is the one I had in front of me—illegal entry through a tough lock, with no partner to watch your back.

I set to work. That Hotchkiss took me exactly two minutes and twenty-eight seconds, but it seemed like two hours and twenty-eight minutes. It finally turned, with a satisfying click, and I started breathing again. I moved across the sill like a rabbit, pushed the door shut behind me and took a deeper breath. The door had a safety bolt, which I immediately shot. This was one time I didn't want to be disturbed.

It was definitely a feminine-type set-up. Tastefully feminine. Dr. Sally has shown me a lot about both taste and femininity over the past eight years, and I felt sure that she would have approved. But I spent no time admiring it. All I wanted was a phone number to somewhere in Hawaii.

The most likely spot for a crumpled piece of paper was a wastebasket. After going through five of those, I had one piece of good news and one bad. The bad news: no note in any of them. The good: the maid hadn't been there: still plenty of trash.

The note was in the next place I looked, the plastic garbage container under the sink in the kitchen. Seven minutes, total. A personal best. Smoothing out the note on the kitchen countertop, I read it, first hastily, then more slowly.

Written in a backhand, flowing script, was the following:

> Barbie: Where were you all day, you rat? I've been calling & knocking on your door & you're never home. Anyhow. I'm off at an ungodly hour tomorrow morning & will be thinking about you in the sun of Honolulu. Wish you were coming. I'll do a little *research* on the Hawaiian boys, so you can save time when *you* go over. Thanks for watering my babies while I'm gone—every other day will be fine. See you Sept. 3. Love Ann. P.S. Enclosing your key.

No phone number.

To say I was frustrated would be a huge understatement. I turned the paper over, but the back side was blank. I scratched my head. This wasn't the first time my genius boss had miscalculated, but it was still hard to take.

"If I were a phone number, where would I hide?" I asked myself, using an old trick my mother taught me.

I decided I'd hide somewhere in the garbage. So I attacked that plastic container like a champ. If you're interested, coffee grounds aren't so bad. Soggy corn flakes are worse. And the worst—I'll spare you the worst.

But my guess was right. On a torn envelope, the number "808/251-5000" was scribbled in backhand, flowing script, under the words: "Barb: Hawaii ph. #." I smoothed the envelope, found a clean spot to give it a kiss. Folding the envelope and the note twice, I slipped them with great satisfaction into my card case.

The note's recipient was not going to be watering anyone's plants. I found a pitcher in the kitchen and did the honors. Having taken an interest in plants of various types, myself, over the years, I was able to make an informed judgment about the keeper of the eighteen plants scattered around the rooms of the apartment: she took care.

While checking the plants in the bedroom, I looked closely at several photographs lying on the dresser. One, in particular, caught my attention. It showed two pretty girls, a blonde and a brunette, in their twenties or early thirties, somewhere on a beach. Both wore bikinis. The picture would have caught *my* eye any time, but it did so particularly in the current circumstance. The brunette was, without question, the same woman who had been with Fuller at Carnegie Hall two months before.

Picking up the photo, I looked at the back. In a different script from that on the note and the envelope were the words, "6/28. Ann: Just a couple of bathing beauties! Love, Barb."

This confirmed my speculation about Barbara McClain being the brunette I'd seen. Knowing I'd been right, needless to say, brought me no particular joy.

Turning the photo over, I paid close attention to both faces. It was hard to believe that someone as comely as that brunette could have been brutally murdered. I put the photo in my card case next to the note and envelope.

Then I made one more pass through the apartment —first, to tidy up, and second, to see if there was anything else I should look at.

There wasn't.

Out on the sidewalk again, no one seemed to

take an interest in my presence. I was strongly tempted to stroll back to Thirty-seventh. The clouds had moved on to bother someone somewhere else, and the sun was shining.

I decided to favor a cab. I needed to get in touch with Ann Shields, and I thought it just possible, as I considered the time difference between Honolulu and New York, that she could be back in town by the following day. But first I had to get her on the phone and give her the bad news.

That was the rub. I didn't relish informing the writer of that note what had happened to her friend.

In the cab I struggled to think of some way to break the news. A thought suddenly hit me. How about finding a patsy to do the dirty work for me? And I thought I knew just the one.

"Pull over at the next phone booth you see," I told the cabby, who was breaking all speed records getting to Thirty-seventh.

"Make up your mind, Mac," he commented with typical New York friendliness. We squealed to a stop next to a booth at Broadway and Sixty-eighth. I rotated my head, checking for whiplash.

Having dialed the number of St. Bede's parish just the night before, I didn't need to look it up. My main concern was, would Fuller be there? That issue was settled definitively when I heard his voice on the phone: "St. Bede's."

Quickly identifying myself, I outlined what I wanted him to do. He was none too happy. I couldn't blame him. He first said he might have to do some schedule adjusting, but finally decided he could work it out. He gave me directions and said to come ahead.

I needed to make one more phone call. For that

one, I had to look the number up in my notebook. Mary Cowan is my travel agent, and a good one. She's also a friend and dancing partner, when that's what I need. Fortunately, she was in.

Mary told me what I needed to know, then put me on hold while she verified a couple of things with the airline. The reservation she made came with one slight obligation.

"You owe me dinner at Sarto's for this," she warned. "I'm not getting a penny of commission!"

"Followed by a bit of boogie-ing afterwards?"

"I could be persuaded."

Phone calls completed, I jumped back in the cab. "Your lucky day, pal," I told the friendly cabby. "Forget Thirty-seventh. Get me up to 108th and Crotona in the Bronx. And take this thing out of low, willya?"

Naturally he grumped. He was a cabby after all. But he made good time.

He wasn't particularly elated at the five-buck tip but didn't throw it back at me, either.

XXI

St. Bede's parish turned out to be a set of ancient but well-constructed red brick buildings in a decaying neighborhood. The few trees remaining on the street were still fighting the good fight but total defeat seemed imminent. Next to the church building, there was a three-story house, with a sign saying "Rectory" over the front door.

The chimes had barely stopped when the door opened. Fuller appeared in full clerical attire—long black robe, Roman collar. I realized I had never seen him in the full gown of his order, nor on home turf. My mind flashed back to our golf game—then, inexplicably, to the bon vivant in the Sulka tie I'd seen with the beautiful brunette. The contrast with the monkish figure before me was striking.

"Come in, Dave," he said, shaking my hand. "It's a quiet afternoon, so we should be able to make the call. When I'm on parlor duty, I often do my outside reading for the week. Not much happens at St. Bede's."

He led me into a tiny office adjacent to the parlor. Sitting behind the desk, he left me the only other chair in the room. "I think I can handle breaking the news—after all, it's supposedly my line of work." He smiled wanly. "You want me to introduce you?"

"I might need more than an introduction. We've got to sell her on the idea of coming back here right away. She needs to talk with me before she says anything to the police."

He frowned. "I'll do what I can, Dave." From the furrow in his brow, Willie obviously had a lot to worry about in this upcoming conversation. I strove to reassure him.

"Remember," I said, "at the moment, Ann has every reason to trust you. Once she gets back, your reputation may be in jeopardy, but—" I stopped. "Well, let me ask you, Willie. Does she have any reason not to like you?"

He looked uncomfortable. "No, she doesn't. I'm just imagining what she's going to be thinking later. Either that I'm a murderer, or, at best, that I'm a sneaky, lying—" He looked at me and asked for the first time, "What do you think about all this, Dave?"

"What difference does it make, Willie? I know damn well you're not a murderer. I'm determined to clear this thing up, and clear you, too. Let's leave it at that."

But he wouldn't. "I just know you must be contemptuous of what I've done."

"No, no," I said, "but I do have a question."

"Oh?" he said, warily. "What is it?"

"I'm just curious how you manage it. The double life, I mean. Oh, I'm not talking about changing from your priestly duds to a shirt and tie in a train station men's room, or wherever." Fuller blushed, suggesting I'd guessed right. "I'm talking about how you deal with your own conscience. How can you face your parishioners, give them personal advice, when you're spending a good part of your time, well, cheating on them? Doesn't that get to you?" I shifted in the chair and looked away. "I'm sorry. Maybe that's too personal."

"No," he said, frowning. "It's not too personal. Besides, I invited it. Actually, I've puzzled over the same thing. How can I go on with my life? As a priest.

"I guess I really don't have any faith, any more. I guess it's just eroded, over the years. I don't believe in God, Jesus, the Church, any of it. I guess it was reading Unamuno that started me down this road. Are you familiar with his—?" He'djust lost me, and he knew it. He laughed. "I guess you're not. Anyway, suffice it to say, I don't believe in very much. Except the Human Spirit. I guess I'm really a Unitarian at heart."

This was a new twist: a priest without faith. Kind of a contradiction in terms. I wondered if he could really mean what he was saying.

"So, in my sermons and counselling, I try to stay away from anything that might disturb people's faith. I'll bet I haven't preached about the resurrection of Jesus in five years or more. Instead, I talk about human concerns." He looked at me to see if I understood. I sort of did, so I sort of nodded.

"As for my private life, I consider it my own business." He smiled. "Anyway, I try to keep it quiet, but it's my life." He reddened. "Well, that's been my attitude up to now. With what's happened, 1 don't know, I've been thinking a lot about that. I wonder if God, maybe, not only exists but is trying to tell me something."

"What about your mother?" I asked, thinking of my own. "What does Marguerite think about all this?"

He frowned, squinting at nothing. "Marguerite doesn't really have any idea what's going on. At least I don't think so. She's kind of a hard lady to read." Another thought struck him. "I'll tell you something funny, Dave. What Jack and I were doing was really pretty innocent. All I ever got was some feminine company. Just being with women—attractive women—and having them like me, was exciting enough. Believe it or not, there never was any real sex in it. Of course," he added with a shrug and a grin, "that would probably have come in time."

We sat looking at each other for a moment till I broke the silence. "Let's call the lady."

He nodded grimly and turned the phone around to face me. I punched out the number and in a mere ten seconds was informed that I'd reached "The Sheraton Royal Hawaiian!" The name rang a bell somewhere in the back of my mind. I knew someone there, but who? I asked for Ann Shields, still trying to remember.

In a moment, I heard a warm, friendly, female voice—this one throaty and rather sexy—telling me "Aloha!" Sounded like Ann Shields was having a good time.

I mouthed, "It's Ann," and handed the phone to Fuller.

Willie handled it pretty well, a lot better than I would have predicted. It was tough duty—far tougher than his regular afternoon "parlor duty." I empathized as he talked.

"Ann, it's Charles," he began. "Yes, I'm still in New York. Oh, Ann, I really wish I could, but . . .

No, I . . . Yes, she sure would!" He grimaced and shook his head. "Ann—listen, I've got some bad news. I'm afraid you'd better sit down."

A brief pause, while something was said on the other end. "No, no, Ann. Look, Ann, it's Barb. I'm afraid she's—" A couple of tears were slipping down the priest's cheeks. He rubbed at them with the back of his hand; but he kept his voice going, low and steady.

"It's terrible, Ann, but someone got into her room Sunday night and—murdered her . . . With a knife . . . They don't know, Ann, they're looking for him. They just don't know."

A longer silence on our end. As Fuller listened, he first reddened, then paled. He licked his lips and said, "No, Ann, I haven't spoken with the police. A friend of mine is with me, Dave Goldman, and he can—'Goldman.' Ann, I don't think you know him. He can tell you more about it than I can. I'm going to put him on, Ann. I love y—" With that last, his voice finally got away from him. He tossed me the receiver, swivelled the chair and showed me his back.

"Miss Shields?" I heard sobs. She wasn't doing well. Hoping she was at least able to listen, I went on, "As Charles told you, my name is David Goldman, and I'm a former policeman, now a licensed private detective."

She mumbled something in a strangled voice.

"I have decided to take an interest in the case, Miss Shields, and I would very much like to meet with you. If you should decide you want to come back immediately, I'd be happy to meet your flight in the morning. I could take you directly to my office, then home from there. But that's up to you."

She found her voice at last, but it was still unsteady. "I've *got* to come, if I can get on a flight."

"I can help you there. Got a pencil?" I proceeded to give her the flight information Mary Cowan had given me.

"The reservation is in your name. Just report to the ticket counter by two o'clock, give them your return ticket, and they'll exchange it for today's flight. Departure is 3:00 P.M." I glanced at my watch. "You have three hours to get yourself together and out to the airport. I'll meet the flight at Kennedy tomorrow morning."

"But, you don't have to do that." She stopped. When I heard her voice again, it sounded wary. "You say you're a policeman?"

"*Former* policeman. I'm mainly a friend of Charles and, I hope, of yours. Look, Miss Shields, I can't tell you how sorry I am that you have to get hit with this all at once. Let me say this: I'll be there at Kennedy. You don't have to decide now. But I'll meet the flight. If you can't make it, don't worry. But if you do want to talk to me for any reason, you can call." I gave her my number. "I'll be at the airport, regardless."

"Thank you. It's very kind of you. But—how will I know you?"

"Don't worry." I visualized the blonde in the photo. "I'll know *you.* Remember the name: David Goldman. I'm—terribly, terribly sorry . . . Now, here's Charles to say good-bye." I handed Fuller the phone, wiped the sweat off my brow, and went out into the parlor for awhile, to give Willie a chance to wrap things up. When I came back, he was off the phone.

"I won't thank you for the help, Willie, because

it was for your own sake. But, for what it's worth, speaking as a layman, I thought you handled that very well."

"Thanks for that, Dave." He looked me in the eye. "I've learned one thing. I never should have let myself get into this—double life. I'll never be able to see Ann again. That makes me feel awful."

"Appreciate your frankness, Willie. As I said, I'm all for you, and I'm going to do my best to get you out unscathed. But I've got to warn you, it's a long shot. You'd better get ready for contingencies, because I don't know if I can pull it off."

He nodded.

"Now, I've got to go, Willie. I'll be in touch. Can you call me a cab?"

I didn't tell Willie I had another call to make to Hawaii. I'd finally remembered who I knew at the Royal Hawaiian. But the call could wait till I got back home.

A cab pulled up in less than ten minutes. As it turned out, the cabby had something I wanted: Tuesday's first edition of the Manhattan *Dispatch*. He was delighted to sell it to me for thirty-five cents.

It was a wasted thirty-five cents. The story added nothing to my knowledge of the case. That was both disappointing and surprising, since crime is the life and soul of the *Dispatch*.

The story was six paragraphs on page seven, unaccompanied by photos. Nor did it carry Rozanski's byline. In fact, I think it was written by one of Chet's cubs. It covered the late Miss McClain's job—teaching seventh graders at a private, non-denominational school on Riverside Drive. A couple of quotes from the youngsters indicated she'd been well-liked.

Arriving back at the mansion, just before six, I went straight to my office and called the Royal Hawaiian again. If Ann Shields was to be our ace in the hole, we ought to be certain she was really in the clear on the murder. It wasn't pleasant to imagine that the pretty blonde in the bikini might have jammed a knife into the brunette, but stranger things have happened, some of them in my own experience.

When I got the switchboard at the hotel, I asked to speak to Jacky Wu, the hotel security guard I'd met three years previously at a law enforcement convention in Las Vegas. I just hoped he was still the house dick at the "Pink Lady," as he termed the Royal Hawaiian. He was.

"Jacky, m'boy! How's things in paradise?"

"Aw, it's hell, man. It's awful. You know, yesterday, it actually *rained?* Awful! So, what's up, Davey?"

"You can do me a big favor, friend, if I could pry your mind off the weather. You've got a young lady staying there. Ann Shields, from New York, checked in yesterday. For a funny reason, I need to know her exact check-in time. Could you get that for me?"

"Trust me enough to tell me why you want to know, Davey?"

"Just get me the info, buddy, and I'll tell you everything."

"Gimme a min, friend." It was closer to ten "min" before Wu returned, but the results justified the wait.

"Got it, Dave. Incidentally, for what it's worth, the lady just now checked out. That's why it took me so long, she was there at the counter. Possibly a good looker, but hard to say, because she was standing there bawling. Not good for our image, man—just as well she's leaving. She got problems, Davey?"

"Yeah. How big they are I'll tell you after you tell me her check-in time."

"O.K. Here it is." I jotted times in my notebook as Jacky talked. "Check-in yesterday, 12:57 P.M. Scheduled for seven nights' stay, but checked out early, like I said, just now. Lost seventy-five bucks in early departure penalty. Say—you don't think that's why she was crying? Because, if it was, she don't belong on the islands, my friend. Hell, daily cab fare'll run you more than that."

"Naw, Jack, she's got bigger troubles than seventy-five bucks. Her best friend was just iced with a kitchen knife. I was the lucky lad who got to give her the bad news. But I wanted to make sure she wasn't the one who did the icing."

"You've got a nasty mind, Davey. Did my information help you decide?"

I referred to my notes. "Settled it in her favor, I think. The killer phoned the police at 11:33, yesterday morning, our time. That's what? 5:33 A.M., your time, Jacky. We know she was at your hotel at 12:57 P.M. No way she could have been anywhere but up in the sky at 5:33 A.M. Am I right?"

Wu took a minute to think. "Sure you are. That's six and a half hours," he said. "Unless she caught an earlier flight and called from here." He thought some more. "Nope. That 11:50 A.M. flight from New York is the first arrival of the day from the mainland. She couldn't have done it, man. No way. She's clear."

"So, you've settled my problem, Jacky. Let me

know, any time I can return the favor. In fact, if you need me to come over to the islands any time . . ."

"Forget that action," he interrupted. "We've got plenty of troubles already, my man, without adding you to 'em."

"Thanks a whole bunch, Jacky. Just see if I ever ask you for any more favors!"

Wednesday. August 24

XXII

Wednesday morning, sitting at the kitchen table, sipping coffee, I studied the story of the murder as presented by The New York *Times*.

It was fairly well covered, with six paragraphs on page eight of Section One. But no photo of the deceased, which was a little arrogant, and no identikit picture of Fuller. "Charles Ryder" wasn't mentioned by name. The only reference to him was in the coy, *Times* style: "A friend of Miss McClain is being sought for questioning. Police are withholding his name until more is known."

A point I found of interest, in view of my trip to Alsip the day before, was what the article had to say about the bank and its ownership. The relevant paragraph read:

> Miss McClain, with her brother, Robert, Jr., was co-owner of Alsip Traders Bank, Alsip, N.Y. This three hundred million dollar (total deposits) institution was founded by the late Robert McClain, Sr., father of the deceased, in 1960. An executive of the

> bank, who spoke on condition he not be identified by name, dismissed the possibility of any connection between the murder of Miss McClain and the death of her father earlier this year.
>
> "Barbara was heartsick about her dad," the anonymous official said, "but she had got over it. Anyway, Barbara was murdered, she didn't commit suicide."

The *Dispatch* was sure to carry a longer and more sensational story than the one in the *Times,* but it wasn't available yet, being an evening paper. Days when there might be something worth reading, I usually wander over to the newsstand on Tenth in the late afternoon.

I planned to do that after picking up Ann Shields, assuming all went well. Little did I know that I wouldn't be seeing that day's *Dispatch* for twenty-four hours. In the end, I was lucky not to be reading it in a jail cell.

The night before, after dinner, I had waited patiently for the Bishop to invite me into his office and question me on how my lady-search was proceeding. Nothing doing. He may have been waiting for me to broach the matter, but if he's too proud to ask, I'm too proud to tell. I don't know, he was probably ticked that I hadn't told him about my apartment visit as soon as I returned. My position was, he could have asked.

So the deep freeze was on. When he's like this, it's not the same as one of his depressions, though it's depressing to me and to Sister Ernestine. My trouble is, I get my back up. Then we've got two stubborn hardheads sitting there in one house, refusing to speak, while Ernie flutters back and forth from one to the other, trying to make peace. I don't know why she bothers trying. Her fluttering never helps, we just eventually get over it.

So, I'd sat in my office after dinner, feet up on the desk, thinking about the situation. I really needed the Bishop's advice, not knowing quite how I was going to handle Ann Shields. She was the new element in the situation. I wished I knew exactly why the Bishop had suggested I bring her to my office "in as receptive a mood as possible." Receptive to what? Visualizing the blonde in the photo I had some vivid ideas of my own, but was sure they weren't what Regan had in mind.

I sat there filing my nails and considering various brilliant and not-so-brilliant ways of letting him know I'd actually talked to Miss Shields. I was pretty proud of myself. I'd found her phone number, and got her on a flight to New York. All this I was ready to tell him, but was he going to budge? Apparently not. And was I going to up and tell him without being asked? Not on your life.

So we had both gone to bed dissatisfied. At least I had, and it made me feel better to think he had also. As I headed for J.F.K. at 9:00 A.M. with no clear idea of what I was going for, the Bishop was up in his chapel, praying or saying Mass, totally ignorant that he and I were probably going to interview Miss Ann Shields at eleven o'clock when he came down from his prayers.

Since I didn't care whether the police knew I was going to the airport, I made no effort to shake the tail, which had become a Chrysler. Maybe they'd rammed their Fairlane into that truck in the alley.

I had allowed plenty of time to get to Kennedy,

but had a devil of a time finding a parking place. I finally found a spot about a mile and a half from the terminal and hiked in from there, arriving at the gate with no time to spare. Passengers were coming off the ramp as I rushed into the gate area.

From the photograph in her apartment, I had memorized the features of the blonde, so I didn't expect to have any trouble spotting her when she came off the ramp. But I damn near missed her. My eyes swept briefly over the tall, classic figure of the brunette who passed me with her red-rimmed eyes open wide, looking for someone. I continued to scan the travel-weary crowd, looking for the blonde.

Fortunately, my memory took over in time to catch a second look at that brunette. She was now standing in the middle of the gate area. The eyes confirmed what the memory knew. This was the brunette in the photo—the same brunette I'd seen with Fuller at Carnegie Hall, two months before.

My mind went into overload. Lights flashed, switchboards lit up, circuit breakers blew. Then I began to sort things out in a semi-rational manner. Wake up and smell the coffee, Dave. The *blonde* was Barb. The brunette was *Ann*.

Then, what the hell had Fuller been doing with *Ann* at Carnegie Hall? The answer came slowly. I recalled Fuller telling the Bishop and me, "Jack and I *doubled* with Barb and Ann all spring." So I had just happened to see the couple when their respective dates were elsewhere. In about five seconds, the mind was under control again. Oh, I'm a quick study, no doubt about it.

Even in her present state—bombarded by the news of the hideous death of her friend, sleepless from a long, hard night on a plane—Ann Shields was easy on the eyes. Wearing a nicely fitted green silk dress—currently a bit wrinkled—and high-heeled black pumps, she had the aura of certain immortal goddesses. I caught her eye and waved. As we neared each other, her fatigue became more apparent. Her mouth was drawn and her shoulders sagged.

"Miss Shields," I said, "I'm David Goldman. My sincerest sympathy." Which turned out to be all it took to break the dam. Her eyes welled up with tears. The least I could do was offer her a shoulder. She accepted, and put her arms around my waist. We stood there a while. Very comfortably, in my opinion.

We weren't a spectacle. Maybe a dozen other couples were engaged in similar activities around us—at least, the hugging part. Oh, it's possible the others had known each other longer than thirty seconds. But who knows? Or cares?

After Miss Shields had herself under control, we headed for luggage claim. I broached the subject of the next stop; her place or mine?

"You've been so kind to come get me . . ." Her voice, low and husky, sounded even better in person than it had over the phone. "If you have some questions, I'll try to answer. I want to help you find Barb's murderer, if there's anything I can do. I may be able to sleep later on, but right now I'm wide awake."

After we collected her luggage in the claim area, she insisted on toting her fair share, and matched me step for step, all the way to the car.

The ride from Kennedy to Thirty-seventh Street was pleasant for both of us, even under the strained circumstances, and even with the Chrysler on our tail. She was nursing some very heavy grief pangs, but talking seemed to help. Also, she had some natural curiosity about where I fitted into the overall scheme of things.

"So you're a friend of Charles? I never heard him mention you. By the way, do you know Jack Lester?" When I answered in the negative, she explained, "He's a friend of Charles. But I don't think either of them ever mentioned their friends. They said they were strangers in New York. You're the first person I've ever met who knew either one of them. Do you know Charles well?"

"Not really." I was pushing vagueness today. "I've only known him a few months."

"Me, too," she laughed, then sobered. "Oh, God. Poor Barb. She was a very special friend. All the way back from Hawaii, I was thinking about her. I was so lucky to live right next to her! And now this . . ." She started crying, and I resisted a very ambivalent desire to comfort her.

"I want to see Charles," she said, after a minute, dabbing at her eyes with Kleenex. I said nothing. Who "Charles Ryder" was had to be dealt with, but I wanted some consultation with my guru before deciding. Fortunately, for the moment she didn't insist.

We rode in silence for a while. Ann had her memories to contemplate. For my part, I was contemplating a soon-to-be realized moment of personal satisfaction. I couldn't wait to see the look on the Bishop's face when he came down from the chapel to be confronted by a strange woman, none other than Ms. Ann Shields, delivered in person from five thousand miles away.

I'd unquestionably pulled off a coup. Forcing Regan to see Willie on Monday had jerked him out of a week-long funk; bringing Ann Shields in today would shake him out of his latest whatever-you-call-it.

Full of anticipation, I rolled up to the mansion at exactly 11:00 A.M. The Bishop's schedule being what it is, this was perfect timing. I did notice, with mild surprise, that the Chrysler left us as we came west on Thirty-ninth.

I double-parked in front of the mansion. My idea was to escort Miss Shields into the Bishop's office before returning the Seville to Fred's. I couldn't wait to see the look on Regan's face.

I was already out of the car, preparing to slam the door behind me, when I saw the two uniformed policemen on the sidewalk in front of the mansion, looking at me. To enhance my reputation as a wild and crazy guy, I was about to tell them to watch my car, there'd be a nice tip in it for them, when I saw Lieutenant Charlie Blake of Homicide climb out of a patrol car down the block and start walking toward me. He gestured to the two patrolmen and they moved too. The gloating look on Charlie's face told me I had a problem a bit more serious than a double-parking violation.

XXIII

"If Dante had been acquainted with that man, he would have added several cantos to his *Inferno*. Lieutenant Blake deserves something lower than the Lowest Circle of Hell." Thus Regan, immediately following Blake's departure from the mansion five months previously. It had been Charlie's first visit there.

I've never read *The Divine Comedy*, being that the only copy in the mansion is in Italian, but I agreed with whatever Regan meant. Especially that Wednesday morning in August when all my best-laid plans got changed by the same lieutenant.

The instant I saw Blake, I realized the urgency of the need to get Ann the hell away from there. Whatever Charlie currently had planned for me was nothing compared to what he'd do if he got definite proof, from Ann, that I was a friend of the elusive Mr. "Ryder."

The instant I grasped what was up, I changed gears. Instead of closing my door and heading around the car to open hers, I spun and leaned back into the car, leaving the door ajar. Ann's eyes widened.

"Miss Shields!" I said forcefully, reinserting the

key in the ignition. "Have you any desire to talk with some policemen right now?"

"No!" she said emphatically, looking over my shoulder. "What do they want? Are you—?"

"No time for questions," I interrupted firmly. I pulled my card case from my pocket, without taking my eyes from hers. "Time for action. I have a feeling they're going to insist I go with them. If you want to avoid them, slide over here, behind the wheel." She looked at me, and I raised the intensity level a notch. "Now!"

Once she understood, she didn't hesitate. She slipped behind the wheel in one economical motion, her skirt sliding up to offer a fleeting view of a silk-sheathed, smoothly muscled thigh. Irrelevant, but I couldn't help noticing.

But this was no time for vagrant thoughts. One of the cops was nearly upon us. I rested a hand on Ann's shoulder in a way I hoped was reassuring, put my face an inch from her scented, pleasantly formed ear, and murmured, "Drive around for five minutes and come back to this spot. Then go up to the door and identify yourself." I dropped a business card onto her lap. "Address and phone number are there. Now, go!"

As I stepped back and slammed the door, she turned the key and went. No questions, no hesitation. I decided to marry her at the first available opportunity.

As the Caddy moved, Blake went into a fit. First he started running after it. That lasted about a second and a half. Then he swung around to the two stunned cops and yelled, "Go after her!" They gave that bit of idiocy the treatment it deserved. They just stared at him. Then he started hustling back to the patrol car, but, seeing the Caddy swing south on Eleventh, realized that was wasted effort.

He rounded on me in frustration. "Who was that, goddammit, Goldman! What I just saw is obstruction of justice, you son-of-a—!"

"Please! Lieutenant! This gentleman here"—I gestured at one of the patrolmen, the one with a paper in his hand—"has something to say to me, and it looks important. I think I should hear him out, then you and I can talk at leisure."

Blake turned red and sputtered. I looked at the patrolman holding a paper, which was undoubtedly a warrant for my arrest. I wondered who had seen me break into Ann's apartment. My next question was, what would be the charge? Breaking and entering? Obstruction of justice?

Turned out, I was way off.

The cop with the paper was looking at Blake for guidance. Blake pointed at me dramatically. "This man is David Goldman, Officer Steadman. Go ahead, read him his *Miranda* rights. We'll worry about the woman later."

"What are you going to charge her with, Lieutenant?" I inquired. "Being in the vicinity of a Catholic establishment without authorization?"

He ignored me. "Read him his rights."

The young patrolman recited, "Mr. Goldman, you are under arrest. You have the right to remain silent. If you choose to speak, anything you say will be taken down, and can and will be used against you in a court of law. You have the right to an attorney. If you can't afford—"

"That's O.K., officer," I interrupted. "I have a lawyer. Just one thing you left out. What's the charge?"

Blake was so tickled, he had to tell me himself.

"G.T.A., wise guy! Grand Theft Auto!" I stared at him. *Grand Theft Auto?* Charlie Blake had finally dumbfounded me. What the hell was he talking about?

"Charges have been filed," he was continuing in triumphant tones, "by the owner of a year-old Lincoln, valued in excess of twenty thousand dollars. You were positively I.D.'ed Monday, at 12:11 P.M., by an officer of the New York City Police Department as the driver of the stolen vehicle. Cuff him, Farnham!"

I couldn't believe it. That damn, unlucky albatross of a Lincoln! Boy, was I ever being taught something about sticking to your principles come hell, high water, or non-existent taxicabs. Next time I was near a blackboard, I would make myself write, five hundred times, "*I Will Never Again Borrow Someone Else's Car; I Will Never . . .*"

The second cop unhitched his handcuffs from his belt and approached me. Not wanting to make things tougher for the greenhorns, I didn't insist on seeing the warrant. I knew the drill. Turning my back, I offered both hands.

What I would really miss was the expression on Regan's face when he realized I'd brought in Ann Shields. That was going to be something to behold and I wasn't going to behold it. Thanks to Blake.

"Handle this right, gentlemen, and you'll be in line for a reward," I said to the rookies. "The Lieutenant might give you an autographed copy of the shortest book in the world, *The Wit and Wisdom of Charlie Blake.*" Not very funny, but I had a lot on my mind.

XXIV

Charlie Blake has a sneezing problem which might or might not be directly related to allergies.

Something, probably ragweed, reaches out and bites him every year in summer and fall. Personally, I'm convinced his obnoxious personality has a lot to do with it. Back when I was on the force, several of his fellow rookies discovered that we could trigger his attacks by getting him riled up. Intense irritation or frustration had about the same effect as ragweed.

One day, the year before I left the force, Blake was really on my nerves. I decided to see if I could predict exactly when his first sneeze would come. When I judged his level of frustration was high, I'd say, "For God's sake, Charlie, don't sneeze!" And that did it—off he'd go in a regular fit.

All right, it wasn't exactly Bob Hope, but it killed some time around Headquarters. After that, whenever he got too much for me, I'd play the game.

After I left the force, Blake had a couple of opportunities to grill me during cases where I came into conflict with the Homicide boys. Charlie is such a bum interrogator, I decided to try the old game of "call the sneeze." Both times I was able to predict it so well that when I shouted "For God's sake, Lieutenant, don't sneeze!" he went into a paroxysm that damn near prostrated him.

But this day I misjudged. Maybe the handcuffs screwed up my timing.

After cuffing me, the squad car took me downtown. The two rookies sat in front, leaving me in the back with Blake. Conversation was minimal. Once, I asked Charlie to scratch my back in a spot I couldn't reach, and he told me to shut up. Call me sensitive, but I took that for a turndown.

They brought me to Twentieth Street, which was wrong in the first place, because Twentieth Street is Homicide, and I was Grand Theft Auto. But that's the police for you, make up the rules as they go along. Once there, booked, photographed and fingerprinted, I was permitted my mandated phone call.

First, however, Blake insisted on putting me in a fresh pair of cuffs. Strictly against regs, of course.

"Since when," I objected, "are you putting cuffs on people who've only been booked?"

"New regulations," he declared. A bald-faced lie. "I'll lock your hands in front, so you can dial. Though a wise guy like you should use his nose."

He made sure he got them on too tight. To show you what a prince he is, he watched my face for a pain response as he did it. Of course, I wasn't about to give him the satisfaction. I just grinned. But I've got to admit, it hurt like hell. There's no bruise quite like the bruise you get from metal grinding against bone. Trouble is, when they put the cuffs on you that way, every hand movement gives you pain.

You get to the point where you don't want to do anything but sit there without moving. Charlie's expression let me know that he knew what he was doing. And enjoyed it.

"Make your phone call, Goldman," he urged. "You've got three minutes. Then I want a word with you."

Dialing the old-fashioned rotary phone brought tears to my eyes. It's impossible to dial a rotary phone without rotating your wrist. Try it sometime. But the pain proved worthwhile. I got the Bishop right away.

"It's me. They've brought me to Twentieth Street, and you've got to get me out of here, Bishop. I've had this grub before and you wouldn't feed it to your worst enemy's cat. I'm convinced that's why Kessler's always in such a foul—"

"David," Regan interrupted genially. "May I be permitted just a word? A certain person is in my office, listening as I speak. The two of us will be adjourning for lunch soon. Amazing job, David."

My wrists still hurt, but I was feeling a lot better. That he was pleased with my performance was nice. Even nicer was knowing that Ann Shields had found her way back to the mansion.

"As for your arrest, it is, of course, outrageous. I knew Mr. Kessler was capricious, but had no idea he was capable of this kind of vindictive harassment. I shall—!" He stopped. Then: "David, is it possible that Mr. Kessler has a listening device on the telephone you're using?"

"Highly possible," I grinned. "They'll deny it, but it was there six years ago, and I bet it's still there today."

"Excellent." His tone was ominous. "Then the following is for whoever may be listening.

"I have spoken with Mr. Rozanski of the Manhattan *Dispatch*. The gist of this conversation will be in this evening's late edition under his byline. In it I have branded the Homicide Bureau of the New York Police Department a sorry collection of inept charlatans, more interested in capriciously harassing innocent citizens than investigating murders." I grinned. If someone was listening in, he was getting an earful. But Regan wasn't through.

"I have told Mr. Rozanski of a witness in the McClain affair who holds vital information. This witness, whose identity I am not at liberty to divulge, is fully available to the police, but totally overlooked by them. Mr. Goldman found this witness by dint of diligence and investigative skills. His success has so embarrassed the police, they have rewarded him with arrest and the threat of imprisonment on charges so contrived as to be risible.

"Mr. Rozanski said he would not print the story without soliciting some response from Commissioner Rawlins. I told him I neither demand nor expect to control how he uses the opinions I express. I will stand by my statements, and welcome all comments by any other interested parties, including the Commissioner."

Regan paused for air—also, perhaps, for an admiring look from the brunette, who I could vividly imagine perched in the black velvet chair. Polysyllabic invective, as he once called it—I had to look up both words—is something he tends to use extensively in the presence of someone young and pretty. I sure hoped Kessler, or some official, was listening in. It would be a pity to waste all that oratory on just Ann and me.

I expected some more three-dollar words from

the Bishop, but he was through. "Mr. Baker has been notified," he concluded, more calmly. "He said you will be hearing from him shortly." The phone went dead.

Aside from the heat and the invective, his report of the conversation with Chet helped me understand why he'd suggested I locate Ann Shields. We needed to let the police know about the missing key ring, but without implicating Fuller. Regan had realized that Ann was the one person who could, with impunity, tell the police about the missing key ring.

The "Mr. Baker" Regan had referred to was, of course, Dave Baker, my fellow golfing Irregular and counsel of record. It was good to know he'd been made aware of what had happened, but, from similar experiences in the past, I wasn't counting on a quick rescue. Cops have some ingenious methods of keeping arrestees away from their lawyers. I have to admit I once used a few of those methods myself.

Blake, meanwhile, had disappeared. I requested lunch, and finally a cop took my order. Forty-five minutes later, he brought me a liverwurst on white bread with mayo, which was close. I'd asked for kosher corned beef on rye with mustard. The cop also brought the carton of buttermilk I'd ordered. It was fine, which was lucky since it turned out to be the only nourishment I'd get till dinner.

I was just finishing the buttermilk when Blake returned and hauled me into a small, bare room I knew all too well. There, he treated me to another sample of his unique brand of interrogation. Not a word was said about the handcuffs. I simply avoided moving my arms.

The point of the interrogation seemed to be to

find out, (1) where I got the Lincoln, (2) what I knew about Barbara McClain and her death, (3) what I'd been doing in Alsip the previous morning, and (4) anything I knew about anything whatsoever. It was the most inane interrogation I'd experienced since the last time I met Blake. For instance:

HE: So you're sticking to it that no one named Charles Ryder has approached you to represent him?

ME: You're not listening, Lieutenant. I've told you three times that the word "approach" doesn't apply here. What about telephone contacts? In any case, I don't know, or know of, any person whose name is Charles Ryder.

HE: You're lying, Goldman. Why don't you try not being such a wiseguy sometime, and tell the truth for once?

It went on like that for close to an hour. I'd been watching him and waiting for the right moment to tell him not to sneeze, when, dammit, there he went, sneezing without warning.

It came when he was trying to pin down how I'd come into possession of the Lincoln. I was throwing in a gag here and there to keep things light and to keep my mind off my wrists.

But the Lincoln was my area of vulnerability. In the hands of an expert interrogator, I'd have been sweating bullets. In the hands of an inept bully like Blake, it would have been a day in the country, if my wrists hadn't been throbbing. The sneezes came when he finally got to what might loosely be called the point.

"I want to know how you got that car, Goldman. Mr. Vessels maintains that, outside of his son and one or two other Jesuit priests, no one had permission to drive it. We've talked to the head Jesuit at the Edmund Campion House, and he says he doesn't know you, and neither do any of the other priests up there. Now I want to know how you got that car, and what its connection is with the McClain matter."

I shook my head. "Really, Lieutenant, this is sad. The car I was driving has nothing to do with you, so I'm not telling you a darn thing about it. As to the Vessels car, you've admitted that it's right at the House of Studies where it belongs. According to you, the Fathers say it might have been sitting there in their parking lot all day Saturday."

I made a gesture with my cuffed hands, immediately realizing that was a mistake. "So what have you got? A pitiful I.D. by a cop who can't see straight, and this guy Vessels that you've browbeaten into bringing charges. This is the saddest excuse for a charge I've seen in all the years I've known you. In fact, it sets an all-time low."

"Oh yeah!" Blake countered. It was then he showed how badly I'd underestimated his frustration level. "If you th-th-think . . ." And that was it. Explosions of sneezing—five, six, seven times in a row. Why hadn't I seen it coming? I was losing my touch, and that was depressing. Since I'd only played along in the hope of winning my "Call the Sneeze" game, I unilaterally terminated the interrogation.

"Look, Lieutenant"—it was a challenge, getting the words in between sneezes—"I've now told you everything. I'm not saying another word till my lawyer comes. I've just turned into a clam. Believe it or not, the lip is zipped." He asked a few more questions between sneezes, but I just made zipping motions across my lips.

"Y-y-y-you can't"—loud sneeze—"get away with it"—two more sneezes—"Goldman!" Handkerchief out, much blowing of nose, four more sneezes. "If you think . . ."

He finally walked out in disgust, leaving the door ajar, which did me an accidental favor, giving me a view of the outside world.

Fifteen minutes after Blake's departure, about three o'clock, things started happening. Through the open door I saw uniformed and nonuniformed cops, some of whom I knew, moving up and down the hallway. A few looked worried. I guessed that a certain Commissioner had received a phone call from a certain reporter, and had descended on Twentieth Street.

Then the flurry of activity eased. Time slowed. It was close to four o'clock, and I'd been reduced to counting the number of wrist throbs per minute, when Blake came back with a scowl on his face, and two words for me: "C'mon, Goldman."

He turned and headed down the hall, possibly expecting me to follow. Not wanting to disappoint him, and having nothing better to do, I followed. He led me from a room I didn't like to one I liked even less: Inspector Kessler's office.

The interview with Commissioner Rawlins and Inspector Kessler—also attended by Charlie Blake—went just about as smoothly as I could have hoped.

Just for starters, they insisted that Blake take the cuffs off me, which told me that someone (either my pal Chet or, more probably, my boss) had been complaining about my treatment. Blake fumed and sneezed, but he'd been violating procedures and he knew it, so there was nothing he could do but unlock me. When I thanked him for giving me my circulation back, he acted like it didn't matter. To my fingertips it did. A lot.

Commissioner Rawlins made a few remarks that indicated he knew the Bishop and I were in touch with a witness the police department wanted to find. He claimed he'd heard this from Rozanski, but by the time he was done asking me about it, I was sure that the pay phone was definitely tapped and that he'd listened to the tape. I didn't make a big thing of it, but I felt kind of sorry for the poor saps who thought their calls to their attorneys were private.

As it turned out, Rawlins was reasonable and we struck a deal. The deal was, they'd drop the charges against me, if the Bishop would prevent Chet from running the story of my arrest in the *Dispatch*. On top of it, Kessler even offered me a ride home. I figured his main reason was, he wanted to talk to Regan, in case I couldn't persuade the boss to drop the story in the *Dispatch*.

I accepted the deal. Since I was going to need the police later on—possibly on this case—I couldn't really afford to be other than gracious.

I told Rawlins, "O.K., I'll try to stop the story, but you have to understand how stubborn the Bishop is." I looked pretty doubtful, like this was going to be the toughest thing in the world. "I'll try to call him off, but God knows how he'll respond."

Under the circumstances, it was the most Rawlins could get out of me, and he knew it.

"Inspector Kessler," the Commissioner recommended, with more than a tinge of frustration in his voice, "let's get this man home. Now!"

XXV

I saw, that afternoon, how an Inspector can make things hop around Police Headquarters when he's of a mind to. I'd have wagered a buck that we'd never get away from that place in under thirty minutes, but we were out of there in twelve.

My old friend Polly is normally a by-the-numbers kind of desk sergeant, as stubborn as any other female, ninety percent of the time. But she had no problem at all, on Kessler's say-so, with filing "Goldman, David" under "Charges, Dropped." Normally a two-hour job, it was done in minutes, and we were on our way in Kessler's four-year-old Chevy.

Kessler tried to use the short trip to Thirty-seventh to discover something about the Lincoln.

"Hell, Davey, the charges are dropped and they're staying dropped. Just between the two of us, you were right. It was Charlie's idea. He wanted to pressure you about the McClain thing. I should've known better but, frankly, I wanted to teach you a lesson." Kessler grinned, one friend to another.

"What I'd really like to know, just between the two of us, is how you—or, more likely, the Bishop—got possession of that car. Just out of curiosity."

I wouldn't play, which he found a little irritating.

So he took another tack. "O.K., so you don't want to talk about the Lincoln. I guess that's your right. How about the woman? Ah, don't give me that raised eyebrow, Davey. The one in the Bishop's car, this morning. Who is she, Davey?"

I could have stonewalled him again, and for self-preservation, I probably should have. Ann knew that "Charles Ryder" and I were friends, and that was a little fact I definitely wanted to keep from Kessler. On the other hand, I didn't want Kessler mad at me. I much preferred the cooperative mood he was in at the moment. It would be nice to be able to contact witnesses and suspects without the fear of getting my license pulled. I even had hopes of looking at some police files on the murder.

So I made a snap decision. I'd open up on Ann. But I also made a mental note to brief her before Kessler got the chance to interview her.

"O.K., Inspector. Her name is Ann Shields. She's the victim's next-door neighbor, and probably her closest friend."

From Kessler's expression, I could tell he already had her name—naturally, since she was next-door neighbor to the victim.

Kessler was skeptical. "Ann Shields? But the doorman said she'd gone to Hawaii—"

He was opening his mouth to finish when a sudden thought hit him. He spoke two words, the first of which was "Holy."

"Yeah," I said, confirming his thought. "She was the woman in the Bishop's car."

Naturally, Kessler had a question. A big one. "What does she know?" He was pulling up in front of the mansion. As Police Inspectors always do, he found a parking space only twenty feet from the front stoop.

"If you don't mind, Inspector, I'd just as soon let her tell you that herself." I got out of the car. "But I guarantee you, it'll change your viewpoint on the case. After you talk to her, I hope you won't forget who found her for you." I slammed the door somewhat harder than necessary.

As I walked around the Chevy, I noted the unmarked Chrysler parked across Thirty-seventh—same spot where the Fairlane had been, the day before. Kessler threw a glance the same direction. I went ahead of him up the steps to the front door. As I pulled the door open, I waved ostentatiously to the two in the Chrysler while murmuring, "Aren't you going to say 'Hi' to your boys, Inspector?"

Red-faced, Kessler growled, "When are you ever going to grow up?"

But he must have called a halt to the surveillance that afternoon. I never saw the Fairlane or the Chrysler again.

XXVI

The Bishop was at his desk, working diligently, and he looked up over his reading glasses as he waved us in. The papers he was working on were the Archdiocesan personnel forms, twice redesigned by him over the years. Staffing the four hundred-plus parishes in the Archdiocese, with the number of priests ever dwindling, was a never-ending struggle. It was good to see him coping with his work load again.

Looking at me, he said, "What? No chains?" Then, to Kessler: "Are you certain you should be permitting a dangerous felon to be walking the streets unencumbered?"

Whereupon Inspector Kessler walked to the Bishop's desk, looked down at him and did something that seemed to be becoming a habit for him—he apologized. But his voice was dry.

"Your sarcasm is merited, Bishop. I didn't know Blake was going to handle it that way. He was wrong, but I can't lay it all off on him. He works for me. I've said it to Davey and I'll say it to you—my apologies."

"Accepted." Regan gestured toward the Inspector's favorite chair. "Please take a seat—if you can stay?"

Kessler sat down. He was opening his mouth to say something when I cut him off.

"Whoa, Inspector." Kessler scowled at me again. "Sorry to interrupt, but I need to ask the Bishop something, before you start." I turned to Regan. "On behalf of Commissioner Rawlins, I'd like to ask you to call Mr. Rozanski and kill that story. You and I both know the police are rats, but why let the public in on the secret?"

Bishop Regan half-closed his eyes and murmured, "I take it you join in this request, Mr. Kessler?"

Kessler was still looking at me, but with a different expression. "Yes, I do. I don't see how that kind of public squabbling helps anyone."

Regan leaned back comfortably in the wheelchair. "How did they treat you, David?"

I involuntarily rubbed a wrist, but jerked my hand away. "Darned well," I answered quickly. "They even had my favorite brand of buttermilk."

The Bishop grimaced. He considers my fondness for buttermilk appalling. "I see. How fortunate for you. And you received apologies?"

"Well, I'd have appreciated one from the desk sergeant. Her name is Polly and she looks—"

"Without persiflage, please, David."

"Apologies from all—Kessler, Rawlins, even Blake. Of course, Blake's was given under duress."

"Yes. Not a genius, your Blake, Mr. Kessler. But, David, you are satisfied they have learned their lesson?"

I grinned. The Bishop was reverting to what Ernie calls his "rector of the seminary" mode. Up in Boston, before he made bishop, Regan was the kind of seminary rector who was feared by all. I've experienced that side of him, and it's no fun.

When I assured the Bishop that everyone in the station house had become very well-mannered, he said, "Very well, use my phone to call Mr. Rozanski. You can talk to him."

Getting him wasn't easy. But finally a familiar voice came on the line. I explained the Bishop's request.

"It's too late for today, anyway," Rozanski said. "It's not even set in type." He paused. "Oh, I get it. You want me to play hard to get? Well, put the Bishop on."

I handed the phone to Regan. "You'd better talk to him, Bishop." Regan listened for a moment before he spoke.

"That would be most unfortunate, Mr. Rozanski," he said grimly. I glanced at Kessler, who was getting a bit pale.

"No, Mr. Rozanski," Regan said, interrupting an imaginary argument, "I have now *withdrawn* my authorization. It is *imperative* that you pull the story. I must insist!"

Kessler was on his feet. "Let me talk to him, Bishop!"

Regan stopped him with an upraised finger. "Yes, Mr. Rozanski?" The Bishop listened to more nothing, then nodded and smiled reassuringly to Kessler.

"Thank you, Mr. Rozanski, I appreciate this. I'll let you know when I have something you can print." Kessler sighed and resumed his seat, and Regan handed the phone back to me.

Immediately I was hearing Chet's voice. "Finished with the fun and games, Davey? Kessler good and scared?"

"You got it, Chet. Talk to you later."

"Tomorrow night at Kelley's and don't forget to bring money." He was reminding me of the end-of-the-golf-season poker game the Delancey Street Irregulars were holding.

I grinned. "Just don't forget your own money, fella."

That settled, I returned to my chair, to find the atmosphere turned convivial. Regan had rung the bell for Ernie, and she was soon with us, taking drink orders. Kessler let the Bishop talk him into having some bourbon, and I joined him, in celebration of my new-found freedom.

Actually, I had mixed feelings about Kessler staying. On the one hand, I wanted him the hell out so I could find out what the boss had learned from Ann Shields. On the other hand, I wanted Kessler's current good feeling to stay alive and well.

After Ernie had left, Kessler raised his glass. "To friendly cooperation and good citizenship." Regan gave a slight bow as Kessler and I sipped booze. The Bishop wasn't having anything—he never does. I understand he used to indulge in a drink or two—and sometimes more—back before the shooting. Now it's nothing but communion wine. Whether there's any medical reason for his abstinence, I don't know. It's not a topic of conversation between us.

"Now. About Miss Ann Shields."

"Excuse me, Inspector," the Bishop intervened. "I'm sure Mr. Goldman will be able to answer questions about Miss Shields more fully after I have shown him something. David, if you would join me?"

Kessler looked puzzled, as I rose and went around

the desk. The Bishop pulled from a drawer a pink slip of paper, which he unfolded on the desk.

I looked at it, then him, with new respect. It was a Manufacturers Hanover Trust Company check from the account of Ann Shields payable to David Goldman, signed in Ann's backhand, flowing script. The amount was one thousand dollars, and in the space marked "Purpose," she had written "Retainer for professional services to be rendered."

I picked up the check and admired it. That little slip of paper, I realized, established my right to a legitimate interest in the McClain case. The one dollar from Abe had gotten me into the Alsip Traders Bank. And there it ended. But, with Ann as a genuine, bona fide client, I had standing. Not to mention strengthening my anemic checking account by one thousand bucks, which didn't bother me either.

Furthermore, I finally had the full explanation of what Regan had had in mind when he suggested I get Ann in my office "in as receptive a frame of mind as possible." He had realized that she had the greatest potential for becoming a client, and thus allowing me to legitimately pursue the case.

"Nice going, Bishop Regan!" I congratulated him. "If it weren't for the lousy pay scale around here, I'd offer you a commission."

Regan was smug. Kessler, wondering what the hell was going on, glowered.

XXVII

O.K., I'll bite. What've you got there?" Kessler finally asked. "The keys to Fort Knox?"

I grinned at him. "Keys, nothing! This *is* Fort Knox!"

I handed him the check. "I must truly be among the chosen," I said as he frowned at it. "A police inspector for my chauffeur, and a Bishop for my marketing agent. And both working for free! Now I ask you: how many little Jewish kids have it so lucky?"

Squinting at the check, Kessler took a sip of bourbon. "What is this?"

"I assume it's what it says," I answered. "A retainer for one thousand dollars from Ann Shields."

He rolled his eyes in exasperation. "I can *see* that, Davey. But, to do what?"

"What do you think? Investigate the McClain case."

Kessler said a word and immediately apologized to the Bishop. Pulling out his pocket notebook, he copied down Ann's account number. Then he put the notebook back in his coat pocket and looked at Regan.

"It's not pleasant for me to tell a man of God he's playing around with the truth. But I've got to tell both of you, this looks fishy. First Davey tells me he's got Miss McClain's next-door neighbor. He's kindly dug her up for us, he says, and tells me she knows things that can help solve the case.

"And now, lo and behold, you've got a *retainer* for him—from *her!* Look, I want the *full story* on this dame, and I want it now! Never mind these games you two play, with scenes for my benefit."

Holding out the check to me, he sneered, "Take it, Davey. But now I want to know all about Ann Shields, and I want the truth. How'd you find her? What does she know?"

"You'll have to ask my agent," I said, just to buy time. "Believe it or not, I didn't know she was my client till I saw that check."

Regan shot me an irritated look—he obviously didn't care for this little game of hot potato. "I take no umbrage at your accusation of lying," he said to the Inspector, "but, the fact is, everything I've told you has been true. The truth is that Mr. Goldman used diligent effort and brilliant detective work to learn of Miss Shields's whereabouts and to persuade her to return to New York. I don't claim his primary motive was to assist you in executing your duties. But your range of useful knowledge will definitely be increased, once you have the opportunity to speak with her.

"Now you wonder what Miss Shields will tell you. I assume she will tell you how the murderer got in Miss McClain's apartment."

Kessler was skeptical. "Excuse me, Bishop, but I would be astonished if she had such information."

"I see. Then I suppose you are as yet unaware

that Barbara McClain had to awaken Ann Shields last Sunday night to be let in to her own apartment, because her key had been stolen? And that Miss Shields had a second key to Miss McClain's apartment? And that Miss McClain told Miss Shields she discovered her own key was missing when she left her brother's apartment?"

Kessler was startled. "Is this straight?"

"I suggest you talk with her tomorrow and let her tell you herself."

"Tomorrow?" Kessler's teeth gleamed through his beard. "Oh no, Bishop. Hardly tomorrow. May I use your phone?"

The Bishop rolled his chair back. "Be my guest!"

"Just a minute," I said sharply. I was thinking fast. If the Inspector ordered an immediate pick-up on Ann Shields, how was I going to warn her that she had heard nothing from "Charles Ryder" since the murder?

"Let the Inspector make his call, David," Regan intervened. His tone was exasperated, but something else as well. "It is almost time for our dinner, and his too, no doubt. We need not prolong this." He shot me a look I didn't understand, but I caught the import. He seemed to be telling me it was O.K. I shrugged. Maybe he knew what he was doing. I damn sure *hoped* so.

Kessler looked at his watch. "Thanks, Bishop." He punched in a number he obviously knew by heart. "Inspector Kessler here. Let me talk to Harmon." He waited a moment.

"Harmon? We've got a new witness in the McClain case. Ann Shields." He spelled it. "She's in the apartment next door to McClain's: 3B. I have it on good authority that she's got some vital information, and we need to get onto it right away. What?" Kessler looked up at the ceiling and shook his head resignedly. When he spoke into the instrument again, it was with twice the volume. "Of course I mean *now*!" He banged down the phone and shook his head in disgust.

"Inspector, I have a request," I said as soon as he'd hung up.

Looking at me, Kessler picked up his bourbon and took a sip. "What's that?"

"Since I located Ann Shields for you, I wonder if, in return, I could have a look at your files on the case?"

Kessler drained the last of his bourbon, put the glass down carefully, and rose to his feet. "I don't—Oh, all right. Why not? Come down to Twentieth Street tomorrow. I'll see that you get a look at what we've got. Most of it, anyhow. If Shields lives up to what you're telling me, you've earned it."

Ernie appeared in the hall doorway. Usually, she would ask her standard question—whether the guest would stay for dinner. Instead, she stammered, "Er, Bishop Regan, the dinner is, er . . ."

Kessler didn't seem to notice her discomfiture. Already on his feet, he gave her a courtly bow and a smile. "Smells good, Sister. I won't keep you gentlemen. Thanks for the drink." He nodded to Sister Ernestine, left the office, and headed down the hall to the front door.

Raising a puzzled eyebrow at Ernie as I passed by her, I followed Kessler to the front door, wondering what the hell was going on. Ernie seemed very nervous—for no apparent reason.

"I'll see you tomorrow at Headquarters, Davey," said the Inspector as he left.

I nodded, wondering how in hell I was going to get in touch with Ann before Kessler's men got to her. As I closed the door, I was also pondering the odd nervousness of Sister Ernie. My ponderings ended as soon as I turned around.

Peeking around the corner of the stairway was my new, thousand-dollar brunette client, showing the signs of just having awakened from a long nap.

"Is it safe, Dave?" she asked, smiling conspiratorially. "Sister told me I should wait till the gentleman left."

I started to grin, realizing why the boss had allowed the Inspector to send his boys to Ann's apartment.

"No, it's not safe!" I scolded her. "You've obviously bewitched my boss. Do you know the penalty for Bishop-bewitching?"

She just grinned. She obviously felt quite at home already in the old mansion. Was she aiming for my job? Certainly, the Bishop had several good reasons to prefer Ann Shields to Dave Goldman. But somehow, I didn't mind the competition.

XXVIII

But David," protested the Bishop, passing the platter of lamb chops to his guest and my client, "I knew that the police would never permit Miss Shields an adequate interval of rest at her apartment. And I couldn't judge how long you'd be able to withstand the torture of precinct-house cuisine before you cracked. Therefore, I asked Sister Ernestine to provide Miss Shields a place to sleep. Sister was kind enough to offer her own bed."

During this explanation, the client giggled spontaneously at the appropriate spots, while she spooned a hearty portion of green beans onto her plate.

I was having second thoughts about marrying her. First of all, if the pile on her plate was any indication, she'd be expensive to feed. There aren't many women who keep up with me in the eating department, but Ann Shields was holding her own.

Worse yet, she seemed genuinely amused by the Bishop's heavy-handed attempts at humor. How, then, could she truly appreciate the finer, subtler wit of David Jacob Goldman? That defied understanding. But, shaky matrimonial prospects notwithstanding, I had to admit that she was showing plenty of promise as a client. A thousand-buck retainer is nothing to sniff at.

I also had to admit she was decorative. A bit puffy-eyed, perhaps, from the four-hour nap, but she now had more bounce in her walk. Though her eyes were still a bit red, they were pretty eyes—deep blues—and went nicely with the well-rounded rest of her.

As for the Bishop's claim that he'd prevailed upon her to stay at the mansion for the afternoon, Ann later told me the true story. She'd fallen asleep at lunch during a lengthy exposition on ancient Hawaiian culture.

I could empathize.

In the Bishop's office later, with coffee, I thanked her for the retainer.

"Well, I wanted to hire you," Ann answered, in her husky voice. "I want you to get the murderer. Do you think you can, Dave?"

The way she said "Dave" made me blush for some reason. I picked up my coffee, blew into it, and said, "Sure I will. Just look how fast I busted out of jail. Let me tell you about a case—"

But Regan had had enough of my crowing. "Miss Shields. I hate to interrupt this charming tête-à-tête, but you'll need a good night's sleep if you are to be fresh for your interview with the police tomorrow; and I have another question or two, if you don't mind.

"However, I have a proposal. No doubt, Miss McClain's family, as well as Messrs. Masterson and Hastings, will be at the funeral. I suggest, Miss Shields, that Mr. Goldman escort you to the funeral. Attending the funeral should afford you, David, the opportunity to see what Mr. and Mrs. McClain look like. With any luck you may be able to meet and talk with one or both of them. As well as resume 'pleasantries' with Messrs. Hastings and Masterson.

"Following the funeral, Miss Shields, David can escort you to the police, where they will take your statement and ask you some questions. Inspector Kessler has already agreed to permit David to glean what he can from police files. Meanwhile, the two of you will have the opportunity to get better acquainted." He beamed with satisfaction, while I shook my head. I was almost ready to wish for another funk.

Finished with his Cupid routine, he took a breath. "Now. Before you go, Miss Shields, I'd like to ask you about a provocative comment you made this afternoon."

She dimpled. "Honest, I didn't mean to. Sometimes I just come on that way."

"Miss Shields! That is not the type of provocation I meant." He was blushing. "I was referring to your comment about the death, last winter, of Miss McClain's father, and its effects on her. Would you please be kind enough to expatiate?"

She crossed her legs, giving a tug to her skirt. She sure did more for that chair than Kessler. "Barb was devastated by the accident," she began. "It changed her. That was when we became friends. Before, she'd had her own circle of friends. You see, she had been engaged, and she socialized with an older crowd that was more the age of her fiancé.

"Her dad died in February. Shortly after, she dropped her wedding plans and quit seeing the guy.

The two of us started getting together almost every weekend. Sometimes we'd double-date, nearly always with guys I knew. Then, one Saturday night, down in the Village, we ran into a couple of guys who became pretty special to both of us. They were quiet, the right age and just—well, real nice. That was how we met Charles. And Jack. Could I have some more coffee?"

While I was pouring, I wondered how much of this we really needed. Not that I minded listening to her, but she was getting rather far afield. Sure enough, Regan called her back to the point, pleasantly but firmly. "I believe you were going to tell us about Mr. McClain's death."

She nodded, "I was coming to that. It was a ski accident. Barb's dad had a ski lodge up at Northern Springs. Barb told me her dad just loved to ski, and he had the place built about three years ago. Every winter, even back before he built the lodge, he'd have a skiing week up there for the bank's board of directors. Barb was on the board.

"The week before she went up there, Barb asked me to water her plants and said she'd do the same for me when I needed to go away. When she stopped by to tell me she was going to be gone, I offered her a drink. We talked about her upcoming week of skiing. It was the most we'd ever really talked.

"She told me how she was on the bank board, and what total—well, 'bullshit' was what she called it—excuse me."

"I'm familiar with the term," Regan murmured. "I'm also familiar with board meetings generally, and can well believe the experience was disappointing. At such meetings, neologisms abound and verbs are treated abusively. I have heard 'entail' used for 'include,' and 'surface' used as a transitive verb." He shuddered. "I could cite other atrocities. I am confident Miss McClain's characterization was appropriate."

Ann dimpled again. "Barb said the only benefit she got out of the whole affair was a week of winter skiing. She loved to ski as much as her dad did."

"Then, when she returned from that tragic holiday . . . ?" Regan prompted.

Ann put her empty cup on the small table at her elbow and directed her gaze toward the Bishop. "She was different. It was very hard on her. She and her dad had been close. She told how it happened. As I remember, her dad was skiing with the bank president—"

"Theodore Masterson," I supplied, happy to be of use.

"Yes, Ted Masterson. He and Mr. McClain—"

But Ann was interrupted by Ernie, who appeared in the doorway at that moment. "Excuse me, Bishop. The Inspector is on the phone and wants to speak to one of you. Are you home?"

I grinned. "He's probably hopping mad because Miss Ann here isn't where he thought she'd be. And he figures we know where she is." Glancing at the Bishop, I got a bit more serious. "Actually, we should soothe him a bit. I'd sure like to look at those files tomorrow."

Regan nodded. "Put him through, Sister." As she left, he asked, "Want to handle it, David?"

I nodded and grabbed the phone as soon as it rang.

"Hello, Inspector. I'll bet you're calling about Miss Shields."

"Damn right I am, Davey!" His voice was harsh. "She's nowhere to be found."

"I just spoke with her. She—"

"Where is she?"

"She didn't say, Inspector. If you—"

"She hasn't left town, has she?" Kessler sounded worried as well as mad.

"No, no, no. As a matter of fact, I suggested that she join us at Headquarters tomorrow when I look at those files. I suggested one o'clock."

"I want to see her *tonight,* Davey!"

I shook my head. "Wish I could help, Inspector, but like I say, she didn't tell me where she was."

Kessler was silent for a few seconds. Finally, grudgingly, "All right, Davey. Don't fail me now. One o'clock sharp!"

I hung up and grinned at Ann. "We'd better not be late."

"Of course, it will be up to you to see that she's not, David," the Bishop said. Apparently he was in no mood to continue the line of questioning about the ski accident, because he said, "You may use the car to take Miss Shields home, David. Upon your return, I will have a job or two for you. You'll recall that you still owe me some duties."

That was a laugh. It was clear to me why he had "duties" for me. He was afraid Ann would charm me into sticking around and talking for a while.

But I didn't argue. I had some sleep to catch up on, and I was anxious to find out what he'd learned from Ann that afternoon. I also wanted to tell him about my own adventures.

"Miss Shields," he said, returning his attention to her, "my condolences on your loss. I will pray for

Miss McClain's soul—and for your well-being, as well."

"Just don't pray for whoever did it," she answered grimly, "and I'll be fine." Her tone indicated things would not be fine for the murderer, if he—or she—were ever unlucky enough to fall into her hands.

Ann certainly wasn't Jewish, but the look on her face brought back an image from early days in Hebrew school. It was the face of beautiful Yael, in one of my picture books, kneeling over some sleeping enemy chieftain as she prepared to drive a tent peg through his skull.

XXIX

Thursday morning I woke up fully rested for the first time since Monday. I'd returned from taking Ann home at eleven, having insisted on walking her upstairs to her apartment. I wanted to be sure Kessler didn't have some of the boys waiting outside her apartment to drag her downtown. But he wasn't that crass. No cops anywhere.

Back at the mansion, I'd gone to bed disgusted and dissatisfied. The Bishop had actually had the chutzpa to turn in before I got home. Which really frosted me. Quite aside from the fact that he'd specifically instructed me to hurry back, there was the fact that we hadn't compared notes on all that had happened that day. If he was going to be any help to me, he needed to hear everything I'd learned—at Ann's apartment, at St. Bede's and at Headquarters.

His snit was getting in the way of our case. I hoped he'd get over it soon. I needed help in the genius department.

I'd set the alarm for 6:45, and by eight o'clock, I was in my customary chair in the kitchen, downing a second helping of Ernie's special fried potatoes. The special part comes in at the beginning, when Ernie sautés onions and mushrooms in butter. Then she goes on from there. Delicious outcome. Unfortunately, Ernie had some words as well as food to feed me. It seems Ann had called at 7:30 A.M.

"She says she'll be waiting on the sidewalk in front of her building, at nine o'clock sharp. I told her you'd be prompt, David, so don't be late. Very nice girl. By the way, is she Jewish?"

"Don't start, Ernie. I've told you fifty times: one mom is enough—more than enough. So lay off, O.K.? I'm warning you!" I glowered threateningly.

"Well, aren't we touchy this morning? All I said was, 'Is she Jewish?' Is that such a crime?"

I sighed. "Ern, will you kindly leave me alone and let me read my paper in peace?"

I'd picked up the *Dispatch* on Seventy-sixth the night before, when leaving Ann's, but when I found the Bishop had already gone to bed, I stomped upstairs, leaving the paper in my office.

Dispatch editors had finally decided to give the McClain case the full treatment. With a Chester Rozanski byline, the story was on page three, below a two-column photo of Barbara McClain, and above an artist's depiction of "Charles Ryder."

Barbara's picture was a nice one. Portrait-wise, it was nicer than the one in my card case. She looked several years younger.

I studied the identikit picture of Fuller—the one we'd been expecting and dreading. It had two captions, "HAVE YOU SEEN THIS MAN?" above, and "MYSTERY BOYFRIEND" below.

The haircut was all wrong, the part way too high. The nose was too narrow, the jaw too wide, the eyes too close together. That's the good news. The bad was that, as a composite, the pieces came together and made a pretty fair likeness. In total, it actually looked like him. Knowing Willie, but not knowing this picture was supposed to be him, could I pick him out? That question made me crazy, so I quit trying to answer it.

My next thought was a related one: would the author of the story recognize Willie from the picture? After all, Chet and Willie had played golf maybe half-a-dozen times. For the rest of that day I half expected to hear from Rozanski, calling me to task for not letting him in on the secret. But he never raised a peep.

The story was in the *Dispatch*'s sensationalistic style that Chet did so well. The main headline was "McCLAIN MURDER SUSPECT SOUGHT," and, in smaller type, the superhead " 'CHARLES RYDER'—BOYFRIEND OF VICTIM: WAS THAT HIS REAL NAME?"

As I read the story, it became clear that Chet had done a fair amount of legwork. A couple of paragraphs gave a brief account of the father's death in the ski accident six months before.

But the new, sensational element in the story had to do with the deceased's "boyfriend," one "Charles Ryder." According to police, "Ryder" spent the night in Miss McClain's apartment, then disappeared.

Reading the *Times* coverage after seeing the *Dispatch* was like switching from Marilyn Monroe to George Bush. More substance, but not nearly as exciting. The story was on page twelve, five paragraphs, same photo of the deceased as in the *Dispatch*, only smaller. Unaccountably, the *Times* didn't run an identikit picture of Fuller. I guess the portrait of a possible murderer isn't in the category of "All the news that's fit . . ." That was fine with me. It would be nice, I thought, if the *Times never* ran the composite.

I left the mansion before 8:30. Not only did I need extra time for traffic, I also had to check in with the client—the nonpaying one, that is. I doubted that Kessler had managed to put a tap on our phone, but I didn't want to risk it. Finding a pay phone at Seventy-third and Broadway, I pulled over. I was soon speaking to Willie, who sounded apprehensive.

"Anything wrong, Dave? I was just about to go to the library for the day."

"Did you see the picture in this morning's *Dis patch*?"

"Yes." He surprised me by chuckling. "It's funny, I was having breakfast with Father Paul, the Pastor here, this morning. He read the story, showed me the picture, and asked if it resembled one of our parishioners. He was wondering if he ought to phone the police! I told him I didn't think there was much resemblance."

"Good," I answered. But I didn't like the idea of that paper floating around the Rectory. I changed the subject.

"Ann's in town, Willie. I'm taking her out to Alsip for Barb's funeral this morning. This afternoon we have a date with the police. One o'clock. Ann's going to tell them what she knows."

"Did you tell her about me?"

"No. And don't worry. We're encouraging Ann to tell the police everything she knows, so we can't tell her who you are. But she's been asking, and I'll need to think of something good, this morning. Any suggestions?"

Silence. Then, shakily, "Just tell her that I didn't do it—and I'll explain it to her some day."

"Uh-huh. Thanks heaps. O.K., I'll give her your message. My buddies are going to let me look at some evidence down at Headquarters. I'll let you know what comes of it. Meanwhile, don't call us, we'll call you. The very walls have ears."

I arrived at 501 West Seventh-sixth, a place I was getting to know like the back of my hand, at three before nine. There she was, standing on the curb. Very prompt. And even prettier than the night before. The eight hours sleep had obviously done wonders. In a silky black dress with high collar, matching pumps and accessories, she brought a touch of class to the Cadillac. I complimented her on her appearance as she settled into the seat, and everything improved even more. She got a spot of color in her cheek that reminded me of the way women used to blush when they still knew how.

Furthermore, she was considerate enough to delay the inevitable questions about "Charles Ryder" till we were on the George Washington Bridge. "The Bishop told me" (God, I liked that throaty voice) "that you'd tell me all about Charles, Dave. Is he going to be there, this morning?"

"Sorry, no. I spoke with him just before I picked you up." I paused to consider. What I was going to say next wasn't going to make either one of us feel very good.

She slipped off her pumps, pulled her long, shapely legs up under her, and rested her chin in her hand. I glanced from the highway to her face. Her eyes were a disconcerting shade of blue, slightly darker than the sky. Given what I was about to say, they were as hard to encounter, in their own way, as Kessler's.

"Dave. Tell me the truth. You know all about Charles, don't you?"

I signalled and took the Palisades Parkway exit. The Seville settled smoothly into the middle lane of northward-rushing traffic.

"That's right. The other guy, 'Jack Lester,' I *don't* know. But Charles I met about six months ago. Before I say anything more, you should read this article from yesterday's *Dispatch.*" I handed her the newspaper, folded to display the story. "Then we'll talk."

I was assuming she hadn't seen it, and she hadn't. She took the paper, frowned, looked at the article, and started reading. A moment later, she gasped. One second after that, she swung her legs in front of her and jerked her skirt over her knees.

"This says that he—!"

"Please, Ann. Read the whole thing. Then we'll talk."

She resumed reading. Finally she placed the paper on the seat between us, pressed her back against the door, and folded her arms. This was going to be tough.

XXX

Ann's next words came straight from the Arctic Circle. "I think you'd better tell me what's going on . . . Mister Goldman."

I matched her, icicle for icicle. "All right, Miss Shields. I'll tell you everything I can."

"You mean, everything you damn well feel like telling, don't you?"

I turned the air conditioning up a notch and kept my eyes on the road. At these speeds, in all this traffic, I didn't need the additional strain of convincing the lovely brunette that Willie hadn't murdered her best friend.

But I had a job to do. I had to elevate Fuller, myself, and perhaps even the Bishop, up the evolutionary ladder from our current category of "Rat." My work was cut out for me.

"Miss Shields, what we're facing is a horrible problem for a guy you like a lot, a guy Barb liked—"

Using the name of her deceased friend was a big mistake. "Don't con me! You certainly don't give a *damn* about what's happened to Barb. All you care about is protecting this—whoever-he-is!" She swallowed, as her eyes filled up with tears. I glanced over, and noted that the tears didn't interrupt that steady gaze of hatred.

As I handed her a clean handkerchief I'd thoughtfully brought along, in my assigned role as Rat's Accomplice, I asked myself, how do I always wind up with these lousy jobs?

What I said aloud was: "I'm sorry, Miss Shields. I just hope you'll let me explain."

She blew her nose. At least she was willing to use my handkerchief.

"What I'm trying to tell you, Miss Shields, is that Mr. Ryder is my friend. The *Dispatch* has it right, up to a point. He *did* spend the night in that apartment on the couch. He got up Monday morning and discovered—the body. He found her in the other room, her bedroom, in her own bed. That's when he came to me for help."

Ann's eyes were narrowed.

"Since then, I've learned certain things that tell me he couldn't be the murderer. Both the Bishop and I are convinced he *couldn't* have done it."

"Does the Bishop know Charles?" Ann asked. "Is he intent on *shielding* him, the way you are?"

I thought fast. "Well, the Bishop's *met* him and—yes—he approves of what I'm doing. In fact, he's helping me on the case." I paused a moment to figure how I should say what I had to say next.

"It's essential at this time to keep Mr. Ryder's identity off the record. Any involvement in a murder case, even though he's innocent, would ruin the man's life." I paused to let those last few words sink in. Ann frowned, looking through the windshield. I went on, "That's why he came straight to me. And I agreed to help him, even though he can't afford to pay me a dime."

I glanced over at Ann, who was still looking straight ahead. The anger was past—for now. It seemed safe to presume she'd be willing to answer a question.

"I'd like your opinion, Miss Shields. You know Charles, in a way, better than I. So tell me what you think. He says he spent the night on Miss McClain's couch and never heard a thing. He'd had a lot to drink. He says he heard nothing—even though the murder occurred in the next room. You saw him that night. Do you think that's possible—that he slept through the whole thing?"

It was nearly a minute before she answered, in a small voice, "Charles is a nice guy. I don't think he could have done it—sober. But, Dave, he has a real problem with booze. I *warned* Barb about that.

"Barb liked her booze, too. I think maybe that's why she and Charles got along so well. I sometimes told her to watch out for Charles's drinking. She'd tell me 'Hey, it's a summer romance, don't worry about it,' and that was it. But I never saw Charles abuse her—I certainly never heard anything. But, God, he drank a lot!"

"So . . . ?"

"So . . . I guess it might've happened like you're thinking. Charles *was* drunk that night—very drunk. A murderer could've gotten away with anything, with Charles like that." She paused. I waited.

She looked at me. "He's a very gentle guy, Dave. I'm glad you're helping him."

She was calling me "Dave" again. I liked the sound. But I was still wary of Miss Mount St. Helens.

"Are you willing to go on helping him?" I inquired. "You've helped him already, more than you know. And I'd like you to keep on helping. But we have a couple of items to discuss."

"Like what?" she asked suspiciously.

I pulled her check from my pocket and held it out to her. "This is your check." She looked at me. I found I could steer confidently with one hand.

"This amounts to some substantial dollars. Assuming it's a true representation of your desire to find the murderer, I have two potential problems. First of all, I was already committed to that before you paid me a penny."

"Why is that a problem?"

"Maybe it's not." I kept my right hand out there, so she could grab the check if she felt the urge. "I'd like it not to be. But in all fairness, you should know, before I deposit this, you could get the same results for free. On the other hand," I interjected quickly, "if you're a generous woman who wants to pay me for my good deeds, I'm not about to object." I flashed a smile. To my relief she smiled back. Prettily.

"The second item's more serious." She looked at me with those big blue eyes. I swallowed and tried to watch the road.

"I've got a second goal in mind in this case. To be perfectly honest, that second goal is pretty important to me—to keep Charles's name out of the limelight and away from the police.

"That's a secondary goal. But to the extent it doesn't conflict with the first, I'm committed. You should know that."

Ann pulled her knees up on the seat again, in a way that was both nice and sort of torturing. She pitched the newspaper into the back seat and smiled at me. "Put the check back in your pocket, Dave.

You look silly holding it out there." I nodded gravely and returned it to my pocket, breathing a little easier. She went on. "Well, if you two are really good friends, why can't you tell me anything about him?"

"I can, but I won't." Seeing her start to flush again, I hastened to add, "Please, let me explain. You're going to be interrogated by the police this afternoon. They'll want to know everything *you* know about Miss McClain and her friends. I want you to be as honest as you possibly can. As of this moment, you can tell the police everything you know without hurting Charles. But if I tell you anything about him, you'll either end up lying or compromised. Putting it bluntly, the less you know, the better for Charles."

"Oh, I get it. You don't think I'm smart enough to keep it to myself. Or else you don't *trust* me." Fortunately, her tone was still calm. A second blow-up wasn't in prospect—yet.

"I think you know the answer, Ann. Sure I trust you. But I also know the kind of grilling that goes on. Believe me, it's better for you if you simply tell them truthfully you don't know."

She frowned. "I see—I guess. I do want to help him." She didn't seem to notice that I'd glided back to a first-name basis with her. Smooth guy that I am.

"He'll appreciate it. Me too. This morning I asked if he had a message for you, and he said to tell you he's sorry—about everything. I promised I'd tell you." I tried to think of how to say what I had to say next, and decided to just say it.

"There's also something else you can do. Not to

help Charles, but to help me. If you'd be up for that."

"What?" Her tone was encouraging. The "ALSIP: 1 MI" sign was just flashing past.

"I'm going to contradict what I just said about being honest with the police. I'd like you to forget that I know Charles. They'll ask you about my calling you. It's O.K. to tell them I called, but say nothing about Charles. Please."

She looked puzzled. "Why?"

"If they find out Charles was with me when I called you, they'll be all over me like fleas on a dog. Right now, they suspect I know Charles, but they don't have anything to base that suspicion on. So there's nothing they can do. When they arrested me yesterday, they thought they had a solid charge—but they couldn't make it stick. But if they hear the full story about that phone call, they'll have me. I hate their accommodations. The food's lousy, and their manners stink. But once they put me in, I'll probably be there awhile. I'm not going to tell them anything about Charles, and that they won't like. They want him bad."

"But what if they ask me how you found me?" She frowned. "How *did* you find me, by the way? Come to think of it, *Charles* didn't know where I was."

I gave her a brief description of how I'd got into her apartment, found the note and the envelope and watered the plants. Her eyes got bigger while I talked. "I *wondered* about those plants!"

I handed her an envelope. "What's this?" she asked.

"Some things of yours that I took from your apartment when I entered it illegally."

From the envelope she pulled the things I'd removed from her apartment—her note to Barb (I'd ironed out the crinkles) and the bathing-beauty snapshot of Barb and her.

She smiled. "Thanks for watering my plants, Dave. And for saving this note. You can break into my place any time. And I'm sorry for getting mad. I shouldn't have blown up that way. I didn't know the whole story."

I could have told her "You still don't," but didn't. Feeling much lighter of heart, I made a right turn, and steered the Seville down a tree-lined street with large, handsome houses on either side. I glanced over at my smiling passenger. Excellent dimples.

We rolled into the parking lot next to the large, red brick church. It was now confirmed. I was getting paid for the case. Time to start earning my fee.

XXXI

The funeral was plenty grim. Lots of damp handkerchiefs. Center right, filling five or six pews, was an entire bus-load of thirteen-year-olds in bright blue uniforms, students of the deceased Miss McClain. The sniffling that came from that section of the church showed that the *Dispatch* was probably accurate with at least one maudlin detail: Barb had been a a popular teacher.

At one point in the ceremony, when the sobs were near their peak, Ann leaned over to me and whispered, "Some of our friends wondered why Barb worked, with all her wealth. I think these kids are the answer." I nodded, not caring to speak at that point. When you're the strong, manly type, you have a certain image to maintain.

Fuller's decision to stay away had been a wise one. I recognized four Homicide plainclothesmen in the crowd. Well, I recognized two and suspected two others. None of them seemed to recognize me, which was just as well. Had Fuller shown, he'd have found himself behind bars even before the funeral started.

Ann introduced me to an attractive young couple that was part of a group she and Barb had run around with. John Boyd was tall, dark-haired, about thirty, in blue serge. Judy Ransome, off-blonde, plump, was also in serge, hers a slightly darker blue. Both appeared appropriately somber as they joined Ann and me in our pew.

I picked out Bob and Missy McClain from Fuller's description. They were in the front pew on the right.

Strangely matched couple. He, obscenely obese, and she, tiny enough to pass for one of Barb's students.

Masterson was a few pews behind, next to a small, attractive blonde. I recalled the family portrait in his office; she was his wife. Hastings was more toward the back with two other gentlemen his age. All three, it appeared, shopped at Brooks Brothers, or someplace like it.

I didn't listen much to the service. At least the sermon was mercifully short.

When the ceremony was over, Ann and I joined the motorcade to the cemetery. After hearing a few more words from the priest, we waited in line to express condolences to Bob and Missy. Ann told them her name, which obviously meant nothing to them, and then introduced me.

Robert McClain was suffering from a bad case of bloat. The two hundred and fifty or so pounds distributed over a frame designed for a hundred and seventy at most, gave him the appearance of a beached whale. While his weight tended to block other details from the mind, I did observe that he had sandy hair, freckles and little green eyes, nearly hidden by the encroaching flesh. His voice was the baritone of a puberty-stricken fourteen-year-old, self-consciously low and cultured, but constantly threatening to crack into a girlish treble.

Was he capable of killing his sister? Hard to say. But one thing was sure. I couldn't picture him tiptoeing through that apartment without waking Fuller. This had to be a man with a rhino's footstep.

Missy was about a third the size of her husband. Attractive, if you like them skinny, which I don't. Her features were regular, but could have used lots of softening. Limp handshake, no eye contact. As to how she talked, just think of finishing schools in the fifties, and you've got it. Neither lips, teeth, or tongue moved much, and the eyes never looked much above your collarbone. Missy had it down pat.

After muttering condolences, I asked about the other two suspects, neither of whom I'd seen at the cemetery. "I wanted a word with Ted Masterson and Norm Hastings," I murmured to her. "Have you seen them?"

Missy didn't seem to hear me. In fact, she sniffed and turned her back. I gathered the conversation was over.

"Was it my deodorant?" I asked the top of her head. Receiving no answer, I added, "I am not a policeman." That drew a shrug of the shoulders. But there was still no indication the conversation was going to freshen up.

I guess Missy had seen all she wanted of strangers the previous three days. I really couldn't blame her for rudeness, especially if one of her visitors had been Blake, which was probable.

While the crowd did its official mingling, I looked for Hastings and Masterson anyway. I wondered if

Hastings held a grudge about the Tuesday dust-up. While Ann chatted with some friends she'd located, I searched, and finally found, Masterson. Hastings, apparently, had decided to skip the cemetery.

The tanned banker and his somber-looking wife were chatting with a small clump of mourners. Masterson shook my hand as though the unpleasantness in his office was a thing of the past. His wife's name turned out to be Cathy. She was nearly as small and slender as Missy, and much prettier, with a heart-shaped face and big, brown eyes. A highly photogenic couple, the Mastersons.

"Could I have a word with you, Dave?" Masterson smiled apologetically at Cathy. She was smack-dab in the middle of a cliché, but stopped dead when her husband spoke.

With a nod to Cathy, Masterson steered me by the elbow. Her big eyes followed us anxiously. When her husband was being masterful, she knew what to do. And what not to do.

"I'm sorry for that scene in the bank the other day," he said, with a confiding look. "I'm afraid Normie's a little touchy. He and Barb were once—well, he was feeling just terrible. I know he regrets what he said to you. He admitted he was out of line, the minute I got back to the office."

"Don't worry about it," I answered. "I probably reminded him of some kid he once gave a bloody nose to. My failing."

Masterson wasn't sure how to take my reassurance, but he went on anyway. "That's not why I needed to talk to you. I'd really like to speak with you frankly about this whole mess.

He quickly continued. "Let me explain. Frankly, Dave, I took the trouble to check you out, Tuesday, after you left. The two people I talked to say you're tops. I'd forgotten—it was you who got that Jenkins fellow put away when that child was murdered." He tried to look admiring. I smiled noncommittally.

"Anyway, what I'd like to tell you is that I'm delighted to know you're working on Barb's murder. Frankly, Dave, I don't have much confidence in the police. I wanted to ask you: in your investigation so far, have you come across the name, 'Charles Ryder'?"

I nodded.

"I thought so. Well, I met the man, Dave. I believe he spent the night with Barb, the night she was killed. That night—Sunday—we were together at Junior's apartment—" He shook his head ruefully. "I mean 'Bob's apartment,' of course. I've just got to quit calling him 'Junior'!

"Anyway, that man, Ryder, had way too much to drink that night. He didn't strike me as a very stable character. Others felt the same way. We told the police about him and helped put together the drawing that was in yesterday's *Dispatch.* I guess they're looking for him."

He shook his head. "I've got to tell you, it's a lousy likeness. But with your expertise, I'd think you could locate him."

Masterson glanced around quickly, then moved closer. This was going to be *highly* confidential. "There's something else I wish you'd look into, Dave." He glanced around again. "Mr. McClain, Senior, died in a skiing accident last February—so the state police said. I was never satisfied that it was properly investigated. Bob, Senior, was a fine skier, Dave, a *very* fine skier. I can't accept that he just stupidly skied into a branch. That was the coroner's finding, you know—based on the State police investigation. It was twilight, but he and I knew that run like the back of our hand. I just don't believe it was an accident. Dave, I've never told this to anyone else." He glanced nervously at his wife, who was twenty feet away, and gave her a big smile. Then he turned confidentially toward me again.

"My first thought was that he must have had a heart attack. Something made him lose control. The autopsy ruled that out. As long as you're working on Barb's murder, you have a legitimate reason to investigate this other death—am I right?"

"I'll keep an open mind," I said. It was the best I could do.

He smiled. I smiled. We joined the company of the others. Two minutes later, with considerable relief, I collected Ann and we took off.

On the way to the police station, I let Ann pick a roadside eatery. That was a mistake. The service was atrocious. By the time we got out of there, I was convinced we'd blown our one-o'clock with Inspector Kessler.

By luck, the traffic cooperated. Ann and I walked through the front door of Headquarters on Twentieth Street at exactly two minutes after one—close enough, even for a fussbudget like Kessler.

XXXII

The first person we ran into at Homicide was Blake. As soon as he saw me, he scowled, glanced at Ann, took two more strides, and did an about-face. Accosting the two of us, he glared at me.

"This the woman you were with yesterday, Goldman?" he barked. This guy could write a whole book on etiquette. Called *The Art of Boorishness.*

"Nice to see you again, Lieutenant." I nodded. "May I introduce my client, Miss Shields? We'd love to chat, but she has an appointment with Inspector Kessler. I don't think we should keep him waiting, do you?"

A sneeze threatened, I could see. He wheeled and strode away.

Kessler only kept us waiting six or seven minutes. Then Polly sent us in. During the wait, I introduced the two women. I also teased Polly about all the regulations she'd broken by letting me go the previous afternoon. On the say-so of a mere Inspector.

"Keep talkin', Davey," she warned. "Next time, we're throwin' away the key. Then when your buddy Kessler comes to get you out, where'll you be?"

"Simple, Pol. I'll just pull my Houdini stunt. You've seen that one, haven't you?"

"The only trick I can remember you doin', Davey, was gettin' the Commissioner on T.V. that time to explain your screw-up."

It ended in a draw, provided you give me the benefit of the doubt, which is only fair. Later, Ann said Polly had the last word—but it's a well-known fact that women always stick together. I'd have aced Polly easily if Kessler had only made us wait a little longer.

Kessler called Records before starting his interview with Ann. I left Ann on-deck, confident she could handle whatever he might fire at her, be they curve balls, sliders or smoke.

At Records, I had to wait around for ten minutes while they rounded up someone junior enough for the lowly assignment of keeping an eye on me while I went through the McClain Case files. They finally found a warm body, and I use the term deliberately. I spent the next two hours in a small room with three thick folders and a gorilla who was totally entertained by a monster wad of gum the entire time I was there.

When the snap, crackle and pop began to get to me, about forty minutes in, I said, "Excuse me, officer, would you mind chewing with your mouth closed?" At that, he looked at me and said, "Wha?" without missing a single pop. I gritted my teeth and tried to work faster.

The first folder was filled with photographs. I scanned them all, some carefully. Several showed the apartment.

I spent as little time as possible examining the photos of the corpse, though there were plenty.

Clothed, as found, and unclothed, plus close-ups of the wound, both with and without knife. Considering the knife got her in the heart, there was surprisingly little blood. My guess was, the killer knew what he was doing.

One shot showed the knife by itself. In another, the murder weapon was lined up alongside the other four knives in the matching kitchen set. All in a row. The killer used the second longest, and the thinnest. What I mainly got out of the photos, besides a slightly sick stomach, was confirmation that Barbara McClain had indeed been the blonde in the bikini.

A second folder contained a lengthy medical report with lots of technical jargon. I tried to wade through it. Having coped with similar reports, I was able to grasp the essentials. Death was instantaneous, or nearly so, when the heart was punctured by a sharp instrument to the depth of three inches—fifty-nine millimeters, if you want to be exact. Stab wound was eighty-seven degrees to the left with respect to the longitudinal axis of the body, eighty-four degrees to the top with respect to the latitudinal. Rib cage undamaged.

Time of death was determined to be 1:15 A.M., plus or minus an hour or so. Source: contents of stomach.

I won't go into the various tests they did to determine whether or not the victim was sexually molested. All were negative.

On the medical front, there was some fascinating discussion of such popular topics as "aortic function," "cardiovascular viability," "ventricular . . ." —but you get the idea. Fancy ways of saying what I already knew: the lady was killed by a knife to the heart.

The third folder contained reports of the officers and scientists who had been on the scene, from which very little new information could be gleaned. Not surprisingly, Burke's was the least scientific, least grammatical and the most helpful. He described the evidence that someone had spent the night on the couch: cushions dented and coffee table in a slightly altered position, as indicated by carpet prints. Someone had put the table back, but hadn't succeeded in finding the exact spot.

Burke had also discovered the print of a man's bare foot in the heavy living-room carpet. Measurement established that the print belonged to a man with a shoe size of nine or nine-and-a-half.

Fuller's shoe size was a nine. I'd already checked.

"I conclude," Burke had typed in the space for Officer's Remarks, "that a male subject, the probable perpetrator, probably of slightly more than average height and substantially more than average weight, slept on the couch. He tried to fix it up to look otherwise by moving the coffee table back into its previous place and putting the cushions back where he thought they belonged. Based on descriptions furnished of Charles Ryder, I found nothing inconsistent with him being the perpetrator."

Attached to Burke's report was an inventory of personal effects found in the apartment. Part of the inventory was the deceased's purse, and contents thereof. I glanced through, turned the page, stopped, and went back. There it was, part of the purse inventory: "One key ring, with five keys." I sat there a while, looking at it.

Returning to the first folder, I found the photograph of the bedroom. The purse was on top of the dresser, just an arm's length from the bed. In my imagination I saw the killer come into the apartment, go into the kitchen for a murder weapon, move silently past the drunken man snoring on the couch, and go into the bedroom. The knife strikes the woman's chest. Into the purse on the dresser goes the key ring. The killer departs as silently as he—or she—came.

Burke's report, and a few others, showed that the cops hadn't totally neglected the possibility that the boyfriend might *not* have done it. They'd done research on forced entry. All four windows had been examined. All were locked tight: no signs of tampering. The police had removed the lock of the door to the hallway, and had examined it microscopically. No evidence of forcing.

The third folder contained references to some eighty-three fingerprints lifted. After eliminating the victim's, duplicates and unusable partials, a total of twenty-two prints had been faxed to Washington for F.B.I. tracing. No checking, first, of local files, just let the Feds do it. That attitude of Leave It To Uncle Sam is what got us into all the trouble we're in, in the first place, if you ask me. Cops.

The above is what I got out of my first hour-and-a-half with the McClain file in the sonorous vicinity of the gum-chewer. There were two interruptions. I would never have thought that Blake would be a welcome sight, but an hour with the wordless wonder made the Lieutenant seem like a relief. I was just starting on the medical folder, jotting terms into my notebook, when he exploded into the file room.

Blake took up a position about six inches off my

starboard bow, glared down at me, and demanded, "On your goddam feet, Goldman!"

Before I could respond, he spun on the moron. "What the hell is he doing in here with these files, Hampstead?" Hampstead actually stopped chewing for a moment as he stared, open-mouthed, at Blake. I was hoping Charlie would give the guy a chance to demonstrate that his vocabulary went beyond "wha," but of course Blake couldn't wait.

Wheeling on his primary target, he growled, "I said, 'On your feet.' "

"I needed to stretch, anyway," I obeyed, yawning.

"Hampstead, I want to know how this shamus got access to this confidential information! Who the hell authorized it?"

Hampstead's eyes widened slightly, and he resumed chewing, allegro. It was time for me to intervene. "If you're going to sneeze, Lieutenant," I said, "you'd better leave us. The Captain here was just telling me how susceptible he is to germs."

Blake opened his mouth to comment—then closed it. I had him. Next time he opened his mouth, he was going to sneeze. His choices were limited.

He left. No doubt to report to Kessler what I was up to. I hoped Kessler would appreciate his devotion to good order.

Hampstead closed his mouth and grinned at me, presumably to show he shared my opinion of Blake. Then he resumed popping.

The other interruption, twenty minutes later, though less fun, was more productive. A plump, young, uniformed woman came into the room, took one look at Hampstead, and turned to me.

"Goldman?" When I nodded, she continued, "Put this with the McClain files, and turn 'em in together." She slapped a folder on the table and took off.

Friendly bunch.

I had nearly finished at that point. The fresh material prolonged my stay by twenty-five minutes. A well-spent twenty-five minutes it proved to be, too.

The folder contained notes on interviews with several people who were the last to see Barb, including our four suspects. I read those four interviews with intense interest.

Junior and Missy's statements hung together nicely: probably too nicely. It made me wonder whether they'd been interviewed together. That would be a breach of department regulations, but it wouldn't be the first time.

Both reported that "Ryder" and Barb had been the first to leave, a few minutes before twelve. They said that Masterson left twenty minutes later; and Hastings somewhere in the middle. After all were gone, Junior and Missy had cleaned the place up and gone to bed—apparently in separate rooms.

Bob sept late—till about noon, though he was a little vague. Missy was up at eight. She met a taxi that came for her each morning at 8:40. She kept the cab waiting five minutes. Apparently she had been in her office all day, though that wasn't confirmed in the records.

Norm Hastings had gone straight home to Alsip. According to him, he'd left five minutes after "Ryder" and Barb, at a quarter to twelve. He told the police he arrived at his townhouse just outside Alsip at 12:30. By 8:30, he was awake, and he was in his Alsip office sipping coffee at nine. At 10:00, he went to court, only to find that the case he was involved in had been continued. He returned to his office and stayed there till one.

Ted Masterson said he left at 12:30 and was back home at 1:30. Up at 6:00 he ran for an hour (usual routine), arrived at the bank at 7:45. He was supposed to attend a seminar in White Plains (twenty minutes away) at nine, but he got there half an hour late, due to pressing matters at the bank. The rest of the day, he was at the seminar.

So the information about Monday morning was all there, but sparse in places. I knew the killer had probably used a phone at 9:30, 10:30, 11:30 (presumably), and 11:33. None of the reports were detailed enough to check on the suspects at those times.

After returning the folders to the Records desk and bidding a fond farewell to Hampstead, I headed back to the front desk.

Polly greeted me with a derisive grin. "Sorry, Davey. Your chickadee ran out on you. Left you a message, which I was tempted to steam open and read. But a young thing like me can only stand so much stimulation."

I took the sealed envelope. "Dave Goldman" was written on the outside in a handwriting now as familiar as my own.

> Dave, dear. Though he doesn't approve of my hiring you, Kessler was very nice. He even arranged for a policeman to take me home. All is well. You're still my guy. Get the son of a bitch. Call me.
> Love, Ann.

"I'm her guy, Polly," I said, in a commiserating

tone. "Just when I was going to propose to you. I hope you're not brokenhearted."

"If her taste is that lousy, she can have you."

"That statement proves what I've always said," I retorted as I turned to go. "Desk sergeants have no soul."

She hooted. Soullessly.

XXXIII

Back at the mansion, I went through my mail. Finding no checks or other good news, I pitched everything in the round file, called my other office, and bandied a few words with Dave Baker, my personal counselor-at-law. I'm afraid I was a bit sarcastic.

"Thanks so much for all your help, Dave. I'm out of the slammer, no thanks to you."

"Hell, Davey, there hasn't been a jail built that can hold you. We both know that. Oh, your ecclesiastical friend did call and ask me to spring you. He just doesn't realize how resourceful you are. I went right on with my duties, and sure enough, here you are."

"Appreciate the vote of confidence, pal. Now I've got a favor you can do me. Consider it atonement."

"Now, listen, I'm already *doing* you a favor, letting you have the prestige of sharing offices with me."

"Just shut up and listen. I need a line on a couple of shysters—excuse me, eminent lawyers. The first is with—is it 'Anderson, Lamberson . . .'?"

" '. . . Morgan and Lamb,' " he finished for me. "Down on the Street. Good ones, too. They represented G.T.C. in that biggie, last year. Remember?"

I was silent.

"I forgot," he concluded, wearily, "you live in your own world over there with the Bishop. What about 'em?"

"I understand they've got a young female attorney who's supposed to be a hotshot. Melissa McClain. Can you find something on her for me? It's worth some nice flowers for Miss Grossman."

"I'll check her out. You said there's another one?"

"Right. This guy heads up his own firm, out in Alsip. Name's Norman Hastings. Don't know the name of the firm."

"Just a sec, and I'll find it for you in Sullivan's. Uh . . . yeah, here it is. 'Tobin, Corrigan and Hastings,' in Alsip. Want a check on him, too?"

"Please. *Any* dirt you can find through that circle of stoolies you call the legal community would help. I'll be properly grateful, you may be sure."

"Sure you will, Davey. Some day."

"Going to be at Kelley's tonight?" I asked, drawing his attention to the Irregulars' poker game.

"Can't make it," replied the counselor. "You guys get enough of my money on the golf course. I don't need you figuring out new ways to pick my pocket."

"Hell, just send over your money. We can get along without you!"

"Yeah, I know. Look, gotta run. Every minute we talk, some poor sucker's getting entrapped, bamboozled and bum-rapped. I'll get back to you in a day or two."

He rang off.

I stuck my head in the Bishop's office where he was happily rattling away on the word processor. He looked up.

"Ah, David," he said genially. "You're back. Anything that can't wait till dinner? I'm making excellent progress at the moment."

"Yeah, I can see that. I was wondering if I should bring a pail of water, and cool that machine down." No reaction. Why do I even bother trying to maintain a friendly, cheerful atmosphere around the place? The Bishop waited so I obliged with a few more words.

"I wondered if you had any suggestions for how I can waste my time till dinner. I'm considering writing a book on the Torah, but, so far, the words just won't come. And if the words won't come—"

"The words won't come, David, because there are none in your head. They're all in your mouth, preventing me from putting my own in the proper order. Fortunately for both of us, I do have a suggestion . . ."

Boiled down, his suggestion was that I obtain more background information on the death of Robert McClain, Sr. So it was unanimous: everyone from Masterson to the Bishop agreed that I needed to look into that ski accident. Of course, the night before, the Bishop had sent Ann away just as she was about to tell us. But I didn't call that to his attention.

As a matter of fact, I had remarkably few details on that skiing accident. Getting what I needed would be a piece of cake if I could get Rozanski in a cooperative frame of mind.

Chet was in, but not feeling very friendly.

"What is it with you, Davey? Since this McClain

thing started, I get a call a day from you with gimme gimme gimme. But what do you give *me*? *Nothing* is what I get, on or off the record. I don't even know who your damn *client* is. Why don't you go give that Bishop of yours a ride in his wheelchair and let me get some work done?"

"Temper, temper. If you're going to pout, I guess I'll *have* to give you something. It's off the record for now, but I've been retained by Miss Ann Shields, a close friend of the decedent."

Silence for a moment. "Shields? That's a new one. I hadn't heard that name, and I've done a lot of research. Who is she? Where does she live? How do I get in touch with her? *Give,* Davey, *give.*"

"Tell you what, Chet. If I can talk her into it, there's a good chance you'll get an exclusive interview with her. In return for which, how about telling me all you know about the death of McClain, Senior?"

Another pregnant pause. When he finally answered, Chet had a new tone. "Interested in the senior McClain, hmm Davey? You know what they say—'Great minds . . .' I've been wondering myself. Two deaths, both violent, same family, same year . . . That got me to wondering. Just today I've gone back into the files and looked it up. Hold on." He was away for about twenty seconds, then returned.

"O.K., here we are. 'Robert J. McClain of Alsip passed away Wednesday, of injuries suffered in a skiing accident at the Majestic Ski Resort, near Northern Springs, New York. Mr. McClain, a banker, fifty-nine, had the reputation of being an expert skier. He is survived by a son, Robert . . .' Blah, blah, et cetera, et cetera."

Long pause, much rustling of paper. "That's all I

can find in the *Dispatch.* Here's the Alsip Village *Reporter,* weekly edition. 'Mr. McClain, owner and chairman of the board of the Alsip Traders Bank, had arranged for a week of skiing for his family and friends at the bank's lodge, located halfway up the slopes at the Majestic Resort. In the party were the deceased's son and daughter-in-law, Mr. and Mrs. Robert J. McClain, Jr., the deceased's daughter, Ms. Barbara C. McClain, the president of Alsip Traders Bank and his wife, Mr. and Mrs. Theodore C. Masterson, and attorney and friend of the deceased, Mr. Norman R. Hastings, partner with the local firm of Tobin, Corrigan and Hastings. The board of directors of the bank had combined their annual meeting with a week of skiing. For the eighth consecutive year . . .' And so on. Nothing here about how the accident happened." More paper rustling. "That's it. Satisfied? And now, I wonder what you've got. You must know more than you're saying—huh, Davey?"

"Could be, friend. If so, I'm not giving that out. But, as always—"

"Yeah, I'll be the first to know." Chet was disgusted. "Aren't you worried you're going to weigh me down with so many favors, I'll never be able to pay you back?"

"Hey, not so sarcastic. It ill becomes your stature as a whatever it is you are with the *Dispatch.* I'm going to get you an interview with my client, aren't I?"

"So you say. Unfortunately, I know what your promises are worth. Just remember who knew you when. See you tonight?"

"I'll be there. After I win my third pot, I'll give you everything I've got on McClain. That ought to be an incentive for you to let me win back some of that money you've taken from me at golf."

I put the phone down, scratching my head. How very interesting. Not only two violent deaths in the same family in the same year, but the same four people on the scene in both cases.

Intrigued, but needing lots more detail than Rozanski had been able to give me, I decided to try elsewhere. Ann's knowledge was strictly secondhand. Still I needed an excuse to call her.

From her muffled answer, I knew I'd awakened her out of a sound sleep.

"I'm *very* sorry," I apologized. "I should have known you'd need sleep, with the jet lag, and a tough morning."

She yawned in my ear in a way that made my left lobe feel very warm. "I'm glad you called. I wanted to tell you about my session with Inspector Kessler. He wasn't tough at all!"

"Yeah, he's all heart. What did he want to know? Was he curious about how I got hold of you?"

"You *might* say that, Dave." She laughed, then filled me in on what she'd learned and what she'd given him. Most of the interview had dealt with the events of Sunday night/Monday morning up in the hallway, outside apartment 3B, with special emphasis on the missing key ring. He had made her go over that a couple of times.

Unlike Willie, Ann couldn't be positive that the keys had been left in the brother's apartment, since she hadn't been there. But at least Kessler now realized that Barb had lost her key ring. I wondered how he would resolve the discrepancy between Ann's testimony and the fact that the key ring was in Barb's purse when the police found the body.

Thanking Ann for her report, I asked her to finish what she'd started to tell us the night before about the ski accident.

"You got interrupted when you were telling us what happened when Ted Masterson got to the lodge, Ann. I guess Bishop Regan was just too tired to listen any more. Can you finish telling it, now?"

"Sure, Dave. I was starting to tell you about the 'secret' trail back to the lodge that Barb said her dad and Ted Masterson had figured out.

"See, last summer the park service didn't clear out the trees and underbrush near the lodge, so it was declared off limits. Barb's dad and Masterson had made a path so they could ski down to the lodge through the trees and underbrush, and they used it every day. Barb said everyone told them it was unsafe, but those guys kept using it anyway. Nobody else would go near it.

"Well, the third day they were up there, Mr. Masterson didn't ski with them. In the evening, Barb's dad apparently tried to make it through the trees to the lodge on his own. It was at twilight, I guess, which made it really dangerous. The rest of the group had no idea he'd try it. They were all waiting for him in the bar at the big resort at the foot of the run. When he didn't come, they drove back to the lodge, to see if he'd faked them out and skied there, using that secret path. I guess Mr. Masterson had made him promise he wouldn't do it alone.

"But Barb's dad wasn't at the lodge either, so they notified the ski patrol. The patrol got out on the slopes in their snowmobiles, and one of them checked the secret run.

"That's when they finally found him. He'd run

into a branch going full speed. It hit him right in the neck. Barb said he'd choked to death, all alone up there on the slopes. She cried and cried, telling me about it. It really tore her up." Ann stopped. I gave her a moment, and then I had a question.

"Ann, do you happen to know if the police investigated Mr. McClain's death at the time?"

"No, I don't know. Dave—do you *think*—?"

"I don't think anything, Ann. The police always check out an accidental death. I was just wondering if Barb ever said anything about it."

"No, she just told me there was some sort of official inquiry. She and her brother—maybe some others—had to answer some questions. It didn't sound like anyone was *suspected,* though."

Something that Ann had mentioned previously suddenly came to mind.

"You told me yesterday that Barb 'changed' after her father's death. *How* did she change?"

"Well, see, that was when she broke it off with Norm Hastings. He'd pretty well dominated her life till the accident."

I was momentarily confused. "Wait a minute. I thought she was engaged to someone. When did Hastings get involved?"

"I thought you knew that, Dave. Hastings was the guy she was engaged to."

"Hold it! *Barb* was engaged to *Hastings*?"

"Dave, I thought you knew that! Of course, I only heard about it from her. As I say, the engagement ended after the accident and Barb started on a different kind of social life. That's where *I* came in."

I was stunned. I thought back to the character I'd met in the bank on Tuesday—the paunchy, middle-aged lawyer with the superficial charm. I pondered how a man whose ex-fiancée has been murdered could, calmly and unemotionally, discuss the sale of her property the very day after her death.

"Dave? Are you there?"

Ann's voice brought me back. "Yeah. I was just thinking, that would have been a convenient thing to have known yesterday."

"I'm sorry." She was hurt. "I thought you already knew that. It seems like you have all the facts."

"Not nearly enough, Ann, not nearly enough. But I'm not blaming *you.* I've just been asking the wrong questions."

Prompted by former negligence, I asked more questions about the other suspects. But nothing emerged that I didn't already know. The Hastings-Barb McClain engagement overshadowed everything.

"Well, Madam client," I concluded, "how would you like to combine some business with a little pleasure? Since you've decided to take the rest of the week off to help me solve this case, what would you think of a trip to the Catskills tomorrow?"

She was excited. "I *love* the Catskills! What's up?"

"Well, I've got my doubts about that skiing accident. If Barb's father was murdered, the murderer will almost certainly be the same person who killed Barb. I'd like to go up there to Northern Springs tomorrow. Want to come?"

Fortunately, the idea of spending another day together was no more repugnant to her than it was to me. I told her I'd pick her up Friday morning, same spot, a bit later: 10:30 A.M.

"We've got to stop meeting this way," she breathed,

proving she could be trite with the worst of us. Which led to a further, and more alarming, discovery: I didn't care how trite she was.

I hung up the phone and scowled at it. "I'm in a lot of trouble," I said grimly.

XXXIV

It was that night—Thursday—that the Bishop finally decided to apply a few of his spare I.Q. points to the case. About time, too. After spending over two hours listening to Willie on Tuesday morning, he'd gone into his hidey hole.

O.K., I'll admit it, he did have the backlog of Archdiocesan work that always builds up when he's been in a funk. To give him credit, he'd gotten it pretty well cleaned up. But he'd opted out of the McClain case, and left me rudderless.

Frankly, I'm still not sure why he vacillated. My best guess is that, after he heard Willie tell his story Tuesday morning, he'd begun to regret helping the guy. All well and good to protect the good names of the two thousand priests in the Archdiocese. But in order to do that, we had to protect the *bad* name of the very guy who'd exercised very poor judgment in the first place. And when Willie had revealed, Tuesday morning, that Barb McClain wasn't the first lady he'd been playing games with, that may have just done it for Regan.

But by Thursday night he was ready to get

involved—"hip and thigh," as old Rabbi Liebowitz used to say in Hebrew school. I'll give Regan this: from Thursday night till the eventual outcome, the man was fully involved. With totally unforeseen consequences for him personally.

To bring him up to date, I had to review nearly three days of activity. I took four and a half hours to review events in detail, often referring to my notes as well as using what he calls, sometimes derisively, my "impeccable" memory. We started in his office, promptly at 6:00, with me describing how I'd broken into Ann's apartment. I was up to Wednesday morning at the airport, when Ernie announced dinner.

By the time we'd finished the bread pudding—mine laced with brandy, his plain—and headed back to his office for coffee, I was revealing Ted Masterson's comments at the cemetery that morning, including his suspicions about the ski accident. And I was finishing with that afternoon's phone conversation with Ann as the coffee ran out. By then, I was two hours late for the poker game, but I didn't mind a bit. It was a relief to have my guru back in the old ball game.

I suppose he's not the best listener in the world, if by good listening you mean empathy. The man's about as empathetic as a lobster. But when he gets it in gear, he can assimilate, collate, and juggle facts with superhuman speed. He can also turn a mishmash into a coherent, logical whole.

That Thursday evening, he was in overdrive.

He had very few questions, mainly, I'd like to think, because I've become a great reporter over the years. I felt drained. As though the total contents of my skull had been airlifted to his.

When I had finished all I had to tell, and drained the last of the coffee, I put down my cup and said, "All right, Bishop. You've now got everything I've got, so I assume you know the name of the murderer. Just tell me who it is, I'll turn the culprit in to Kessler, and Father William can get back to his life as a monk-and-playboy." Believe it or not, I was only half joking. I'd seen the man perform.

The Bishop was sitting back comfortably with his eyes closed and his leg rests elevated for circulation. He hadn't shifted his position once during the previous hour. If I hadn't known him better, I'd have assumed he fell asleep. But knowing him as I did, I knew he was working as hard as anyone can who operates on sheer brain power. Well, actually, I have to admit that when he didn't move for a good thirty seconds after I challenged him to "Name that Murderer!" I began to wonder whether I'd overestimated his powers of concentration. In fact I was about to test him by saying something irritating when he spoke, eyes still closed.

" 'Monk-and-playboy,' indeed. I don't know which is more insufferable, David, your fractured syntax, or the real dilemma to which it points. The idea of rescuing this so-called 'monk' from the consequences of his irresponsible, arrogant, immature—" He stopped, opened his eyes, and glared at me. "Words fail me, David, and you know that doesn't happen often."

I nodded, and he continued with a sigh. "Nonetheless, I suppose we should proceed, for the sake of the Archdiocese. I am committed. And so, thank God, are you." He favored me with a slight smile. "I congratulate you, David, on persevering with the case—and quite effectively, too—in the face of my own abject withdrawal. I assure you, that won't happen again. As I said, I am committed." He put his fingertips together, tipped his head back and frowned at the ceiling.

"As to naming the murderer, you must have omitted something because the name eludes me. Nonetheless, you have provided some very interesting and provocative information. I have a suggestion or two. But first, what conclusions have *you* drawn?"

"Well, there are two obvious areas to explore. The ski accident—if it was an accident—and the four people up at Bob McClain's place last Sunday night."

"Agreed. And of the two areas, which will Mr. Kessler be pursuing?" His eyes were again closed, his body still.

"Oh, I don't think he's going to be bothering with the ski accident. I doubt if he's got the same underhanded proclivity you have, of suspecting every innocent accident of being a homicide."

His eyes popped open. "Your use of words, David," he grumbled, shaking his head. "If I occasionally treat words as duelling swords, as you claim—and I suppose that may be true on certain occasions—then, utilizing a similar metaphor, you wrestle them to the ground and pummel them into submissison."

Getting no rise out of me, he sighed. "Nonetheless, I cannot quibble with your conclusion. I agree. The police will, with the prompting Miss Shields has given them, be worrying those four people like an angry terrier a rag doll. They will try to learn more about that disappearing and reappearing key ring. And, while busy with that, they may overlook the possible connection between the death of Miss McClain and that of her father six months ago.

Indeed, there may be none. But if there is, it's possible we could steal a march on Mr. Kessler. In any case, connection or not, I have formed a conjecture which could stand some testing.

"Your current plan to drive to Northern Springs tomorrow just happens to be admirably suited to test that very conjecture. I must warn you, your trip may prove fruitless. The habitués of ski resorts, I have found, tend to scatter to the four winds in the summertime. But I urge you to find at least a policeman or two to speak with. They are *not* seasonal, I would assume. With luck, you may find others with information as well.

"Of course, with your usual foresight, you have arranged for a suitably attractive escort for the day. I have no objection, though I recommend you take steps to prevent her from interfering. Her words about 'wanting to help' are problematic."

"I'll sit on her."

"To be sure." He gave me the look he always gives me when I play around with my own handy colloquialisms. Then he pressed a button on the arm of the wheelchair and elevated his legs an additional inch. "Meanwhile, it might be useful to obtain further background information on our four suspects. Why not put our friend, Mr. Rozanski, to work on it?"

"Not a bad idea. I've already got Dave Baker working on Missy and Norm—since they're both lawyers." I looked at my watch. "I'm now more than two hours late for the poker game. If I rush, I can play a hand or two. That'll give me a chance to find out if Chet can lend a hand—so to speak—at the same time."

Regan looked at his watch and shook his head.

He can't understand anyone going out after ten o'clock at night, but he's given up on changing me. Wheeling around to his desk, he started on a pile of personnel files he'd been perusing earlier. I was dismissed.

The poker game was a debacle. Though three hours late, and the first to leave, I still managed to be the big loser. When I walked out in disgust at 12:30, I was forty-seven bucks leaner than when I'd arrived. Of course, everyone was sorry to see me go, for purely selfish motives. But no one disputed my excuse: I was tapped out.

The only good thing that happened to me that evening came when I cornered Rozanski in the kitchen. At the time, the two of us were replenishing the beer supply for everyone.

"Got a little job for you," I warned him.

"If you want the murderer's name, Davey, I'm saving that for a scoop on Sunday. But here's a deal. You tell *me,* and I'll tell you if you're right."

I grinned at him. "As a matter of fact, I've got the list narrowed to four, and I'll give *that* to you, if you'll promise to research the people for me."

He raised a quizzical brow. "Hell, I've got a list of *one,* Davey: Charles Ryder. Only, no one knows where he is or what his real name is. I've suspected all along that he's your client."

"Wrong again, Chet. I don't even *know* anyone whose name is Charles Ryder."

Rozanski sneered.

"I'll give you a little hint," I continued, "and this one is free."

He glanced at me suspiciously.

"Ryder didn't do it. And you can take that one to the bank."

Rozanski continued to look skeptical. So I went on.

"Then who did? I'll give you that, too. One of those *other* four folks who were at the brother's apartment last Sunday night. Bet your house on that, and you'll never sleep in the street."

Rozanski's eyes widened. He realized I wasn't playing games. "One of those four? How do—?"

Kelley's mellifluous voice floated in from the dining room. "What the hell's going on with you two in there? Will you bring the damn beer, and let's play some poker?"

"Keep your pants on!" I yelled. I turned to Chet. "The natives are getting restless. We'd better get back in there. Find me some info on those four people, Chet, and you won't regret it. Hell, you're going to need it anyway, when one of them gets arrested."

He gave me a long, suspicious look as I loaded the tray with six cold bottles of beer and a couple of bowls of pretzels. I wondered what he'd say if he knew that "Charles Ryder" was someone he'd played golf and had a few drinks with. I'd have loved to say, "Chet, don't you ever look at your own paper's identikit pictures?" Duty inhibits one's liveliest impulses.

Chet didn't say anything further about my request, but I knew I'd hit home. I thought he'd have a fairly good bag for me by the weekend.

So, despite my flattened wallet, I wasn't feeling all that bad when I got home and set the alarm. Losing fifty bucks is never pleasant, but having the Bishop back in the game, getting another full night's rest, and gaining the prospect of acquiring new data on the suspects more than made up for my financial losses.

Best of all, I had a hot date with a dynamite-looking brunette who was going with me to the Catskills the next morning.

Friday, August 26

XXXV

The drive up, Friday morning, was delightful. The day was hot and muggy, but the Cadillac's interior was an air-conditioned seventy degrees. The picnic basket in the back seat, prepared by Ernie, looked inviting. And the brunette sitting eight inches to my right, bare legs crossed, wasn't getting a bit uglier with age. Her casual outfit included Spandex shorts, frilly blouse, and not a whole lot more. She posed a real traffic hazard. My eyes kept wanting to swivel in their sockets.

Having thought about it during breakfast, I'd devised a suitable way that Ann could help. As we pointed the Seville northward on the parkway, I brought it up. "You'd like to help?"

She turned to me eagerly. "Oh, yeah! Just tell me what you want me to do."

"Now, don't get too excited," I cautioned. "I don't need any crooks tied up, which is a shame, because I know you could do it. I'd like you to nose around the Majestic Resort, and see who you can worm some information out of. I've always heard that ski bums enjoy having information extracted by pretty brunettes. How are you as a sex kitten?"

"Hey! You're looking at someone who sat through *Black Widow* three times! I'll put some moves on these guys they've never even heard of!"

I did my best to dampen her enthusiasm to a manageable level, but she was dying to play. So, with some misgivings, I decided to turn her loose. First I gave her our basic story. We were a couple of high-concept, freelance writers commissioned to do a magazine article on ski safety. We were investigating deaths on the slopes.

"Naturally, given our subject matter, we're looking into Bob McClain's death. If we're lucky enough to find someone who was there in February, it ought to be duck soup." I frowned and shook my head. "I don't know what it says about human nature, but being in the vicinity of a fatal accident seems to be the most exciting thing that can happen to a person. Anyone who was there at the time will be dying to talk about it. I guarantee, you ask a question, and they won't shut up."

I handed her a spare notebook. "Keep this. It's an excellent prop. And by the way, not *just* a prop. Get down everything you can. If you get too engrossed in the story, you might forget what we're here for."

That got Ann anxious. She sat for a moment, watching buildings sail by on either side. "I don't know, Dave. It started out like fun. But now I'm afraid I'm going to screw up." Her voice was subdued, and she looked distastefully at the notebook in her lap.

I patted her on the shoulder. "Don't worry, you'll do fine. Look: think of it as collecting data. We want to talk to anyone who was there last February 3 . . ."

By Newburgh, we had our basic strategy worked out and had progressed to more personal issues. By New Paltz I had learned what she did for a living: something called systems research with an outfit on the Avenue of the Americas, a fifteen-minute walk south of her apartment. By Kingston I had heard plenty about her family back in Oklahoma, which seemed to consist mainly of her father, big oil tycoon.

"I think one reason Barb and I got along so well was that both of us had lost our mothers at an early age," said Ann. "So our fathers had to bring us up. Both our fathers were really successful guys. Of course, I was an only child, whereas Barb had her brother. But we both had loving dads. Mine had only two loves: me and his business. And he never let me doubt that I came first. I don't think many kids can say that, but I could, and so could Barb.

"Course, Barb also had her brother, but he's six years older and she always felt like he resented her. She really didn't get along with either him or Missy."

"Why was that?"

"I'm not sure, Dave. I never met them while Barb was alive. But she told me a lot. Barb felt Bob was throwing his life away, gambling, living in an expensive apartment on Park Avenue and not doing a blessed thing but live off Daddy. And he was always asking Daddy for more. Their dad has provided trusts for both Barb and Bob with a 'spendthrift clause.' My dad has the same thing in mind, though my trust is tiny compared to what Barb's was."

"Spendthrift clause?" I was just waking up to the fact that rich kids have a whole different vocabulary.

Ann looked happy to be able to teach me something. "Just means you can't use your stock as collateral. You can't borrow against it—and any lender has to know that. So your access to loans is limited. Barb told me that *really* bothered Bob. It meant he had to get by on just the dividends from the stock. He couldn't take out huge loans, because he didn't have the equity or income. Lenders shy away when they see that kind of clause."

"How much were his dividends?" I was starting to take notes in my head.

"From little hints Barb gave me, each of them must have gotten something like twenty or thirty thousand a year. Their dad had put a little less than twenty-five percent of all the bank stock into each of their trusts, keeping just over half for himself."

She frowned. "I know one of the fights with her brother began when Barb told him it was ridiculous that he should go after their father for more. After all, he had his trust income, plus Missy was making plenty."

She laughed. "Get this, Dave. Junior told Barb, 'Well, as man of the family, I ought to make at *least* what my wife does.' At the same time, he didn't think it was fair for his dad to even take Missy's income into account in figuring how much money he should have to live on." She shook her head, grinning. "I guess he just wanted it both ways."

"Did Bob ever consider getting a *job?* That's been known to lead to an income occasionally."

Ann chuckled. "Barb's position, exactly. But I guess Bob had all kinds of reasons why no job was worthy of him."

"Did the father's death bring them closer together?"

"Oh my God, Dave, that's when the fights *really* started! Their dad had left each of them exactly fifty percent of his remaining shares: split it right down the middle. So, neither one had control. To make any changes in the bank, both had to agree.

"Their main argument was over the bank's dividend policy. Bob wanted more of the income paid out to the shareholders—him and Barb. And Barb wasn't ready for that. Her position was, why pay the taxes? Why not leave the money there to grow?

"So, with her not agreeing to a dividend increase, Bob wanted to sell the bank and cash in their chips, you know? He couldn't even sell his shares, the way their dad had left things, unless he could get her to go along and sell hers too. And Barb was wavering on that one. She asked Mr. Masterson for his advice, and he definitely told her not to sell. He said if they sold at that point they wouldn't get fair value for it. Still, I know she was thinking about it real seriously the last time we talked, which was just last week."

"So, how did Missy feel about all this?"

"No idea. But I know Missy disliked Barb. Actually, 'hated' was Barb's word for it. I think that had more to do with Barb's being a teacher than anything about the bank.

"I guess Missy made a sneering comment about teachers—something about how little money they made. And Barb really let her have it. She could do that when she got mad, she had a temper like mine." Ann grinned ruefully. "Barb called Missy a snooty bitch who thought more of her five-hundred-dollar suits than about what really mattered—which, in Barb's opinion, was children."

We were now in the Catskills, we skirted the northern edge of the Ashokan Reservoir, and drove through the village of Northern Springs. A mile west of town, we came to the "MAJESTIC RESORT" turnoff.

Emerging from a dense thicket of trees, I could see an open expanse, with a sizable hill sloping sharply upward to our left. The hill was partially covered with trees, interspersed between several wide swaths of grassy slopes. Supported on crosslike pylons, the ski-lift cables snaked all the way from the foot to the peak of the mountain. Of the six or seven lifts, only one was operating.

Nestled at the foot of the lifts were three large buildings with wide, sloping roofs, in behind a several-acre parking lot with a meager summertime sprinkling of cars and vans. In front of the main entrance was a large sign reading "SUMMERTIME RATES." From the looks of abandonment about the place, they needed to reduce those rates even more.

"Want to try your skills?" I inquired.

"I'm game!" It was nice to see her excited again.

"Then you're on your own. Hop out and start worming. I'll pick you up right here sometime before six."

Ann slipped on her topsiders and strode bravely toward the big front door of the Resort. I headed back to Northern Springs, wondering what sorts of adventures she'd encounter on her first day as deputy detective.

XXXVI

As the county seat of Catskill County, Northern Springs houses the local custodian of law and order. The county courthouse on the town square was in the typical, fake-Greek style that seems to dominate every county seat. At ground level were individual county offices, including one marked "Fred. C. Langston, Sheriff." That door also bore a handwritten note reading: "Gone to Phoenicia. Back around 12:30. Fred."

I was looking from the note to my watch and wondering how much later he'd be, when a beat-up black-and-white K-car with "Sheriff: Catskill County" on the door pulled into the "RESERVED" parking space in front of the office. I sized up the khaki-uniformed man who emerged from the car as he unfolded his lanky body and reached into the car for his Smokey-the-Bear hat.

He was a lot of man to size up. About six-six, broad-shouldered, maybe ten or fifteen pounds overweight, he had muscle to spare. This didn't surprise me, in a county sheriff. What *did* surprise me was that he was black.

He flashed a smile as I caught his eye. Stepping onto the sidewalk, he grabbed my outstretched hand. His grip was bone-jarring. "Sheriff Langston," he stated in a gravelly baritone. "What can I do for you?"

"Sheriff, I'm Dave Goldman. And telling you what you can do for me might take a minute or two of your time, which I hope you've got."

He glanced at his watch. "Normally, I'm sitting down to lunch about now."

"Well, Sheriff, I'd be delighted to *take* you to lunch."

"Thanks. I'll take you up on that. Just give me a second to see if I got any messages on the answering machine, and I'll be right with you. My secretary doesn't get here till one."

The Sheriff was as good as his word—back on the sidewalk inside his promised minute. "Let's go down to Frieda's, Mr. Goldman. They have a decent salad bar."

"Make that 'Dave,' would you, Sheriff?"

Once in Frieda's, and settled in our booth with our salad plates, I confronted Langston straight on for the first time. His strong face with its hooked nose, high cheekbones and muscular jaw gave him the look of someone who enjoys confrontations, and he had a formidable one at the moment. Namely, the salad plate before him—a large platter piled astonishingly high with green comestibles. He caught me glancing at it.

"Now," he said, taking his first bite. "What can I do for you, Dave?"

I pushed a radish around my plate with the fork. "Sheriff, I'm a freelance writer planning an article on ski safety. Several skiing deaths occurred last winter. What caused them? Were they preventable? The National Skiing Association recorded eighteen deaths last winter and I just happened to notice that one of them occurred right here at Majestic."

Sheriff Langston lanced a chunk of feta cheese, pinioned it against a couple of raw cauliflowers, and looked at me impassively, his eyes wary. Something about my story seemed to bother him, but I didn't know what.

I decided to pull out my notebook and consult it, for credibility. Having done so, I leaned forward, using my sincere voice. "This Robert McClain, Sheriff. He died February 3. I have some background data on the case, but I understand you had some involvement as well. I wonder if you'd mind telling me what you know about it."

An uncomfortable silence followed—uncomfortable for me, that is. The discomfort increased as the Sheriff's intense gaze showed no signs of diminishing.

"Interesting story, Dave, very interesting. A freelance *writer,* you say, doing an article on ski safety? And you just *happened* up here 'cause what? —you noticed that Northern Springs was only an hour or so from the city? Uh-huh. And you thought you'd pop up here and talk to the hick sheriff?

"No, don't bother to interrupt. You'll have plenty of opportunity after I'm done. I'll see to that." Langston put down the fork and leaned across the table, glancing right and left, in mock confidentiality.

"Well, *Mister* Goldman—*if* that *is* your name—I've been reading the New York *Times* and, to be honest, I just don't believe a freelance writer just *happened,* accidentally, to pick this week of all weeks to come up here and look into the McClain death—the very same week the old man's daughter gets murdered with a knife. You know what I mean?" He leaned even closer and dropped his voice to a near-whisper.

"So, *Mister* Goldman, I'll just have to look at your I.D., if you don't mind. 'Cause this story about freelance writer just ain't cuttin' it." He extended his left hand to me and snapped his fingers a couple of times. "Let's see the I.D."

XXXVII

I pulled out my billfold and put my private investigator's license onto his waiting palm. "At least I didn't lie about my name," I said with a weak smile.

He squinted at the card, with its lousy photo of me in a sweatshirt. He looked up with raised eyebrows. A patient man, waiting for an explanation. Which had better be good.

"Here's the way it is, Fred." I explained the circumstances as efficiently as I knew how. "Now," I concluded, "may I tell you what I'm *really* after, and why I'm really here."

He nodded, without expression. So I did—explain, that is—fighting, every inch of the way, through the dark, suspicious, steady gaze. Not an easy thing, even telling the truth. I omitted only the unimportant details and, of course, any hint of my relationship with the infamous "Charles Ryder." By the time I had finished, Langston had finished his salad.

Apparently my explanation satisfied Langston. "Thanks for the fill-in, Dave. This time I'm buying it." He leaned back. "Now let me share something with you. I've been looking for someone to arrive ever since I read about Barbara's murder. And as soon as I saw you on the sidewalk in front of my office, I was *sure* this was it. I mean, you got 'cop' written all over you. Well, O.K., let me tell you what I know."

Langston explained to me some of the background behind McClain's purchase of the property. Though adjacent to state land, where the ski resort was located, McClain's property was privately owned. Under its previous owner, part of the land had been leased to the ski resort—and one of the trails, "Lodgepole," was on the McClain property.

"When the property sold," Langston said, "McClain built his lodge on a flat spot about halfway up the run. He had the right to use Lodgepole for access to all the other slopes. That's what's called 'ski-in, ski-out' property. It sells at a premium."

Trouble was, as Langston explained it, the resort stopped maintaining the trail. As the brush grew up around the trail, it got to be dangerous to ski. Eventually, the resort put up a fence to keep skiers off Lodgepole. McClain was hopping mad, but he couldn't do anything about it.

The week of the bank's ski holiday, when all the directors were at the lodge for their annual meeting (Langston explained), Masterson found a way around the fence that blocked the Lodgepole run. He and McClain used the trail—but they were the only two who dared to ski it, the trail was so overgrown. They made an agreement that neither one of them would ski it unless the other one went along.

I complimented Langston on the amount of research he'd done.

"Thanks," he said. "You're the only guy who

noticed. In fact, I'm glad you asked. After the whitewash the state cops did, I made up my mind I was gonna get to the bottom of it. I thought all along there was a good chance Bob was murdered."

At that point, the Sheriff put down his coffee cup and looked me in the eye.

Here it comes! I thought, getting that tingle in the spine that usually meant I was closing in on something good. Obviously, I'd come to the right place.

But when Langston spoke the next words, he had a small, sad smile on his face.

"Only thing is, Dave, when you look at the suspects, it had to be the people staying at the McClain lodge. And every single last one of them's got an airtight alibi. I looked at all the angles, I've gotta tell you. But when I came to the end of it, I had to rule out murder."

I stared at Langston, my heart sinking. It was beginning to look like the trip to Northern Springs had just turned into a gigantic bust.

"Say what, Fred?" I narrowed my eyes at him.

"I know," he nodded mournfully. "I didn't wanna believe it either. Everything smells like murder, but nothin's out of place."

"Well," I sighed, "I was hoping my homework was all done." I pulled my notebook out of my pocket. "Looks like we'll have to begin at the beginning."

The Sheriff grinned at me sympathetically. "Can't say I blame you. I've been there, too. Well, I need more coffee, but apart from that, my time is yours."

It was a lot to cover, but in a lot of ways I was lucky. Without Langston, the groundwork would have taken me months, especially since the trail was cold.

First, I wanted some distinguishing features about Bob McClain, and Fred came up with a good one. Seems the guy was a perpetual cigar smoker. Everywhere he went, even in the slopes, he had a cigar stuck in his mouth. Lit or unlit, it became his trademark—so much so that his nickname was "Stogie Bob."

We went over the events that occurred the evening that Stogie Bob took his last puff. It was already dark, and Langston was having dinner with his wife at the Majestic when the emergency call came through from the station house: McClain was missing. Within minutes, snowmobiles were crawling like bugs over the slopes, headlights blazing.

A key guy in the search was Stub McKay, who was head of the ski patrol and the ski school, as well as year-round manager of the trails. After talking with some of McClain's party—who'd been waiting for him in the Majestic Lodge—Stub concluded that Bob must have tried the Lodgepole trail by himself.

Even in the dark, it didn't take long to find the body. The corpse was lying in the woods directly under a tree limb in about forty inches of deep powder. Stogie Bob's windpipe had been crushed. It looked like he'd run into the tree limb at high speed, probably out of control. Death was quick. Suffocation.

Langston shook his head. "Everyone was pretty shook up, including Stub. The women at the lodge were damn near hysterical. That daughter, Barb, was probably the worst off. I've never seen anyone take on so."

I nodded.

"Well, after the women got settled down, Ted

Masterson and I talked about it. Said he was feeling awful. Blamed himself, 'cause he's the one who figured the way around the fence. Stub was mad as hell about that—talked liability and such—but he eased up when he saw how hard Masterson was taking it. I guess Ted and McClain had been buddies for a long time. I gathered Masterson was sort of McClain's protégé in the banking business."

I asked about the death site. Langston had gone back with Stub at six o'clock the next morning. They'd looked around pretty carefully.

"We could see Stub's snowmobile tracks from the night before, and we made sure to stay on those, so we wouldn't mess up the snow. Up at the top, we saw a number of ski tracks where Stogie and Masterson had got around the fence, then some tracks leading down the hill. Bob and Ted had used that trail at the end of every day, and you could see the turn-marks in the fresh powder."

Langston hesitated a second, and squinted.

"What is it?" I asked.

"Well, there was one thing I couldn't figure out, and maybe it's not important. About those tracks?"

I looked up from my notebook.

"Yes?"

"Well, most of them were short fishtails—you know, the kind of short tracks skiers make in deep snow, doing jump-turns. But one set of tracks were kind of swooping—way off to the left and the right. Like one of them had really taken his time getting down the hill." The Sheriff considered that for another moment, then shrugged. "I guess one of 'em just decided to take it slow."

I waited a second.

"Anything else?"

Langston looked at me, considering hard. "That's about it. That branch was so low, both guys had to duck it every time they came down the hill. The way it looked, McClain had forgotten—or he'd been moving too fast. Anyway, he didn't duck, I guess—and it caught him right there." The Sheriff pointed to my Adam's apple. I tried not to gulp. "Stub and I looked around real careful, where the body had been. There was no sign anyone else had been there. And like I say, there was plenty of snow. If there'd been footprints, we would've seen them."

There were a few more details, in the next hour or so, that ended up in my notebook—but mainly because the Bishop asks me about *everything* when he's in an asking mood, and I don't like to be ruthlessly interrogated without a script in front of me. But if there was anything to find in those notes, the Bishop would have to do the finding. I was high and dry, and just about convinced—though I hated to admit it—that the state cops had done their job. Taken on the evidence, this case had "accidental death" written all over it.

Langston and I were on good terms by the time we got back to his station house. But like everything else, good terms are never eternal, and it wasn't long before my reputation was under stress again.

It happened just about the moment Langston pushed open the door of the Sheriff's office and invited me in.

"This here's Marilyn O'Donovan, my right-hand person," he said, introducing me to a pretty, plump, red-haired secretary. "Whatta we got, Marilyn?"

"Stub just called, Sheriff," said the redhead. She

turned out to be one of those secretaries who turns every statement into a question. "He needs you to come up to the McClain lodge right away. Says there's a woman up there giving him a false story? Ummm . . ." She looked up from her notebook. "This woman told Stub she and some fella were doing an article on ski accidents? Wanted to know about that McClain thing last winter? I guess she got Stub to take her from the resort up to the McClain lodge, and they were looking around when Mr. and Mrs. McClain, Jr.?—they came driving up, and said they knew the woman, and that she wasn't any magazine writer. They think she's some smart-alecky reporter or something, trying to nose around, get some dirt on something or other?"

I felt my face getting redder with every question Marilyn asked.

Sheriff Langston had been holding his hat since he came in the office. He now flipped it onto a chair and turned to me, hands tucked into hip pockets.

Smiling a mirthless smile, he spoke softly. "Well, well, well. Seems like you didn' tell me quite everything, *Mister* Goldman, even *now.*"

XXXVIII

"Well, what a coincidence!" I exclaimed, glancing back and forth from the girl to the large, angry Sheriff. "*Two* magazine writers showing up at the same time, same place, looking for data on the same subject. Just think of the probabilities of that happening! *The Guinness Book of World Records* should be notified."

"Stuff it, Goldman!" Langston's patience had snapped. "Your humor's wearin' thin. I wanta know what the hell is going on, and right *now!*"

"Look, Sheriff, outside of a little cover story, what lie have I told?"

"You said you came up here alone."

"Hold it right there. I never said I *came alone.* If you assumed it, I can't help that. I had no reason to hide the fact that Ann came with me."

"O.K., you didn't say 'alone,' so scratch that. Does that girl have an investigator's license? If she doesn't, I'm gonna—"

"Give me a *break,* Fred! You can't charge her with anything. You don't need a license to ask a few questions."

"O.K., O.K.," he said resignedly. He grabbed

his hat, put his arm around me and headed me toward the door. "I imagine you want to take a run up to McClain's place."

"Not only that—I'll drive."

As we drove out of town toward the resort, I seized the opportunity to ask about alibis.

"Sheriff, I was damn near convinced that whoever killed Barb must have done her dad also. I mean, we've got the same four people who could have killed the girl, all here at the lodge last February when the dad died. He died in a ski accident that no one witnessed—no one who's talking, that is. Now you tell me that it would have been physically *impossible* for any of them to have done it—and not only that, they all have airtight alibis. I just can't believe it. Tell me about the alibis, would you?"

He declined. "We'll be seein' Stub McKay in about five minutes. Why not wait and let *him* tell you? Then you can judge for yourself whether he's credible."

"Any idea of what the autopsy had to say?" I asked.

Langston laughed. "You just don't give up, do ya, Dave? As a matter of fact, I *did* see the autopsy report, though what it said won't help you much. Death occurred between 12:00 and 6:00 P.M.! That's right, a six-hour window. See, the temp was down near zero that day, which makes the determination of time of death very chancy. But the cause was clear—a ruptured windpipe. Now, that *could* be done by a tree branch. But it could also be done by one quick hand-chop."

We had just reached a level area where a generous-sized A-frame was perched. From the vantage point we had a generous view of the valley below. Sitting on the steps of the spacious porch of the building were two people. One was Ann. The other was a corpulent-looking bruiser with a fair-sized beard, wearing a floppy outback-style ranger hat. He seemed at ease. But Ann, even at a hundred yards, looked like she'd lost her last friend and had just abandoned all hope of ever finding another.

XXXIX

We rolled to a stop next to a shiny, new Porsche that was parked by the front steps. Off to the side was a dusty, battered pickup truck with the words "Majestic Resort" stencilled on the left-hand door.

Ann's face lit up when she saw me. It didn't look like her time with the outdoorsy bruiser had been sheer entertainment.

"How y' doin', Stub?" Langston said as he shook the man's hand. A gleaming set of teeth appeared in the middle of the beard. The Sheriff pronounced my name.

"Hey, Dave, raht prouda meetchew!" McKay allowed. His nasal tenor drawl bespoke a rearing south of the Mason–Dixon line. *Well* south. The Sheriff had a homey accent of his own, but Stub made him sound, by comparison, like a sophisticated Manhattanite.

The skin of McKay's round face, I observed from up close, had a leathery look from much too much exposure to the sun. I guessed him to be in his late forties.

I introduced Ann to the Sheriff, and his quick, shrewd eyes sized her up. "Reporter, huh?"

He grinned at her, then turned to McKay. "What kinda trouble y' into *now,* Stub?" he asked mildly.

"Hey, Freddy, no trouble," the ski pro answered easily, with a shrug of his massive shoulders. "The lady here was asking me some questions about Stogie's accident. We were talkin' about it down at the Resort, and I offered to bring her up here and show her where it all happened. I've got a key, you know, so I can keep an eye on the place while they're gone. Well, we'd no sooner got here when up comes Junior and Missy in their Porschmobile. One look at the lady—who they recognized—and they start their yellin' an' fussin'. They claim she's fakin' this magazine routine."

Ann was pale. I gave her a brotherly pat on the arm and a wink, with a whispered, "Welcome to the club."

After that, I doubted that we'd gain admittance into the interior of the lodge, but I was wrong. Thirty seconds after Langston's rap on the door, the very corpulent Bob, Jr., opened it and ushered us in to what, I later learned, they called "The Great Room."

The title was fairly apt. About the size of a medium-sized bowling alley, The Great Room was filled with rugs, furniture and rustic gew-gaws. The decorator had obviously been overcome by a fit of outdoorsiness; heads and skins of dead animals were everywhere. Over the main fireplace was a huge bearskin, the jaws gaping wide. A pair of crossed snowshoes flanked the bearskin.

Missy McClain was seated on a sofa in the center of the room, looking down her nose at everything:

skins, heads, people, you name it. Though it was probably my imagination, she seemed to have grown smaller, and Bob even fatter, since the funeral just the day before.

Junior asserted immediate control over the proceedings. Standing next to the couch where his wife was seated, he said to Langston, "Thanks for coming, Sheriff. I want you to know I am simply distraught over these people's insensitivity." He waved a vague hand at Ann and me. "Missy and I have lost two close and dear family members this year. And now we find this alleged magazine writer up here, digging up who-knows-what! Well, Sheriff, it's simply an outrage." Taking a deep breath, he shook his head. When he resumed, his somewhat feeble baritone—always on the verge of cracking—sounded hushed.

"At my sister's funeral, just Wednesday, this man was nosing around, asking questions. I later find out he'd barged into our bank just the day before and bothered several officials there in similar fashion. So I checked him out. Through a police official I know, we learned"—Junior's tone grew ponderous—"that Mr. Goldman is a former policeman who was discharged from the force years ago—*for cause.* The New York police have registered numerous complaints about his constant interference with their investigations. And this is his accomplice. She was at the funeral with him! I saw her! Now she comes *here* with some cock-and-bull story about being a magazine reporter. It's an *outrage,* Sheriff, and I want it *stopped!* I'll sign whatever needs to be signed."

Langston had been nodding sympathetically.

"I can appreciate how you feel, Mister McClain,"

he said, looking humbly down at his hat, "but I need to know what law these people are charged with violating."

"Trespassing, for one thing," Missy said in a thin voice. Neither lips, teeth, nor face seemed to move as she spoke. "This woman was on our property without authorization."

I grinned, and patted Stub McKay on his thick shoulder. "You're in trouble, fella. You're the one who brought her up here, right?" That attempt at humor could not really be called wildly successful. Fred and Ann stared, Junior and Missy glared, and Stub looked embarrassed.

"Mr. Goldman has a point, Mrs. McClain," Fred said. "It does seem she came up here with Mr. McKay, who has your permission to look after the lodge."

"But she *lied* to him," Junior blurted out, his voice breaking into a momentary falsetto. "She's here under false pretenses."

"Not a crime, as far as I know, Mr. McClain," Langston demurred, "unless you can show me some law."

"Well, I just want her *out* of here!" Bob exploded. "And her 'godfather' with her!"

I stepped forward. "I'm terribly sorry about the misunderstanding, Mr. and Mrs. McClain. Let me explain, please." The two of them glared at me.

"Miss Shields, here, was a close friend and neighbor of your sister, Mr. McClain. She told you that at the funeral, but maybe you didn't hear her. I am a licensed private detective, and Miss Shields had hired me to investigate the death of her friend."

"You what?" Missy glared at Ann. "You dared

to hire this *man,* to investigate? How *dare* you usurp the authority of the police?"

Ann looked at me with helpless eyes. I turned my attention to the attorney. "Look, Mrs. McClain. There's nothing illegal in what Miss Shields has done. All she has asked me to do is assist the police in their investigation."

"Sheriff, excuse me," Missy snapped, "but we're expecting weekend guests. Mr. McClain and I don't have time now to come to the courthouse and sign charges. We'll rely on you to do the right thing regarding these people. I hope that's understood?"

You haven't lived till you've seen a four-foot-eleven-inch woman look down her nose at a six-foot-six-inch sheriff. And, to give her full credit, she did it with ease.

"Mrs. McClain," I intervened, "we're already on our way. You've got a beautiful place here, and I think your guests are going to have a whale of a fine weekend."

We were a couple hundred yards down the road, with McKay right behind us, when the Sheriff spoke. "Pull over a second, Dave." I complied. "Do you have a few more minutes to waste up here in God's country?" Langston asked.

"What have you got in mind, Fred?" I wondered. I noted that McKay's truck had pulled to a stop behind us.

"If you've got another fifteen minutes, I expect I can get you that talk with Stub you wanted along with a drink on-the-house at the Resort."

I glanced at Ann, who nodded. "Don't ask *him,* ask me. I'm the client," she said to the Sheriff, "and the answer speaking for both of us, is 'Yes, thank you very much.' "

Langston walked back to the truck and exchanged a brief word with McKay. He returned, climbed in the back seat, and said, "To the Resort, Driver. There'll be a sizeable tip for you, if you get us there in thirty seconds."

"Best offer I've had today!" I said.

And burned some rubber.

XL

The bar at the Resort was as rustic, in its own way, as "The Great Room" of the McClains' lodge, though much more understated. Looking at those walls made you feel like Abe Lincoln all over again. Logs everywhere, big ones. Sunlight streamed in through the glass wall behind the bar. As we entered, we had a vista of the green, sweeping slopes of the mountain, rising in tilted acres of waving grass.

The bartender looked like a college fellow. McKay called him "Ralph," as in "See what my friends'll have, Ralph, and rush 'em over here."

Ralph was eager to please, since his boss was playing host. He put us in a large booth in the darkest corner.

Ralph brought the drinks and distributed them around the table.

"Well, Stub," Sheriff Langston opened the conversation, "these people run a con on us good and proper, both of 'em. Though I imagine Miss Shields, here, was a little smoother with you than old Buster with me." Fred gave me a big smile. "I've already told what I know, Stub. Now it's your turn."

McKay nodded, took a hefty slug of his beer, and looked at Ann and me. "I'm the one to talk to," McKay began, " 'cause I was the guy that found the body. But I gotta tell you, you're not gonna get anywhere lookin' to make this into a case of murder." He looked at me defiantly.

"If it's not, it's not," I shrugged. "But I'd like to hear what you know about it. The Sheriff's already got me ninety-five percent convinced it had to be an accident."

Stub proceeded to describe the fatal Wednesday much as Langston had described it earlier. But he had one important addition—the alibi for the residents of the McClain lodge.

McKay began his story with the sighting of McClain, Senior, from the chairlift toward the top of the Iroquois run.

"I was on the lift heading up for my last checkup of the day skiers, and he was just startin' down," McKay recalled. "I waved and he gave me his standard salute." Stub demonstrated, putting the tips of the fingers of his right hand near his forehead, and sweeping the hand grandly out into space. "And of course he had a cigar in his mouth.

"Bob was a funny guy. He was real patriotic, loved the military, always using salutes and whatnot. And he sure loved that damn seegar—I think it made him feel like Gen'ral MacArthur. You know, he was lots of fun to have up here.

"Anyhow, as I was sayin', Stogie and me waved to each other at 4:30. He was just starting down Iroquois, going like a bat outta hell, the way he always did. I was just about to get off the lift. I chatted with a couple of my kids—the ski patrol—up there on Iroquois for a few minutes, then skied on in. The lights had just come on, the night skiers were gettin' ready to come onto the mountain, so I decided to take a couple of minutes for a beer or two before gettin' back out there again." He took a big swig of his beer, wiped his mouth, and continued.

"So I went in the bar. It was 5:02. I can tell you I'm absolutely positive 'bout it, 'cause I checked the clock here"—he gestured at the large clock above the bar—"and I see the McClain bunch, sittin' right over there." He pointed to a round table, with six chairs around it, commanding a view of the slope through the picture window.

"It was Junior, Missy, Masterson 'n' his wife, Cathy, and a guy named Hastings that I didn't know too good. Barb was there too. They'd pulled a seventh chair up to the table for Stogie, but he hadn't got there yet, so they invited me to have a seat till he came. I had a beer with 'em, before going out to get the night bunnies going. As far as Stogie bein' late, I thought nothin' of it.

"I checked the time again when I left 'em to go back out, and it was 5:31. I noticed, 'cause I'm supposed to do the first nightcheck at 5:30, and I was a little pissed at myself for getting out there late. One minute ain't bad, but I don't wanna set a bad example for the kids."

"I'd better explain something here," Langston cut in, turning to me. "What the state police eventually established, with lots of help from Stub, is that Bob, Senior, couldn't have got from the top of Iroquois over to Lodgepole—where he was found—in under twenty-five minutes. To get there, he had to take two lifts and two trails. We timed it, so we know it takes twenty-five minutes, minimum. So whenever McClain died, it couldn't've been before five o'clock." Langston looked at me for my reaction. I was thinking hard and fast. Stub knew Bob pretty well; and he'd seen him at 4:30 . . . I had a question for Stub.

"How close were you to Bob when you saw him at the top of—Iroquois?" I asked.

"Not very close—Stogie was takin' off, I was up on the chairlift. He musta been, oh, maybe thirty, forty yards away. But I knew it was him, not only by the seegar and that salute of his, but by the godawful chartreuse outfit he had on! Worst looking thing I ever seen. Hell, I didn't even know what 'chartreuse' was till he wore that damn thing. Now I wisht I'd never found out."

Langston shook his head. "Yeah, that chartreuse—" He turned to me. "Later on, Stub and I both heard how he happened to be wearing it. It seems Barb had given him a whole outfit—pants, jacket, and cap—for Christmas, last year. It was all this godawful chartreuse. Apparently everyone but Barb had teased Stogie about it. The day he died was the first day he'd worn it."

Stub picked up the narrative. "When I was with the rest of 'em in the bar, everyone was laughing about Bob's 'neon' outfit. Barb came in for some heat, 'cause she's the one who'd given it to him. They were laughing that he'd never put the dang thing on till Barb come up, and, only then, after two days of nagging by her.

"Anyhow," Stub concluded, "you can take my word for it, there wasn't anyone else, anywhere on the mountain, wearing anything like what Stogie had on. That was *definitely* Stogie I waved to."

I was pondering what a fruitless mission to ski country this had been. It was now the bottom of the ninth, the home team three runs down, two outs and the batter down two strikes. I decided I had to try for something—maybe just a scratch single up the middle.

"O.K., Stub, I think I got the picture. We're dealing with an accident. But just for the record, and to fill up the last two pages of this notebook before I throw the damn thing in the Hudson River, tell me about the rest of the evening."

McKay put down his nearly empty glass and gave me his full attention. "I was getting the night skiers goin', and I was just going over to take the lift up Iroquois again, when one of my instructors came charging up and said there was a problem with the McClain group. I was surprised, because the last time I'd seen 'em they were in the bar, relaxed and happy. Well, it turned out they'd gotten worried about Bob a couple minutes after I left 'em, so they drove back to the lodge to see if he was there. When they saw he wasn't, a couple of 'em went out and began shouting up the slope. They didn't get no answer. A couple more came back to the base of the lifts to get us and start lookin'.

"Normally, with something like that I don't get too excited, but this one scared me right away. Hell, I *knew* Stogie, and he was a wild man. I thought about Lodgepole, and how he'd paid no attention to my warning him about it. So, I told one of the kids to have everyone git out there and start lookin', while I grabbed a snowmobile and took off on a beeline for Lodgepole.

"I went by myself. I got to the Stoge—his body, that is—right at 6:20." Stub glumly finished the last of his beer, glanced over at Ralph at the bar, but made no motion. Then he looked at me inquiringly. "Time for another, Dave?"

"Thanks, but no," I answered. "That seems to tie it up with a ribbon. He must have died sometime after 4:55; you found him at 6:20. And, I take it, none of those people at the lodge were out of sight between 5:30 and 6:20."

Langston and Stub just shrugged. "That wouldn't add up, Dave," Langston said. "Stogie had to be dead by 5:30: he was already missing. But, no, for your notebook, none of the party split up after that. Every one of them was accounted for, the rest of the evenin'."

Ann and I bade the gentlemen a not-so-happy but friendly farewell. Although they'd shot down our dream of tying a second murder into the first—or rather, chronologically speaking, a first into a second—they'd been kind enough to buy us a drink to drown our sorrows.

As I opened the door of the Seville for Ann, I said, "That's how it goes with detective work. Some you win and some you lose. Now, we've got to go back to the city and solve the one murder we've got left to solve."

She settled into the seat. "Just *get* the son of a bitch, Dave. That's all I ask."

XLI

Driving back, Ann began to worry about starving to death. As soon as we left the Resort, she'd realized that her body had been deprived of sustenance since breakfast—unless you counted the mai tai just consumed, which she didn't.

Prompted to plunder the lunch basket, the lady immediately set out to prove that her performance at the Bishop's table Tuesday night had been no fluke. She wolfed down the entire lunch Ernie had made, both her portion and mine. Before she tore into the third cold chicken breast—Ernie had intended two of those for me—she said, "Are you *sure* you don't want anything, Dave?" There was a note of longing in her voice.

"You're still a growing child," I told her, translating one of my mother's favorite expressions from Yiddish to English. "Enjoy!"

Though I had now kissed off today's expedition, I was still fascinated by the descriptions of the ski accident. I related to Ann a few of the things I'd learned from the Sheriff at lunch.

Then Ann filled me in on what she'd learned

from Stub about the activities of the suspects on the day of the accident. She proved she'd followed my instructions to use the notebook, referring to it constantly.

"Masterson was the only one who didn't go skiing that day. His wife had just come up that morning. She hadn't planned to come at all, since they had a sick child at home. But he got better, apparently, so she decided to come. Masterson said he'd just skip that day and let her use his lift ticket. He spent the day cross-country skiing and swimming in the indoor pool at the Resort. Later, he met the rest of them for après ski in the Resort lounge.

"All the others went downhill skiing. Mr. McClain had promised Ted he wouldn't ski Lodgepole that day, since he wouldn't have company. Stub said Ted started cursing after they brought the body down. Saying things like 'Why did the S.O.B. have to go off on his own like that?' I guess he was really upset. According to Stub, everyone was."

"Was Bob, Senior, skiing with any of the others that day?" I asked her.

"Stub says not. He was up on the expert trails all the time, and the rest of them weren't up to that. Wait—I guess he had Norm Hastings with him for a while, some time during the afternoon, giving him a lesson. Norm did give one of the steeper runs a go," she continued, "but he fell a few times and didn't enjoy it."

I still wasn't getting anywhere. No matter which way you shuffled the evidence, this ski accident still didn't look like a murder. So I changed the subject.

"Let's talk about Barb," I said, as we sped past Newburgh. "Try to think of any other little thing you haven't already told me, that might relate to one of those four people."

Ann gazed at the highway for a minute before answering. "Going back to last spring," she said, slowly, "she was talking about her brother, one day, and how he was always in need of money. Umm, she said that he—Oh!"

I gave her a quick glance; her blue eyes were startled. "What have you got?" I demanded.

"My *God!* I'd forgotten all about the *envelope!*" She paused, no doubt trying to recall. I gave her time.

Three or four seconds later, when she did speak, her voice had a breathless quality. "One night last spring, we'd been out to a tavern, just the two of us, Barb and I, for some mai tais and conversation. We got back and she invited me in for a drink."

"I take it," I interjected ironically, "you're getting to an *envelope*?"

She reached over and mock-slapped me on the cheek. At least I *assume* it was meant to be mock. My eyes teared up and my vision blurred. I made a mental note to avoid ever starting a real fight with this lady.

"I agreed to come in," she went on, completely concentrated again. "I only had a Coke. Barb fixed herself a strong rum and Coke. After she made the drinks, she went into her bedroom and came back with an envelope. It was all sealed up with lots of tape, and addressed to herself, in her handwriting.

"She told me she wanted me to guard it for her, somewhere besides my apartment. She'd just been robbed a second time, so she didn't trust apartments as a place to keep things. She told me she wanted me to keep it in a safe deposit box. I told her I didn't have one and asked her why she didn't keep it in hers. And then she said a funny thing, when you think what happened to her. She said, 'I don't want to keep it in mine, 'cause you know what happens if you die?' I told her I didn't have a clue; and she said, 'The state opens it, and all your secrets come out. And this has got to stay a secret!' I asked, 'What *is* it, Barb?' but she wouldn't tell me.

"Well, I *did* take the envelope back to my apartment that night. I figured she would get over it in the morning and probably not even remember giving it to me—and I could just give it back to her somehow.

"But, next morning—it was a Saturday—she was tapping on my door at ten o'clock, wanting to know if I've thought about what to do with the envelope. We talked some more. Even cold sober, she still wanted me to take care of it.

"Finally, we drove out to Alsip together, to her dad's bank. Well, actually, I guess by then it was *her* bank. She had me open a safe deposit box. She even paid the rent on it for a year—fifteen bucks, I think it was."

I drove a few more seconds and, just then, noticed the sign, "ALSIP: 1 MI." As I saw it, so did Ann. We looked at each other.

"And it's still there?"

She nodded slowly, her big eyes looking right through me. "Yes. I hadn't thought of it in months."

"Real quick, now, where's the safe deposit box *key* right now?" The "ALSIP: 1/2 MI" sign was coming up, and I was starting to slow the Seville.

She frowned, thinking. A semi behind me gave a toot on the air horn and I responded by flipping on the right-hand turn signal. I normally would have flipped him something else, but I was preoccupied.

"Let me see"—she was pawing through her purse—"I just don't remember where I put it . . . Yes!" she exclaimed triumphantly, holding aloft a bunch of keys on a ring. "Here it is!"

"Good," I muttered, pulling onto the exit ramp as the southbound semi hit the accelerator and blew by with an angry blast of air. "Now, if it only stays open till 4:00." The watch on my wrist read 3:52.

We discussed the situation as I tore down tree-lined streets. It was fortunate that I'd been to the bank just three days before. I didn't have to stop and ask directions. Ann could remember where the safe deposit section of the bank was, though not what its hours were.

Key firmly clutched in hand, she got out of the car as I pulled up to the front door. It was 3:58. From the scowl on the face of the guard, I gathered we'd just beat the deadline.

Five minutes later, Ann came through the door, triumphantly waving a large, manila envelope in her hand. I hurried to open the car door for her.

The guard had his suspicious look back as we drove away. Had he just watched a hot car while the driver's partner-in-crime committed the robbery inside?

Judging from his shrug, he didn't really care a whole lot, either way.

XLII

By the time we pulled away, we were already discussing how to handle the new development.

"Did Barb give you instructions what to do with it, in case of her death?"

"She said, 'Open it, and use your own good judgment about what to do with what's inside.' "

We drove through Alsip in silence before I gave her my considered opinion. "Well, it's now your property, as nearly as I can tell. I'd lay you odds it's got something in it that would help us. But it's not only your property, it's your case. I mean, you're the client. So, it's up to you."

She looked at me. "What would you advise, Dave?"

I glanced back at her briefly. We were approaching the parkway on-ramp.

"My advice," I said, turning onto the ramp, "would be for you to open it right now and read to yourself. From that point, you can use that good judgment to decide what to do next. And after your best judgment kicks in, read it aloud to *me*."

The car grew quiet. I glanced over to see Ann

looking down at the envelope and frowning. "Open it and take a look, Ann. Then you can make a decision."

She obeyed, slitting the envelope open with her thumbnail. As it turned out, there were two envelopes, one inside the other. The inner one, no doubt, contained whatever Barb had wanted to safeguard. I drove in silence, keeping my eyes on the road, while Ann took a good ten minutes to read whatever it was. Without turning my head, I kept track. There were three sheets of paper. When Ann finished, she put the pages on her lap and looked at me. I glanced over. "Well?"

"You need to read this, Dave." She was very quiet, and her voice shook. I glanced again and saw she had tears in her eyes.

"Read it to me."

So she did. The three sheets were written on both sides—all in longhand, from Robert McClain, Sr., to his daughter, Barbara. This is the document that subsequently became "People's Exhibit Number Six" in the celebrated trial, where two experts established to the jury's satisfaction that it was in the senior McClain's handwriting and written the week before his death. What became of the original letter after the trial, I don't know.

But I've still got the xerox I made that evening in my "McClain Case" folder in the office safe. So here's what Ann Shields, in a sometimes quavery voice, read aloud to me on the Palisades Parkway southbound, that Friday afternoon in late August.

> My dearest Barbara—
>
> You may be wondering why you're getting a letter from the old man at this time,

when we just saw each other this afternoon & will be spending an entire week together up at the Lodge next week. But some things are easier to write than to say.

Barb, you know how disappointed I am in Jr. I now have to tell you confidentially that I'm not only irritated with him, I am frightened *for* him. He is in trouble with certain gamblers; he owes over $130,000 that I'm sure of; & it's probably closer to 200.

Of course, Melissa makes big bucks with her law firm. But my sources there tell me she's on thin ice. Something about falsification of her records at Michigan. Of course, Bob has his trust, but that brings in less than 30. Which will be all they have, if Melissa loses her job. And, you know as well as I, they can't live on that, or twice, or 3X that. Not the way they live.

I had a long talk with Jr earlier this month, & both of us got a great deal off our chests. Jr feels I have always favored you & I had to admit he's probably right. You were an easier child & you have certainly been a finer adult. Of course, my disapproval of his marriage didn't help matters any & he still feels bitter over that. But one result of our talk was he agrees to give serious thought to divorcing Melissa & I agreed to help him with that any way I could.

You know how I feel about her, tho of course I didn't tell Jr: that woman is a she-devil. She'd do anything she could to make the divorce as mean & dirty as possible but I believe we've got the tools to fight her with & that he can come out of it without taking too much of a financial licking. I've discussed it, confidentially, with Norm & he's already working on it.

& speaking of Norm, I've got a couple of Personal Observations, Barbara, & I hope you'll take them in the spirit in which they are made. First of all (putting Norm on the back burner for the moment) your drinking. I know: I share the blame for a lot of your problem (& whether you want to admit it or not, Darling, it *is* a problem). I like my booze all too well, *myself,* God knows. But, Barbara, dearest, I really can take it or leave it *alone*. You can only *take* it. & too much of it. Please think about it & don't hate me for telling you about it; I only do it because I *love* you.

Of course the second personal observation I have for you concerns Normie. Since you two are engaged, I have to be more honest with you than I've been up to now; & believe me, it's the only time I'll mention it. I have no intention of disowning you, or anything stupid like that. But Barbara, darling, Norm is a charming, debonair, totally sociable man, *without a heart.* I trust Norm as a lawyer, but, Barbara, he is the most ruthless, vindictive person I've ever met. (It occurs to me, that may be part of his success as a lawyer!) I haven't wanted to be so frank with you in the past & have simply pressed the issue of the age differential, an issue where I'm on very shaky ground, as you have amply demonstrated in our discussions (okay, arguments) of recent weeks. You must have thought me an old fogy with my objections, but now you'll understand my *real* reasons. Pls think about this: I've known N longer than you, by some years & marrying him would be the biggest mistake you ever made, I promise you.

Finally—believe it or not, all the meandering so far is only prelim. to the reason I'm writing this letter. I haven't told Jr & don't want him to know, but I have agreed in principle with an outside group to sell them the Bank. I want the matter kept quiet til the fourth quarter of this year, at which time the sale price will be determined & the first installment paid. Ted is handling it for me, along with Norm; he (T.) is delighted about it. He's always been a bit unhappy, despite our great friendship, that I've insisted on keeping the bank stock within the family. Yet he has been intensely loyal. Now his loyalty will be rewarded, because I've made it an integral part of the deal, that he be kept on for a minimum of five years as CEO, at a fifty percent boost in pay to start, with further escalators in later years; plus stock options up to 5% of total ownership. T. was effusively grateful when I outlined it for him, but he shouldn't be: if anyone deserves it, it's him. He's more responsible for the Bank's success than anyone & I include myself in that.

I *don't*—repeat, *don't*—want Jr to know about this sale! & have instructed T. & N. accordingly, because I'm hopeful that, after our discussion of two weeks ago, he may be in the process of getting his shit together. I think it's important that he get his debts taken care of first, rather than just counting on a bailout from me: I think that may be what got him into all this trouble in the lst place. But more importantly, if the divorce could be finalized prior to year-end, as Normie thinks it should be, Melissa would have no action against the sale or its proceeds: at least, that's N's opinion.

You will benefit from the sale, to the tune (after paying off holding company debt, and after capital gains taxes) of roughly $4 million. So will Jr. I'm not worried about how *you* will handle this sudden windfall, but I am worried about *Junior*. N tells me the trust language permits either of you to invade principal, once the trusts have some cash instead of stock only. Which is why I'm telling you & not him. My fond hope is that he will get his shit together in time to deal with this in the way that he should.

Should, God forbid, anything happen to me (& nothing *better* happen to me, I'm having too much fun) I ask you to carry on for me. You know I'm leaving an equal number of my shares to both you & Jr. It would be my preference to leave the majority to you, because I trust *your* judgment far more. But I just couldn't do that to Jr & I think you understand. Which makes it hard for me to put *you* in charge—you'll have no more shares than Jr—and you'll have to do it by gentle persuasion. It'll be difficult for you, and I'm giving you no ammo, if it comes to a fight, but I trust you. I know you'll do the right thing, for Jr & all concerned.

I have just reread this long, boring epistle (forgive me, my Barbara) & realize what a buttinski I am, in my children's affairs of the heart. But, honestly, I don't think it's because I put either of you on a pedestal—I think I just have Norm and Melissa pegged right. She certainly hasn't made *Jr* happy &, I'm telling you, N won't make *you* happy either.

We can, I hope, talk all this over at our leisure next week, relaxing, up at N. Spgs. I'm still hoping to get you up to Mohawk basin to try the moguls. *I know you can do it!* But I'm saying no more about that—I've already given about three times as much advice as most daughters would take from their dads in one short (?) letter.

All my love,
Dad

Ann's voice cracked a few times in reading. We were in the middle of the George Washington Bridge before she finished, and she had to speak up a bit, at the end, to be heard above all the blaring horns of drivers going the other way.

After a long silence, I took a breath. It seemed like the first in a long time. "Amazing," I said. "Now, how about letting the Bishop read it?" I glanced over at her. "What do you think? You're the boss."

Ann frowned at me for a moment, then handed it

over. "I want you to handle it, Dave. It's too hot for me. Just don't *lose* it!"

"If I lose this," I told her, placing it carefully in my notebook, "you have my permission to stop payment on my retainer and burn my license."

By now it was pushing five o'clock. I was in her block. I pulled up to 501 and let her out, in too much of a hurry to even walk her to her door, but she didn't mind. I promised her I'd call, and hustled back into the rushing rat-race of midtown Manhattan madness.

Half an hour later, I walked into Regan's office. My tap on the door was as perfunctory as they come. I was hot to show him the letter. One look at his face banished all thoughts of letters from my mind. The Bishop was pale as a ghost. He was doing something I didn't recall ever having seen him do before—running his fingers through his hair. He looked up with a wild expression, bordering on panic.

"Father William called two minutes ago, David," he said, sounding out of breath. "He is now at the Fordham University Library." He propelled himself a couple of rolls in my direction without taking his eyes off my face. He looked so totally helpless, it was scary. "An hour ago, two Homicide plainclothesmen came looking for him at St. Bede's. They are there now, awaiting his return. They told the parish secretary they want to interview him—in the matter of the *Barbara McClain homicide.*"

I felt the blood drain from my face and I momentarily forgot where I was. "Jesus Christ!" I said and apologized immediately: "Excuse me, Bishop; terribly sorry."

"Don't be," he answered fatalistically, glancing at the crucifix on the far wall. "He may be our last hope."

XLIII

My mind was a jumble. I looked at the Bishop. "O.K., how did Willie hear about it? What did you tell him to do?"

The Bishop wheeled away nervously. "He just happened to call the parish to see if they needed him for anything. He had told them this morning he'd be home for dinner. An hour ago, he was making so much progress with his work at the library, he decided to skip dinner and spend the evening there if he could. So he called the parish to see if he was needed. That was when he learned the police had come. He called here forthwith." The Bishop pulled up in front of the south window. His back was toward me, and his shoulders sagged.

"As for what he should do, what could I tell him? I told him I was beyond my depth. I suggested he call back in ten minutes. I hoped that you would have returned by then." Regan spun his chair and wearily wheeled back to his desk.

"I greatly fear this finishes any possibility of sparing the Archdiocese the public obloquy we have been trying so hard to avoid." Behind his desk again, he faced me and swallowed hard. "Do you see any way to avoid it?" It was an appeal, not a question.

It was up to me to put some uplift into the atmosphere. I tried to come on more optimistic than I felt.

"O.K. First, let's see if I can find out what the boys have got. Meanwhile, you pray. *Hard.*"

I thought about going outside to a pay phone, then realized, if we were tapped, Willie had already blown his cover by calling here. I decided, the hell with it, we were way past worrying about a tap. I went into my office, picked up the phone, punched the number for Homicide and asked for Sergeant Parker. Joe Parker was the last kid I trained in Homicide before I got the boot, and we'd kept up our friendship over the years. At the moment, he owed me one, though not one *this* big. Nothing *like* this big. But I was desperate.

Also, I was lucky—because I got him right away.

"Joe, I'm not going to identify myself," I said guardedly. "You know who this is, don't you?"

He must have caught the concern in my voice, because he answered in uncharacteristically serious tones. "Yep. What can I do for you, friend?"

"Do me a favor and call me from a different instrument, will you, pal? And soon?" He didn't even bother to say "good-bye" as he cut the connection. I went to the doorway.

"He'll call me from a pay phone," I told the Bishop, who was still slumped behind his desk. The eyes told the story: he'd cut himself out of the loop. He was so low he'd lost interest in the whole proceeding.

"Hey! Don't quit on me *now!* We're going to need your fancy intellect if we're going to keep our buddy out of the slammer and the Archdiocese out of the press. *Think! Think! Think!*"

"About what?" He was grim.

This wouldn't do. My man was going to pieces on me. "Come on! I've got a call coming in here in just a minute. Then, we'll know what the cops are up to." I hoped. "Meanwhile, *you* think about what excuse a priest would have for getting the hell out of town for a while, without leaving a forwarding. You've got ten seconds. Maybe less." My phone buzzed in my office, and I went. Fast.

"Ya sound breathless, Davey," came Joe's voice. "Didn't know ya cared."

"Thanks for the quick call back, friend. As for the wisecracks, better save 'em. Are you in my debt at the moment?" He'd know I was referring to our delicate bookkeeping arrangement of hot tips given and received.

"Hell yes, man! Hey, you clued me on the Carlson murder and the—"

"O.K., O.K. Nice to know I'm appreciated. This is your lucky day, Joe. Right now, you're in a position to pick up two points for a reversal. I need a big one."

I heard the sound of the wheelchair. The Bishop appeared in the doorway. Well, at least he was alive and listening again, if not yet thinking. An encouraging sign.

"Lemme hear it." Parker was wary. I couldn't blame him.

"The McClain thing . . ."

"I *heard* you were on that. The word around H.Q. is that—"

"I could care less about the word around H.Q., Joe. You and I both know who's pushing that: Blake. Right now, I'm in need of a little info. But do me a favor. Before I tell you more, you've got to agree that whether you help me or not—and that's your choice—you forget what I'm about to say as soon as you hang up the phone."

"Hell, you know you don't hafta ask *that,* Davey. What do ya wanna know?"

"O.K., Joe, here's my question. Why are you guys looking to interview a certain priest up in the Bronx on the McClain thing?"

A prolonged silence. Then Sergeant Parker broke the silence, fairly loudly, with the same word I've omitted from this account before, and will again. Having said the word, he went on, "Are you representing Father Fuller? My God, Davey! Now I don't know if I can forget we had this conversation!" We tried some meaningful silence while each of us tried to wait the other one out. Finally he went on, wearily.

"O.K., Davey, I'll give it to you. But, brother, you owe me a dozen for this one, and I'm gonna expect payment, too."

I waited.

"What we got, Davey, is this. We've had exactly a hundred and thirty-eight responses to the identikit of Charles Ryder. Got the exact number right here on my pad, 'cause I'm the guy in charge of the identifications. Ain't that a kick? You really called the right guy *this* time, buddy." He waited for a response, so I grunted. He was right, I had been lucky. But I was too worried to feel elated about it.

"Most of 'em are fruitcake stuff as usual. You know the way that goes. And leadin' the fruitcake parade—I *thought,* till just now—with eight supposed I.D.s is a *priest,* for God's sake, up in the Bronx. You got it—Father William Fuller. He's way out ahead of the pack, Davey. Number two only has four responses, and no one else has more than two.

"We kissed off the first couple on the priest, but three more came in late yesterday. Then, when we got three more today, we just *had* to go see the man. In fact, we still aren't takin' it serious—look-alikes happen all the time, you know that. But *you* callin'! Jesus!"

I tried to ignore the way he threw around the name of my boss's boss. I'd done the same, more than once. "What's the current status?" I asked.

"Hell, Davey, a couple of our guys are up at St. Bede's Parish right *now.* They called in a half hour ago. The priest is due back from somewhere, and they're just gonna talk to 'im. A five-'n-dimer, Davey, the ol' 'wuzzy' routine, where wuzzy that night, who wuzzy with. There'll be your run-of-the-mill alibi-checkin', the usual crapola." He paused, then asked soberly, "What's goin' on, Dave?"

"Not a thing, Joe. Nice talking to you, and I owe you. In fact, you get a cool dozen favors if you forget this conversation. A contract on your life if you don't."

"Look, don't worry about my memory. I don't even remember who I talked to tonight. And, by the way, you owe me *more* than a dozen, kiddo." He rang off.

I looked at the Bishop and he looked at me.

"They've had eight reports that Willie's the guy in the identikit," I told him. Silence. "When's he going to call back?"

"Father William?" Regan shook his head. "Any minute." He went into a silence infected with gloom.

I suppose he was hoping that I'd clear the whole thing up—brilliantly. I'd have loved to, but he's the brilliance department around here, and at the moment his brain cells were on strike.

Meanwhile, my own mind was racing, though at its own meager bumper-car racing speed. The most we could hope for was to gain the weekend. *If* we could keep Fuller out of sight for the weekend, and *if* we could find the killer in the meantime, then maybe, just *maybe,* the cops could be appropriately redirected. But that meant finding the *real* killer over the weekend.

The odds were somewhat worse than the New Jersey Lottery. I'd just wasted the day in Northern Springs on a red herring, the Bishop's brain had gone into hibernation, and, of the four suspects, none looked any better than anyone else. The letter from papa had been a hell of a find, no doubt about it, but it didn't narrow the field any.

The phone shrilled—this time, it was the Bishop's line.

I grabbed the phone from my desk and punched the flashing button.

"Bishop Regan's office," I said in my official, church-secretary voice.

"Dave!" Father Willie's voice was tense and hushed. "Thank God you're back! Did the Bishop tell you what happened?"

"Yeah," I said, calm of voice but all nerves around

the edges. I looked up to see Regan sitting nearby, doing nothing. When I waved at him savagely to go into his office and get on the line, he blinked once, got the message, whirled and rolled.

"The Bishop is picking up," I said, affecting calmness. "Let's have a three-way conversation here and come up with a solution." I heard the Bishop pick up.

"O.K., here's where we are," I stated, taking command like Crockett at the Alamo. "You can't go to St. Bede's, Father. But you also don't want to alarm the police by taking a run-out powder. Which gives us a dilemma. Now, tell me exactly who you talked to at St. Bede's just now, Willie. What did they tell you? And what did you tell them?"

"I talked to the housekeeper, Mrs. Keebler." Willie was being very quiet—almost whispering—and very intense. "I told Mrs. Keebler I was planning to stay at the library and work through the evening. Were there any messages? That's when she told me the two policemen were waiting for me."

"What did you tell her to tell them?" I held my breath and crossed my fingers.

"Nothing. I told her not to say anything to them, not even that I had called. I said I'd call her back in fifteen or twenty minutes." I let the air out of my lungs, gratefully, but didn't uncross my fingers.

"She sounded suspicious, but I think she'll do what I said. Actually, I think she was a bit put out with the cops, waiting there in the parlor while she tries to get dinner ready. Oh—I told her not to plan on me for dinner."

"You handled it like a pro, Willie," I assured him. "I'll now give you a chance to continue handling it that way.

"Call Mrs. Keebler back and tell her you've been called away—out of town. In fact, tell her you're calling from out of state. And you won't be back till Monday morning."

"But, Davey, that'll never work. Mrs. Keebler knows I've got to take confessions tomorrow afternoon, I've got masses Sunday morning. She'll raise Cain!"

"O.K., O.K., let's try this, then—"

"Just a minute, David," the Bishop cut in, with an encouraging crispness to his tone. "As it happens, I have met Mrs. Keebler. She's a harridan, by the way, but that's neither here nor there. What if I call her—?"

"No," I interrupted. "We've got to keep you out of this."

"If you'll permit me to finish, *Mister* Goldman!" he cut in sharply. First crispness, now irritation. Things were looking up.

"I can phone Mrs. Keebler on the other line. Harridan or not, she respects my position. I'll tell her that I've directed Father William not to return to the rectory. I will tell her this must not be divulged to anyone, above all, not the police."

"Hold it," I interrupted, yet once again. "I like it a lot. But let's simplify things. *We'll* call the rectory, Willie. Don't *you* do anything. Just hang out at the library till it closes late tonight and then go back to the rectory. Everything should look normal. And pray hard. The Bishop and I will take care of the police."

"But, wha—?"

"Just trust us, and do what I said, Willie. It's going to be fine."

He had another comment, but I cut him off with an instruction to call me from the rectory as soon as he got back to St. Bede's. Then I hung up and walked into Regan's office.

"What are you up to, David?" the Bishop asked, suspiciously.

"Ever heard a Catholic priest with a Jewish accent?" I responded. "Well, keep listening, Bishop, because you're about to hear one."

XLIV

Bishop Regan blinked at me at least a couple of times. Maybe more. "David, I cannot permit you to—"

"Don't give me that, Bishop! What's our alternative? We're in *too deep*. You don't have to lie. All you have to do is—"

"—materially assist you in your lie," he finished in disgust. "I'm not going to do it, David."

Five minutes later, he had Mrs. Keebler on the phone while I listened from the extension in my office. As delicately as possible, the Bishop explained that Father Fuller was on a confidential assignment, one that could under no circumstances be divulged to anyone, least of all to the police. Regan ended the explanation as follows:

"Now, Mrs. Keebler, I would appreciate it if you would ask one of the policemen to pick up the phone, simply tell him that Father Fuller would have a word with him. Thank you, Mrs. Keebler. I look forward to seeing you again, soon. And if you are ever in the vicinity of West Thirty-seventh Street, I hope you will drop in and see me."

He grimaced. I couldn't see him, since I was

sitting in my office, but I know the man. He grimaced.

I heard nothing for thirty seconds, then the sound of a second phone being picked up. Mrs. Keebler's voice came on: "Father William?" I shook my head resignedly. Why couldn't she just follow directions?

Mentally I was consigning the busybody to the nether regions of whatever hell there be. Fortunately, Regan was right there. "Mrs. Keebler," he said through his teeth, "*please* put the policeman on. Father Fuller is ready to talk!"

"Oh! Er, Father William. This is Officer Grady." At last, Mrs. Keebler had done *something* right—given me the name of the cop. I was aware of Grady's existence, but we'd never met. Or talked. Thank God.

"Yes, Father?"

"Yes, Officer Grady." I sounded, I hoped, exactly like a priest. I just hoped the guy wouldn't challenge me with some Latin phrases, my Latin being all but nil. "You wanted to see me, Officer?"

"Ah, yes, Father, our apologies, but we have a couple of questions we'd like you to answer. We expected you some time ago. Would it be too much trouble for you to come right now, Father?"

"Well, Officer, I'm afraid we've got a problem, and I'm terribly sorry about it. Mrs. Keebler didn't know that I was going out of town. I'm in New Jersey for the weekend. *Terribly* sorry. Can't I answer your questions over the phone?" Of course, I knew the answer to that one as well as Grady did.

"No, Father, we're not permitted to do that. Department regulations, don't y' see." Grady paused, thinking. I started to suggest a Monday morning meeting, then decided to wait him out. "Well, Father, I don't reckon a couple of days are going to matter a great lot. Would ten o'clock Monday mornin' be good fer you, Father?"

"Fine," I answered, withholding a sigh of relief. We arranged to meet at the rectory and said our good-byes; his were regretful, mine cheerful.

After taking three deep breaths, I got up and walked back into the Bishop's office. His face showed the same relief my lungs felt. But I wasn't expecting what came out of his mouth.

"How about ordering us an anchovy pizza, David? I feel like celebrating. And you can tell me about your day at the ski lodge."

I looked at him for a moment, then slowly shook my head. "Boy, what a difference a phone call makes! I'll admit I approve of your change of mood, but I'm afraid I need to point out a thing or two.

"First of all, you know perfectly well we're going to be in trouble with Sister if we don't eat the stuff she left for us in the refrigerator.

"In the second place, and more importantly, we've got no reason to celebrate. All we got out of that call is a two-day reprieve. On Monday, Grady's going to be back at St. Bede's for sure, and Willie better not miss *that* appointment, or he'll find out the real meaning of 'trouble'!

"Finally, boss, I've got to tell you, my report is going to make those anchovies taste like boiled newspapers. Not to say I got nothing. Right here"—I showed him the envelope—"is the last letter McClain, Senior, ever wrote the daughter. And it's a pip. The only trouble is, it points at *everyone*. As far as the ski accident being a murder, forget it. We can kiss that one off. It was an accident."

He was unfazed. "Now, now, David, let's not be

hasty. I'll have to be shown convincing proof before I believe Mr. McClain died of an accident at the precise moment he was putting the bank up for sale. I don't believe it.

"As to the two-day reprieve, I believe we will find it quite sufficient. I spoke with Mr. Rozanski this afternoon. He will be here at ten o'clock tomorrow morning with what he referred to as a 'full bag' of information on our four suspects. Then, we shall see what we shall see.

"And as to Sister Ernestine, I have every confidence that you will finally be able, by dint of superior wit and ingenuity, to take care of the simple matter of concealing all evidence of our 'crime.' "

I should interject a word about Ernie, who was spending the night at the Staten Island convent. Somehow, she's got it in her head that pizza is bad for the Bishop. So there's this constant tug of war between them, and I'm of course caught in the middle. She'll invariably leave the refrigerator full of what she calls "good, nourishing food," whenever she's going to be away. And the Bishop, almost as invariably, orders in pizza. Being a detective, my assignment is to hide the evidence, but, somehow, she always, always, figures out what we've pulled, whereupon she raises holy hell.

"So, David, if you will be kind enough to order our dinner—I would recommend Milazzio's, but will rely on your judgment—I will be ready to hear what Goldman hath wrought today. You say you have a letter from the senior McClain which you refer to as a 'pip'? I'll admit, David, I am intrigued."

I approved his suggestion of Milazzio's, and placed the order from my office. They promised it would be on our doorstep well inside of half an hour, which, from past experience with Milazzio's, meant somewhere between forty-five minutes and an hour. But Milazzio's quality is worth the wait.

I returned to see Regan at the south window, craning to look down the alley to his right. "Afraid Ernie might be sneaking up on our blind side?" I asked.

He wheeled around, reaching his desk with three powerful pushes. "Not at all, David. I was checking the sun's position. Due to your inattentiveness during the private banking seminar Mr. Nathanson held for you in my car on Tuesday, I need to have a further word with him. I must reach him by sundown or, as you know, he will be incommunicado till tomorrow night. And that may be too late for our purposes."

Regan was giving me too much credit. It actually took me a few seconds to realize that Abe, as a highly observant Jew, would not use a telephone on the Sabbath. From sundown Friday to sundown Saturday, he was useless to us.

Thinking about the tradition of Sabbath observances took me back to the days of my childhood. Friday dinner, every Friday night, right after sundown—the start of Shabbat—the candles, the wine, the challah. And, above all, the Sabbath greeting, *Shabbat Shalom!*

"I'll place the call, David," the Bishop said, interrupting my thoughts. "Why don't you listen in?" He was in a good mood. He likes Abe.

Abe was just answering with a "*Shalom,*" as I picked up.

"*Shalom,* Abe. Frank Regan, here. Mr. Goldman is listening in, with your permission."

"By all means, Frank!" came the piping response.

"*Shalom,* Daw-veed!" I completed the circle of "peace" with my *shalom,* which seemed the least I could do.

"Thank you, Abe, for your help on Tuesday," the Bishop began. "It was good of you to permit David to accompany you to Alsip. From what he tells me, the visit may have harmed your relationship with the bank. If so, my apologies."

"Not at all, Frank. David helped to expose a very arrogant anti-Semite there, and I am well rid of them. What can I do for you this time, Frank?"

"Just this, if I may, Abe. You gave David a brief tutorial in the various aspects of bank transfer-of-ownership. I was intrigued by the roles played by the various regulatory bodies and the accountants.

"But one further question. Do I understand from David's recital of the instruction you gave him, that a certified audit by an outside accounting firm will invariably be performed when a bank is sold?"

Abe's reply was immediate. "Oh, yes. The sale price would depend on book value and/or earnings. In the case of Alsip, the book value will be the operative figure. Without an outside audit, that figure is worthless. One is always performed at the time of a sale."

"But wouldn't the bank's books be subject to annual audit in any case?"

"Not necessarily, Frank, not by an outside C.P.A. firm. And not in the case of Alsip Traders Bank. You see"—Abe was obviously in his element—"all banks are subject to regulation. In the case of Alsip, which is referred to as a state, non-member bank—meaning it is regulated by the State of New York, and is not a member of the Federal Reserve—the bank is visited by examiners from the state and also from the Federal Deposit Insurance Corporation—on both a regular and an *ad hoc* basis.

"But it's up to the bank's shareholders whether the books are subjected to a regular, annual audit by outside C.P.A.s. Closely-held banks often get along without an audit. The examiners take a look at the books when they come in, and that keeps bank managers honest."

"Nonetheless, in case of sale, the books *would* be audited?" Regan insisted.

"Absolutely, Frank. And, if you're thinking of Alsip, yes, there was such a provision in the contract of sale."

"Has any audit been held?"

"Not yet." Nathanson sounded surprised at the question. "Keep in mind, Frank, there has been no sale. Had the envisioned sale gone through, the audit would have been as of September 30."

The Bishop's voice rang with satisfaction. "Thank you very much, Abe. You've been very helpful, and I trust your Sabbath will be joyful and undisturbed. I am in your debt, and hope you will soon give me the chance to repay."

" 'Repay,' Frank? Let there be no talk of repayment among friends. It was a great Christian—at one time, a good Jew—who wrote, 'Owe no man anything, except to love one another.' Your St. Paul is not a favorite of mine, Frank, but that injunction is worthy of Gamaliel. I commend the thought to you. *Shabbat Shalom,* Frank and Dawveed!"

XLV

The pizza was fine, I guess, but I couldn't taste a thing. I was too busy trying to figure out the Bishop's abrupt change of heart. How could he have gone from so low to so high just because of a two-day reprieve? It didn't make sense. I'd seen his mood changes before and didn't trust them.

Furthermore, I had no idea why he'd been pumping Nathanson. So a bank had to have an *audit* when sold: so what? We were after a murderer, not a sneak thief. It didn't occur to me at the time that the two could be one and the same.

As the Bishop and I ate pizza in the kitchen, I filled him in on the day's activities, letting him know the various reasons the ski accident could not have been a murder. He listened carefully, as always, while scarfing pizza.

He probed deeply into the details of the accident that had killed McClain, especially the alibis of the four suspects. He wanted full details about the place where the body was found.

"They said forty inches of powder?" he asked at one point. "There was a time when I skied powder.

It requires a great deal of skill, David, and has its moments of danger."

The Bishop thought a moment. "Tell me about the tracks."

I repeated what Langston had told me. "Apparently, the two buddies came home that way every day, so there were a number of tracks. What did the Sheriff call them?—fishtails."

"Any tracks going off another direction?"

I shook my head. "Not that the sheriff noticed. Of course, the ski patrol had been back and forth on the snowmobiles, bringing the body in." Then I glanced at my notes and was glad I had them. They reminded me of one more thing Langston had told me. "Oh yeah, about those ski tracks. Sheriff says there were a couple of long, loopy turns going out to the sides."

The Bishop looked at me. Hard. "Wide turns, you mean?"

"Yeah. Thinks one of the guys took his time getting down."

He closed his eyes. I didn't want him to get into a prayerful mode—and God knows I didn't want him to flip into a mood for some reason, so I said quickly, "Want me to go on?"

"Yes," he said, after what seemed like a long pause. "Specifically, I'd like to know how McKay recognized it was McClain that he saw at the top of the Iroquois lift."

I explained about the cigar and the salute, but my boss didn't buy that as positive I.D.

"Anyone could stick a cigar in his mouth, David. And as for the salute? Let's be serious."

I then explained about the chartreuse outfit, adding, "I can't believe there were two outfits like that, floating around those hills!"

"Nonetheless . . ." the Bishop went on. And on. And on.

I've got to tell you, it depressed me all over again, to see him pursuing the same fruitless line of questioning as mine. Inevitably I thought he was bound to wind up with the same conclusion. I reckoned without genius.

Conclusions aside, Regan ended, as always, with the contents of my skull residing neatly inside his. As to the letter from daddy, he spent some time with it. Back in his office, he read it through at least twice. I read it again myself. He had only one comment on it, but it proved to be significant.

"As you say, David, the letter points in many directions. But isn't it curious how people fail to see the flaws, and even perfidy, of those close to them, those they love? I sometimes wonder if Jesus didn't suffer from just that form of psychological blindness with regard to Judas."

Jesus and Judas?

In any case, I didn't see that we were making substantial progress toward getting the case solved before Willie's appointment with destiny that next Monday morning. The Bishop obviously disagreed with that assessment. So all I could do was hope he was right.

We both got to bed early that night. Before we went up, I disposed of the pizza remains in such a way that Ernie would never, ever, discover them. I also tried to reach Dave Baker both at his office and his home. I wondered if he'd been able to find out anything about either Hastings or Missy.

No luck, the first two times I tried. Finally I got him at home.

"You know why I'm calling, Dave. What's the

latest on Norm Hastings and Missy McClain?" Turned out, Baker had located a little dirt on each. I got the Bishop to pick up in his office, so I'd be spared more humiliation by failing to grasp some obscure but (to Regan) highly important point.

Dave had a kit bag of facts and innuendo. In brief: Missy was indeed in danger of being fired from her law firm. The reason—falsifying her college records. Seems she hadn't graduated number-one in her class from Michigan Law. In fact, not even in the top half. Her fudging had only come to light a few months before. Her partnership in the firm was under discussion by the firm's managing board.

As for Hastings, he was generally regarded as a tightwad. Dave's informants told him Hastings didn't "keep up" with the law, and therefore he was no longer a competent attorney. Most regarded him as a thoroughly unpleasant fellow, with prejudices going in various directions.

I reflected how well these views—except as regards competence—coincided with the opinion of the late Mr. McClain. They certainly coincided with mine.

As we wished each other good night, the Bishop made a parting comment that was to prove prescient. Wheeling into his bedroom, he announced with a half-smile:

"We are very close, David. Tomorrow is the day that will make us or break us."

His tone was optimistic, but the words could have cut either way.

Saturday, August 27

XLVI

Rozanski was uncharacteristically late—eighteen minutes, in fact—for our 10:00 A.M. appointment. Letting him in, I held the door open with one hand, while ostentatiously scrutinizing the watch on the other wrist. "I'd have *sworn* we said ten o'clock!" I murmured as he brushed past me into the mansion. "The Bishop shortened his prayers by an hour, knowing how prompt you are. And your coffee's been waiting for you for twenty minutes. Don't blame *me* if it's cold as ice."

He waved me away. "I've had three hours sleep, buddy. Don't give me a hard time. Kessler and I were up till four, working on a murder down in the Bowery. Check tonight's paper for all the gory details. I actually thought on Wednesday I might be able to break away for golf. Today's my last chance to play this summer."

I nodded. "Last chance to get the rest of our money, you mean. My heart goes out to you, pal."

Once seated in the Bishop's office, Chet was pleasantly surprised to find the coffee hot. "Mind if I have a cigar with this, Bishop?" he asked. Permission was granted, and I got the ashtray. We were going to have to fumigate the damn place by the time this case was over.

"I used to smoke a cigar once in a while," the Bishop ruminated. "Enjoyed them, too. Since the . . . incident, I try to avoid anything habit-forming. I still enjoy the scent.

"However," he straightened up in his wheelchair. "You're here at my invitation, Mr. Rozanski, because you have some information for us. Please tell us what you've learned."

Chet tossed me a large envelope. "Nance collected these for me, Davey. Some fairly decent data there on all four individuals. You can go through it. Meanwhile, I'll tell you the important stuff." He leaned back in the chair, took a deep puff on the Panatella, and released the fragrant smoke toward the ceiling.

"I'll start with the brother. This kid—and I use the term advisedly, Bishop, because it's not clear he's ever grown up—was raised in the lap of luxury. Lost his mother at an early age, and was brought up, along with his sister, by their late father. Word is, the brother always resented his little sister. There was an explosion of sorts earlier this summer at a charity function. My informant didn't know what started it, but the brother totally lost his head, actually took a swing at the sister, which she luckily ducked. Word has it, the brother looked homicidal at the time. Yeah, Davey, I know; sounds too good to be true. But that's the word they used: 'homicidal.'

"As to motive, it might help to know the kid's personal financial condition. I hear it's not as good as advertised. He likes to play the ponies, and not too successfully, at that."

"How *un*successfully?" the Bishop asked.

"Very. He's reputed to be in hock, big time, to the mob. Could be, I don't know. How do you verify a thing like that?" I said nothing about the fact that the Bishop and I had corroboration, in the form of the letter from daddy.

Chet proceeded. "Something I can verify—at least a little better, I've got two informants for this—is that he was after his dad to sell the bank. He wanted to have the proceeds distributed to the shareholders in cash. He and Barb were both quarter-owners of the bank till the dad died. Then they both became equal shareholders.

"But the trust agreements, already drawn up by daddy and still in force after his death provided that the bank shares of one trust couldn't be sold without the agreement of the other trust. Of course, before daddy died, nothing could be done without daddy's O.K. But after he died, the trust agreement meant no sale without sis's O.K." Chet looked from the Bishop to me. Deciding we both understood the significance of what he'd just told us, he resumed:

"So that's the brother. Now we come to Missy" —he drawled the next word, derisively—"*little* Missy. It's funny, I can't find anyone in town who likes the broad. I've never met her, but the word is, since she married into big money, she's been high-hatting all her old friends. She apparently worked her way through Michigan Law the hard way, then married into the McClain fortune, and went upscale."

"So she never attended any fancy prep school?" I asked.

Chet scowled, and consulted his notes. "Naw, what makes you think that?"

"Just a wild hunch."

"Naw. Uh, here it is. No, public high school, then U.C.L.A. She's a *California* girl." He grinned. "She had no East Coast to her at all until shortly before she met McClain. She came to New York as an associate with Anderson, Lamberson. I understand she and the kid met on a blind date about three years ago. They got married a month later. Everyone had Junior pegged as a life-long bachelor till she came along.

"And, you're wondering, did she have a motive for murdering her sister-in-law? Well, she didn't care for Barb and she made no secret of that fact. Of course, she shared the same money motives as her hubby. Any questions so far?" Chet paused, puffing on his cigar.

"Any military or police background for either?" the Bishop muttered. I looked at him. *Now* what?

"Hmm," Rozanski murmured, looking at his notes again. "Nope. Bob graduated from Cornell two years after the draft ended in 1972. He's been doing what he's doing—specifically, precious little—ever since. As to little Missy, nope, nothing here."

"Any R.O.T.C. or N.R.O.T.C. for either, while at college?" the Bishop persisted—again, to my puzzlement.

"Uh, nope," the reporter said, after checking.

I looked at the Bishop. "No more questions, Bishop? No? Nor have I." I got up. "O.K., Mr. Rozanski, tell us all about Norman Hastings, while I fill your cup with a bit more Java."

"Thanks, Davey. I thought I was going to have to get it myself. Hastings is with Tobin, et al. of Alsip, but you know that. One point on him. He's the only one of the group who might have had a romantic motive. To wit, he was aching to marry Barb. And daddy was dead set against—thought the age differential was too great. Then death took daddy's objections out of the picture."

Chet raised an eyebrow. "Query: did Hastings take *McClain* out of the picture? I know, I know, McClain's death was an accident. Or was it? There's some smart money around that says not, and I own some of it. From what Davey told me earlier in the week, the two of you may have a few doubts about Senior's death as well." He looked for reactions and, not getting any, continued.

"Anyway, if Hastings *did* knock off the dad, it didn't do him a bit of good. Barb ended their romance anyway. I hear she finally decided to honor her dad's wishes in death in a way she never had in life. The question comes up, very naturally: did she break it off with Hastings because she somehow knew that he murdered her dad? That falls apart if you decide the dad's death was an accident."

As Rozanski blew steam off his fresh cup of coffee, I asked, "Why would Barb wait so long to blow the whistle, if she suspected something? And why would Hastings wait so long to kill her? If she suspected him, wouldn't he have been in jeopardy every day she was alive?"

"Hey, I'm just giving you suppositions. Do what you want with them. I'll tell you this, though: Hastings took it *very* badly when Barb broke their engagement in March. I have it on solid authority that there was a nasty little scene. They didn't speak for months afterwards, and the social set in Alsip was all atwitter over it.

"Eventually, it was resolved amicably through the gentle mediation of Mr. Ted Masterson. He was apparently able to convince both of them they were being silly about it, and they became 'just friends.' But Hastings is a deep one. He may have carried a grudge. He certainly didn't seem very broken up over his former fiancée's murder."

Rozanski put his cup down. "Any other questions on Hastings?"

"As before," Regan murmured. "What about military or police service?"

Rozanski consulted his notes again. "Went into reserves out of college—that was in 1954—and served on inactive duty, in the Quartermaster Corps, from 1954 to 1956. That's it. Went for his law degree after that."

With no more questions on Hastings, he proceeded on to Ted Masterson. "Not much *against* this guy. Grew up in Alsip, the poor kid on the block. He's three years older than Junior, and I don't think they knew each other. But the dad knew him. Brought him into the bank as a gofer back when Masterson was in high school. Word is, when Masterson went off to Vietnam, the old man promised him he'd always have a job there. And he kept his word. Masterson never missed a beat. Comes back from Vietnam with a flock of medals and moved back into the bank the same day. Two years later the old man bumped himself up to chairman primarily to leave room for Masterson as president."

Rozanski sipped some more coffee. "Word is, he's done a terrific job as prez. Bank makes lots of money. Only motive anyone can come up with for him, is that he never got any options on shares of the holding company. Here he was, making all that money for the bank, and not sharing in the wealth. Probably got a decent salary and yearly bonuses, but most execs want a piece of the action, and that he never got. Daddy was adamant about it. The bank was a family business and that's where he intended for it to stay."

Of course, what Chet didn't know was, we could kiss that one off, too. After all those years, Masterson was about to get into the big bucks—high salary and stock options to boot.

Chet stretched. His cup was empty, but when I raised my eyebrows, he gave a shake of the head. "Thanks, Dave, I gotta go soon. Today's a day off for clowns like you, but just another day in the life, for a working stiff like me." I generously refrained from pointing out that he hadn't missed many golf Saturdays all summer.

"Anyway. It would be pretty bizarre for anyone to knock off somebody for that reason. Hell, if you're a topflight performer, like he is, you just quit and go somewhere where they'll treat you right. And he never did that. The man was absolutely loyal to McClain.

"Yesterday," Rozanski went on, "I talked to a head-hunter who told me he approached Masterson a couple of times, a year or so ago, because of Ted's great track record. Did Ted want to explore job opportunities at double the money he was getting in Alsip? He was worth it, according to this head-hunter. But nothing doing—Masterson wouldn't even talk. After a while, the word got around, and the head-hunters started leaving him alone. Waste of their time to even talk to him."

Chet chuckled. "In fact, about the only flaw I can find in the guy is, he's a total workaholic. Though everybody's tried, no one has ever been able to get him to take a vacation. He's in the office nearly seven days a week, fifty-two weeks a year. But he's not like most workaholics. He doesn't force his hours on the employees. He never criticizes any of them for taking holidays or vacations. He's a well-loved man in that bank—everyone agrees on that.

"He's always been a superb athlete, too. He was the only twelve-letter man in the history of Alsip High School, legend has it. Apparently he led the basketball team to the state double-A championship, his Junior year." Chet stubbed out his cigar in the ashtray.

"He's stayed in shape over the years, and he's still a fierce competitor in basketball and tennis. Avid skier. It's been said he's sworn off skiing since McClain's accident, but time will tell on that one. It remains to be seen whether he'll manage to keep that promise, once the snow starts flying this winter."

When I saw Rozanski to the door, with more promises of huge scoops, he was distrustful.

"I know, I know, Davey—'Don't call me, I'll call you.' That's your motto. I'll believe this 'if-and-when,' when it happens."

He was already out the door and halfway down the steps when I called after him, "Hey, Chet! You gotta trust, man! The Bishop says, 'All things come to those who trust!' And it works!"

"I'll trust *you,* when you get me something," he muttered without turning around.

Now that's a lousy attitude, if you ask me.

XLVII

At 12:48, Saturday afternoon, the Bishop named the murderer.

We had just finished Ernie's excellent spinach salad. The Bishop rang the little silver bell for dessert, which turned out to be raspberry sherbet, with some kind of sauce Ernie had dreamed up, the total concoction turning out so delicious we both demanded seconds. Ernie beamed. Temporarily.

However, our praise of her dessert didn't spare us our tongue-lashing. She laid it on us when she brought the coffee. "I just want you two to know, you don't fool me one bit. I go away one day, leaving you *nourishing meals* in the fridge, and do they get touched? No, they do *not*. Instead, in Sally Mueller's garbage can down the alley, I find that good food rotting, along with wrappings from a pizza ordered-in from Milazzio's. David, you ought to be ashamed of yourself!"

"*Me?*" I was outraged. "It wasn't even my idea! And why are you rummaging around in the neighbor's garbage, anyway?"

She shook her head in disgust. "What are *you* doing, using the neighbor's garbage cans for your leavings? If you're going to go to all that trouble to hide my food and pizza wrappers from me, I guess I can take a little trouble to find them. And you know how bad that so-called 'fast' food is for the Bishop, David! I rely on you—"

"Enough!" the Bishop roared, stopping even the redoubtable Sister Ernestine in her tracks. "I needn't be talked of in the third person like some pathetic imbecile. You know perfectly well, Sister, anchovies are essential to my health. If I find it impossible to eat them on anything but pizza, allowances must be made."

Ernie, having proven the main point, that we couldn't put one over on her, sniffed and carted away the empty dishes. Put in our place once again, the boss and I departed for our separate offices. How far, I wondered, was I going to have to go to elude her investigative capabilities? Was it possible I was seeking help on my cases from the wrong member of this household?

By the time I'd looked at—and disposed of—the mail, straightened my desk top a tad, and walked through the connecting door to the Bishop's office, he was "pacing" again. His muscular hands whipped the wheelchair from one end of the large office to the other, making a small thump every time he came off the Karastan rug. At each end of a swing, he did a small wheelie as he spun the chair around. Had Ernie been present, they'd have been large wheelies, just to bug her. He was hard at work. And I sensed he was close to a solution.

Checking my watch, I sat down in the black velvet chair and waited, there being little else to do under the circumstances. The rolling lasted another eight minutes. The frown on his face gave him the appearance of a two-year-old, hard at work learning a new trick. Why that kind of physical activity enables his brain to work, God only knows. But it does.

At 12:47 (I had just checked my watch for the third time) he rolled to a point five feet from me, spun the chair in my direction and stopped. As he spoke, he was still panting slightly from the exertion.

"I have devised a plan of action, David, and need your advice. As well as your consent, of course."

Yeah, my consent. As if I had any choice. I shrugged and leaned forward, and he proceeded to fill me in on how we were going to spend the rest of this rather eventful day, and bag a murderer in the process.

XLVIII

So, after three hours and twelve minutes of preparation, we were ready to go. At precisely four o'clock, the Seville, gassed up and gussied up, was brought around to the front door, personally, by Jerry Mangrum, our weekend garage guy. This personal service only occurs on those rare occasions when the Bishop needs to go somewhere. As per Regan's brilliant idea, altered slightly with a couple of unbrilliant but practical modifications by yours truly, he and I were northward bound for the McClain ski lodge. The get-together with our four "players" was to be without forewarning. I couldn't call them "suspects" any more; to my mind they were now three individuals and a murderer. So, "players" seemed to fit them as well as any other word.

The Bishop and I had spent over two hours discussing the plot we were cooking up. Of that two hours, the first half-hour was dedicated to his explanation of who the murderer must be and why. When he finished convincing me, he summarized our position, and I pretty much had to agree: "We now know who committed both murders, how they were committed, and why. We have motive, opportunity and ability. And we fairly well know the means. What we lack is proof."

That was our problem. When you added up everything the Bishop had—and it was plenty good, as far as reasoning went—what it amounted to was a jumble of conjectures, guesses and deductions, all circumstantial, with nothing even approaching any hard evidence.

In a normal case, our procedure would have been simple and straightforward: go to Kessler, empty the bag, and let him round up the evidence. In a normal case. Here, where we had to prevent the public from knowing that a Catholic priest had been in the dead woman's apartment at the time of the murder, our normal disclose-all method wasn't going to work.

Sure, I could have started to hunt up the evidence myself. Only trouble was, the hunting could take weeks, and our boy had a Very Big Appointment scheduled for this coming Monday at 10:00 A.M. That was why we had to devise what the Bishop called "The Program." I preferred to think of it as "The Scam."

We first verified that the four individuals we sought were indeed going to be at the ski lodge that evening. On Tuesday, Masterson had told Abe and me that he and Norm were going up to Northern Springs over the weekend to do some fishing. Friday afternoon, Missy and Junior had said they were expecting "company," which seemed to confirm it. But we needed to be sure. It took me only one phone call to clinch it: they were all up there. All four, plus Cathy Masterson.

The plan of action the Bishop had dreamed up—

the "scam"—was chancy and had lots of possibilities for foul-up. I tried to think of a better one, and couldn't. So I reluctantly agreed to it and tried to plug the gaps, using the knowledge and experience of twelve years in law enforcement.

After we decided on a plan, I had several calls to make before we left.

The first was to Sheriff Langston. I found that he was available that evening and amenable to joining our little game of chance, sight unseen.

Next call was to the garage to arrange for the Caddy to be brought around. After that I tried to call Fuller. He was in church, so I left a cryptic message.

Then I called Ann, and that's where things got sticky. Regan and I had discussed at length whether or not she should be included, assuming she was willing to go. The Bish preferred to leave her out of it, but I pointed out a thing or two, and he reluctantly agreed to have her join us. The program almost got a bit revised, when I finally broke it to her that we wanted her cooperation.

The problem was, she wanted to have the whole story before we left, over the phone, here and now. I told her no, we'd discuss it in the car, and she finally agreed to wait. We left it that we'd pick her up at 4:15.

But that call was a cupcake, compared to the final one: the one to Sally Castle. As I may have mentioned earlier, Sally and I had scheduled two baseball dates for the week. Our "bookends of baseball," we'd been calling it, a great way to end the summer.

The first was the Monday game at Yankee Stadium, five days earlier. Well, you saw what happened there. We did make the game, courtesy of Mike Burke, my friendly police sergeant, but I made us late. Sally had noted my tardiness at the time, and reminded me since.

The second half of the bookend—the truly spectacular half—was to be that evening's twi-night doubleheader at Shea. Mets versus Dodgers, Darling and Gooden versus Valenzuela and Hershiser, strength against strength, *mano a mano,* to the death. The first game was to start at 6:00, and Sally and I had agreed to meet at her apartment for drinks beforehand, around 4:30. So, it was with a good deal of trepidation that I punched out her number at twenty minutes to four. My trepidation proved to be fully warranted.

"Darling! I'm so glad you called. Be a dear, and pick up some olives—those imported green ones I love. You can get them at Kirschbaum's, it's right on the way. O.K.?"

I groaned, inaudibly I thought. Not inaudibly enough.

"Davey?" Her voice had distinctly ominous overtones. "Did you say something, dear heart? *David!*"

The word "David" in Sally's mouth is not a good omen. "Uh . . ." I said: not a good omen for *her*.

Silence. She was on to me. And more silence.

"Uh, Sally . . ." Still nothing. I was going to have to walk this lonesome road all by myself. "About tonight . . ." Nothing. "Something has come up. I'm sorry, forgive me, but . . ." Nothing. "Aw, come on, Sal, *yell* at me! Say *something!*"

"Something has come up, has it?" Ice. "Well, you'd better *deal* with that something, hadn't you?"

"Listen, Sally, I know it's late, but I could bring the tickets by. Maybe you could find someone else to . . ."

A sharp detective knows it's silly to go on talking into a dead receiver. So I cradled the instrument and sat for a while looking at the floor, thinking. Flowers and candy? Nope. Slash my wrists? Better. I resolved to defer a decision till I was in a better mood.

Then I got an idea. Jerry's Cycling Maniacs was, despite the name, a messenger service that had done some good things for me in the past. And they were handy: virtually around the corner, at Fortieth and Tenth. I called. Lo and behold, they had a messenger sitting in their ratty office with nothing to do.

"How long to get an item from here to East Sixty-fifth?"

"Forty-five minutes," was the snappy response. "You're lucky, the guy we got here is *fast*. He *could* get it there in half an hour."

It was easy to catch the suggestion that a little incentive wouldn't hurt.

My watch said 3:46. "Send him. Put the charge on my tab. And tell him it's a twenty-buck tip if he can get it there by 4:20."

The line went dead without another word being spoken. Now that's action.

I was debating whether to call Sally back to tell her the box seat tickets for the twi-nighter were on the way, or just let her be surprised, when the phone rang, and it was her. I was forgiven—sort of—with the understanding that she wanted those tickets *forthwith*. I gave her the good news about Jerry's Cycling Maniacs, and the deep freeze thawed a little more. By the time we rang off, we were almost friends again. She even said "goodbye" before hanging up on me.

After that, I sat there wondering who she'd found to take my place at such short notice. I'd just decided I didn't really want to know, when the doorbell chimed. It was the messenger, a Chinese teenager whose bike, at the foot of the stoop, looked taller than he was.

His English was shaky, but he nodded frantically when I showed him Sally's address on the ticket envelope. Disgusted at my hesitation, he finally grabbed the envelope and the twenty out of my hand, tore down the steps, leaped on the bike and laid rubber. I looked from his rapidly receding figure to my watch: 3:49. By 4:15 he'd either be at Sally's or dead.

I heard the elevator descending as I closed the door. The elevator descends into the kitchen. The contraption was installed in the shaft of a dumbwaiter by an engineer friend of the Bishop. The kitchen may seem like a stupid place for an elevator to end up, but it actually has worked out fairly well. For one thing, it certainly removes any temptations Ernie might have to be slovenly.

Regan came rolling into the hallway from the kitchen, saw me, and stopped. He was impeccably attired in his finest going-out attire: black, English-cut sharkskin suit, black silk shirt topped by the white Roman collar, pectoral cross neatly tucked in the inside breast pocket of the suit coat so that the silver chain was visible against the black shirt. His usually unruly white hair was under control, and he appeared to have shaved again.

"Ready, David?" He couldn't hide the fact that he was excited. Hell, so was I. I nodded.

"A few more possibilities have occurred to me, which we can discuss in the car."

"Any objections to my carrying iron?" I asked him.

"I take it, you are referring to a firearm? I would prefer not, certainly. If that Sheriff is going to join us, then he will surely be provided with sufficient means of coercion."

I wasn't sure I agreed, but didn't feel too strongly either way. If the murderer was packing iron, which was an outside possibility, one could question the wisdom of a shoot-out in the midst of all those innocent people.

On the other hand, if a gun was flashed and the Sheriff *wasn't* there for some reason, the wisest course would be to let the person escape. With the identity known to the police, arrest and incarceration would be just a matter of time. So Regan was probably right: no hardware.

At 4:00, when the Caddy pulled up in front, we were already on the stoop. I tilted the chair back and bumped the Bishop down the eight steps to the sidewalk. He propelled himself to the curb, while Jerry got out and opened the door. Using the bars installed for his benefit on the side and top of the car, the Bishop lifted himself from the wheelchair into the front seat. Jerry took the wheelchair to the trunk, and I went around to the driver's side. When the trunk slammed down, I started the car and gunned it, waving good-bye to Jerry.

"Here goes nothing," I said, turning uptown on Tenth.

"For Father William's sake and, more importantly, for the priests of this Archdiocese, it had better be *something,*" the Bishop answered grimly.

XLIX

Ann was waiting when we pulled up. And damned if she didn't tug open the front door, stick her head in, and give the Bishop a wet one on the cheek. He didn't treat it as any big thing. He just said, "Nice to see you again, Miss Shields." But I sure wasn't going to ignore it. As Ann climbed into the back seat, I leaned over and pretended to check the Bishop's jawbone for lipstick. He swung around and gave me a look that could have withered an oak tree.

We tried to persuade Ann to forego discussion of the program till Sheriff Langston could hear it too, but she won the battle of wills, and we wound up giving her the full scenario on the way up. Which turned out to be a good thing, because explaining it to someone else revealed a few flaws we'd overlooked. Plus, Miss Ann had a couple of reasonable suggestions of her own.

By prearrangement with Langston, our next stop was his office in Northern Springs. At five minutes to six I tapped on his door. It opened immediately, and the Sheriff filled the doorway. We shook hands.

He peered into the car. "Who's that you've got with you?"

"You met my client yesterday," I replied. "She's in back. Up front is Bishop Regan, my colleague. So try to be polite, Fred. Since he's a paraplegic gentleman, it would be easier to talk in the car. If we don't have time to finish explaining everything by the time we get to the lodge, we can pull over."

His eyes had widened. "Hell, Dave! This ain't no walk in the park. We've got a one-or two-time killer, a very dangerous individual! What the hell are you doin', bringing a woman and a cripple up—"

"Oops!" I stopped him. "Don't jump to conclusions, Fred." I took his elbow and got his eye. "Look, the Bishop is the guy who figured the whole thing out. He designed this evening's scam. It can't be done without him. Plus, he's a man of God, so watch your mouth."

"All right, Dave," he said, resigning himself to the situation. "Let's go."

At first, Fred was clearly uncomfortable sitting in the same car with a high-order cleric. But as Regan proceeded to tell how he'd deduced the identity of the murderer, the lawman's eyes narrowed. After he heard the Bishop out, we parked while the four of us conducted a round-car discussion, chaired by the Bishop, outlining the sting operation.

We nearly lost the Sheriff over the issue of self-incrimination.

The Bishop frowned. "I think you misunderstand our purpose, Sheriff. We are not trying to dupe a criminal into self-incrimination. We are seeking *evidence,* not a confession. This person, I can say with a fair degree of confidence, will never confess, even through inadvertence. Especially not through inadvertence."

Langston simmered down, though he still had plenty of reservations.

It was nearly seven o'clock before we had finished covering all possible contingencies—all the ones we could think of, that is. As it turned out, we overlooked a big one.

Ann was obviously excited. So was I but I thought I'd kept it hidden. Then Ann asked me why I kept buttoning and unbuttoning the top button on my shirt. I told her I always do that. It gives the shirt a pleasant, lived-in look that I like.

Program in place, we finished the short trip up the mountain to the lodge. As we pulled into the clearing we saw smoke rising from the chimney. Two cars were parked in front: the McClain's Porsche we'd seen the previous day, and a Buick, presumably belonging to Masterson or Hastings.

As we pulled up next to the steps, I expected someone to come out on the porch and challenge our right to be there. No one did. I went around and took the wheelchair out of the trunk, sprung it from its folded position, and set it next to the right-hand door of the car. Regan lifted himself out of the car by his friendly bars and lowered himself into the wheelchair. Fred and I hoisted the Bishop up the steps and onto the porch, while Ann closed up the car. For the second time in twenty-nine hours, the Sheriff rapped authoritatively on the oak front door.

In a moment, the door opened. Missy stood in the doorway, taking us all in. I noticed the intense, delicious aroma of grilled steaks. Irrelevant and immaterial, I tried to tell my stomach.

From the look on Missy's face, I would have guessed she would slam the door in our faces, but she didn't. Perhaps she saw Langston place the toe of his boot unobtrusively next to the jamb, the moment the door opened. Good technique. That foot-in-the-door trick is one useful thing—possibly the *only* useful thing—they teach you in cop school.

Instead of trying to slam the door, Missy turned and announced to all and sundry, in a bored tone, "We have company, dear ones. And it looks to me like trouble."

L

I knew it wouldn't be easy to get into the lodge, and it sure wasn't. Bob McClain soon joined his wife in the doorway. He was wearing jeans and a lumberjack shirt so new I was surprised not to see price tags dangling from it. I was tempted to ask if Omar the Tent Maker did his clothes, but stifled it.

Junior quickly located the person who had his foot in the door. He was hard to miss.

"I'm sorry, Sheriff," said Junior, "but you've chosen an awkward moment to drop in. We're getting ready to eat. I'll have to ask you to come back later."

Langston followed the prearranged script. "With your permission, Mr. McClain. Mr. Goldman, here, has something to say that'll only take a second. After that, it's your decision whether we stay or go."

"What's going on, Bob?" Norm Hastings called from somewhere inside the house. No one responded. Junior glanced down at Missy and got some invisible signal from her.

"Well, all right," he said to Langston. "If it's

very brief, Sheriff. I really don't have the time to—"

"Let me make an introduction, Mr. McClain," I interrupted. "This gentleman," I nodded to the Bishop, whose eyes stayed focused on Junior, "is Bishop Francis X. Regan of the Catholic Archdiocese of New York. He has what I think are some interesting theories about what happened to your sister."

People are funny.

Both Missy, then Bob, had given the Bishop a quick glance at first, same as they gave the rest of us. But after the initial look-see, they had avoided looking at him. They seemed embarrassed.

I'm sure Regan has his own theories about why people act the way they do around the disabled. But my boss has never invited a discussion of the matter, and I'm sure not going to bring it up. I mention it at this point, because Junior completely ignored my introduction of Regan. He continued to direct his eyes at Langston and me. I liked McClain even less than before, if that were possible. But we had a game plan to follow.

So I went on, "As a matter of fact, the Bishop is convinced he knows who the murderer is, and it *isn't* Charles Ryder." McClain snorted. I ignored it and continued. "Not only is he convinced of it, he has convinced Sheriff Langston, Miss Shields, and me. I think you owe it to yourselves to hear him out." I looked for some sign of reaction from the McClain pair and got none, which bothered me. I was now at the crucial moment which would make us or break us. It would have been nice to feel I had an edge going in.

I took a deep breath, preparing for the pure

bluff. *How* I said the next piece was at least as important as *what* I said. I had rehearsed it with Regan a couple of times, and neither of us liked it much. Trouble was, we couldn't think of anything better. So I tried to look serious as hell, and gave it the old college try.

"We aren't coming back, Mr. and Mrs. McClain. If you won't hear us now, the Bishop and I will have no alternative but to turn over everything we know to the police. I guarantee you, a ten-minute postponement of a dinner will seem small potatoes—so to speak—compared to the treatment the police will give you after they've heard what the Bishop has to say."

As I spoke, I could see our stock rise, visibly. The change was in Missy. She still had the look of a person who's just caught a whiff of something unspeakably vile. But I could see worry in her eyes—and plenty of curiosity. No way, I felt sure, was this Head of Household going to let us go back to New York without telling our theory.

Just as I finished speaking, sure that we'd won, a new player entered the picture. Norm Hastings, another one of my least favorite people, approached the doorway, peering over Missy's head. He was wearing one of those repulsive chef's aprons, imprinted with the face of a black cook, below which were the words "HEAH COME DE COOK!!"

Raising his chin to get the Sheriff's eye, Norm showed his teeth. "Maybe I can help, Sheriff. I'm Norm Hastings and I'm an attorney and I have a serious complaint. This *gentleman*"— contemptuous nod at me—"has been making a nuisance of himself ever since he saw fit to involve himself in our affairs." In a tone of ill-controlled outrage, Norm explained how I had insinuated myself into the offices of Alsip Traders Bank for the purpose of making an "extralegal" inspection.

"An outrage, Sheriff!" concluded Norm, on a rising note. "And now look at him, shamelessly invading our privacy *here!*

"Sheriff, you're the law in Catskill County, and it's not up to me to tell you what to do. But if you were to ask for my advice, it would be to get this charlatan out of here as soon as you can, and never let him back into your county."

Hastings eased his way around Missy and stepped out on the porch. He took Langston's elbow and lowered his voice, looking up confidently into the lawman's unreadable eyes.

"Now, Sheriff, I don't believe you'd *intentionally* let a shyster like this Goldman, with his shyster tricks, get away with what you've let him get away with. If anyone should know about the tricks Jews pull, it's a guy with your kind of street-savvy. So put this boy in his place, O.K.?" Hastings grinned and winked.

Fred Langston simply shrugged him off like an uncomfortable jacket and lowered his eyes a foot and a half to confront Missy.

"Ms. McClain," he said in a way that brought a new and official tone to the proceedings. "I am here, Ma'am, only unofficially. But I believe you are perhaps more capable than the gentlemen around you of understanding the gravity of this situation. You have seen the effect of damaging evidence—and what it can do to the accused." Langston held her in his steady gaze. "Yes. Well. I think these gentlemen and this lady, who are investigating the death of your own sister-in-law, have solid grounds for their conclusions. They have come all the way here to tell you their story. I think, personally, that your family's reputation may hinge upon listening to what they have to say."

"Now, Sheriff—" Hastings began, but Missy cut him off sharply. And without moving her lips.

"Norm, *please* get rid of that obnoxious apron. Come in, Sheriff. Miss Shields and gentlemen: make yourselves at home. Bob, Norm, some chairs for our guests, please."

Suddenly, I was looking at Missy in a totally different light. As Norm took off the apron and scuffled around getting chairs, I actually felt a certain warmth toward the woman.

I eased the Bishop's wheelchair through the door. He was furious, I felt certain, though his face showed nothing. He's most impassive when he's really angry, and now he had every right to be. He'd been treated like a nobody. The three householders had directed their eyes and their comments to everyone but him. The star of the show and he had yet to open his mouth.

But his moment would come. As he wheeled himself over to the spot we'd agreed on, I breathed a sigh of relief. Step one completed. We were in. I wondered if the rest of the plan would go any easier.

Hah.

LI

Just as we were all getting settled, Cathy Masterson, pretty but puzzled, came in from the kitchen. Unfortunately the aroma of sizzling steaks followed her. I could almost sympathize with Junior's insistence that we come back after dinner.

Ted Masterson was the last to appear. He came in from a hallway across from the kitchen. Missy went up to him at once and conferred in low tones. I saw Masterson flash an indecipherable look in my direction. But finally he took a seat along with everyone else. The desultory hum of conversation gradually subsided.

Bishop Regan had the floor. He surveyed the audience.

"I thank you for your hospitality, Mr. and Mrs. McClain, though it has, in a sense, been coerced. I will not apologize for the coercion, because I have something to tell you about the death of your sister and sister-in-law, respectively, which will more than compensate for any inconvenience we may have caused."

"Would you mind telling me your place in all

this?" asked Hastings. "I don't see where you fit in. A Catholic bishop—?"

"Yes, I would mind, Mr. Hastings. Our time is limited, and I'd prefer to stick to the subject at hand." Hastings reddened but subsided.

"The subject is this: how one of the people in this room brutally murdered, not just Miss McClain, but her father. *Your* father, too, Mr. McClain."

General pandemonium. Hastings blurted out something. Masterson stood up and took a step toward the Bishop, no doubt intending to ask a question. Then he looked around, subsided, and took his chair again.

Tilting back on the two hind legs of his chair, Junior gave a mirthless chuckle. When he spoke up, he had the attention of everyone in the room.

"That's crazy, Bishop. The state police conducted a *complete* investigation at the time of Dad's death, and concluded, beyond question, that it was an accident. You can look at the coroner's report. Just because my sister was murdered doesn't mean that—"

"If you please, Mr. McClain," Regan cut him off. "I anticipated this irruption. I invited it, to get it behind us. If I can prove my assertion, let me. After I expose my reasoning, I will be open to rebuttal. But first you must listen to what I have to say." He paused. Again the room grew quiet.

"I am certain that one of you—the same one who murdered Miss McClain—murdered Mr. McClain six months ago, and for basically the same reason. One of you already knows it to be true. As for the rest—I hope I can convince you. But I must tell you that the person of whom I speak is terribly ingenious. In my opinion, this person will never be brought to justice for the second murder. So it's your father's murder that will snare him, if he is to be snared at all."

"Excuse me, Bishop," Missy said indolently. "I happen to agree with you about Daddy. I have *always* been suspicious of that 'accident.' But in the case of Barb, the police have already identified Charles Ryder. This man"—disdainful gesture at me—"says Ryder didn't do it. But Ryder's the only one who *could* have. He spent the night there, the apartment was locked, and Barbara had the only key. Even Bob and I didn't have one. It's absurd to think this Charles Ryder, whoever he is, also killed *Daddy.*"

"Your deductions are accurate, Madam," the Bishop responded, "but not *ad rem.* Please, let me describe what happened last Sunday night—rather, early Monday morning—without naming the killer. Since I know his identity, I invite him to make corrections in case I err in minor points of fact, but I will excuse him if he chooses to keep silent. He is doomed in any case, though his doom will come from the murder last winter, not Miss McClain's. Ironically, it will be his clever and, up to now, successful efforts to pass off the death of the senior Mr. McClain as an accident which will lead to his undoing."

I was getting nervous. We had agreed on one procedure, but Regan had changed tack by revealing to the murderer that he couldn't be nailed on the second homicide. Was this a bit of hasty improvisation by Regan, in an attempt to trap the perpetrator? Whatever he was up to, we were now committed. I could only let him proceed.

And proceed he did, to the intense interest of all. The sound of a pin dropping could have been heard from one end of the room to the other.

"Last Sunday night," he began, "you four people—excluding you, Mrs. Masterson—were together at the apartment of Mr. and Mrs. McClain. Some time during the four hours she was there, Miss McClain's key ring was removed from her purse."

"So that was why they were asking all those questions about the damn key ring!" exclaimed Masterson.

"Yes . . ."

"But how did they know that? And how did *you* find out?" asked Junior. The rickety-looking straight chair on whose hind legs he was still balancing, seemed barely able to support his eighth of a ton.

"If you please, Mr. McClain, Mr. Masterson. This will go much faster, and you'll shorten your wait for that fine dinner I can smell cooking, if you'll simply permit me to proceed."

Following a short silence, the Bishop resumed. "How I know, and how the police learned of it, isn't important. The fact is, the key ring was taken by the murderer. After Miss McClain and her escort left, he stayed at Mr. and Mrs. McClain's for a time. He no doubt assumed that Miss McClain would discover her keys were missing only when she arrived at her apartment and got the janitor, or whomever, to let her in. Which is approximately what happened.

"When the murderer left the McClains' apartment, he went straightaway to Miss McClain's apartment, let himself into the building with her own key, and into her apartment the same way. He went into the kitchen for a usable knife—the type didn't greatly matter, since he is an expert with weapons of all types. He dispatched her quickly and efficiently, as his training provided, and left her key ring in her purse."

Absolute silence; every face was fixed on Regan. I was surreptitiously watching one face in particular, as I'm sure the Sheriff was, but the murderer wasn't giving anything away.

"But the murderer was lucky as well as clever, or at least so it appeared to him at the time. Sleeping there on the sofa, in a drunken stupor, was Miss McClain's escort. The killer might have been tempted to transport some of Miss McClain's blood into the living room to smear on the sleeping man, rather in the mode of Lady Macbeth, but he was far too subtle for that. Nothing obvious or derivative about this person. He simply departed as unobtrusively as he had come, making certain he left no fingerprints.

"Next morning, he called the apartment three times, starting at 9:30, at one-hour intervals. The first two times, the phone was answered by 'Ryder,' obviously awakened from a sound sleep both times. To the third call, at 11:30, there was no answer. This was the signal for which the killer was waiting. Quickly placing a call to the police, he said just enough to achieve his purpose. He told them of a body, gave the address, mentioned 'Charles Ryder,' and hung up.

"It was, though hastily improvised, a brilliant plan. Had 'Ryder' already notified the police, the anonymous call would not have jeopardized the killer, and 'Mr. Ryder,' given the incriminating evidence, would surely have been arrested.

"If, on the other hand, 'Ryder' had decamped, even better. He would never be able to evade the police-search, and the way he absconded would look very bad in the subsequent trial.

"But the murderer had failed to reckon with one, highly unlikely possibility—that 'Mr. Ryder' would somehow elude the police. How he has been able to do so must be a source of amazement and frustration to the murderer even today. One cannot fault the murderer for his miscalculation. It was simply bad luck. Normally the police are phenomenally successful in finding a person who has been identified, at least if they want him badly enough. But not this time; at least not yet."

Regan looked around the room. All faces were intent. In the hush, he continued.

"Now, let us go back six months earlier. At that time, we had the same five people—plus you, Mrs. Masterson, as well as Mr. McClain, Senior. All were up here at the lodge for a week of skiing. Lovely place, incidentally. No doubt, even lovelier in winter.

"Someone here," he continued, "had already decided to murder Mr. McClain. I will not go into motive, for now. Suffice it to say, he had very good reason to want Mr. McClain dead. Given the circumstances, in fact, he found it a virtual necessity. He faced ruin and probably imprisonment.

"After three days at the lodge, the murderer had perfected his plan. And an ingenious one it was. He prepared well in advance, as we shall see, but—as in murdering Miss McClain—he brilliantly utilized a circumstance that he probably hadn't anticipated.

"His first day here, he discovered that the run to this lodge had been closed by the Resort, due to unsafe conditions. He had the perspicacity to see that the combination of that danger, blended with Mr. McClain's well-known recklessness, offered a perfect opportunity to disguise a murder as an accident. So he deliberately encouraged Mr. McClain in a course of action which contravened the prohibition. He devised a way through the fence, so the run, called 'Lodgepole,' could be opened up. He and his friend skied the run daily, even drawing the attention of officials at the Resort . . ."

I was watching Masterson carefully throughout the last few sentences. The only change I could observe in him was a growing paleness, and a barely perceptible sneer, which seemed to grow as Regan continued. But when the interruption came, it was from a different direction.

"Wait just a minute." The voice was that of Missy, who was sitting next to Cathy Masterson. Cathy was transfixed, very pale, her big eyes staying with Regan. She seemed afraid to look at her husband sitting three chairs to her right.

"You're accusing Ted Masterson of murder!" Missy was saying. "I'm not going to let one of our best friends—!"

"Never mind, Missy," said Masterson very coolly, without a quaver in his smooth, musical baritone. "Let the Bishop finish. He's not going to hurt anyone but himself."

I saw his wife swivel her head. She gave him the briefest of worried glances, then turned her attention to Regan.

When the Bishop continued, his eyes were fixed on the banker directly across the circle. "Naturally, for you, Mr. Masterson, it is better to hear me out, to see how much I know. I'm gratified you want me to continue." Masterson said nothing, just continued to sneer.

"To continue . . ." The Bishop narrowed his eyes. "I don't know when you devised the denouement, sir. I suspect on that final day, Wednesday. No doubt you told Mr. McClain you wanted to meet him, either here at the lodge, or, more likely, somewhere on the Lodgepole run, later that day.

"You told him, and everyone else, that you preferred to do a little rigorous cross-country skiing that day. You did, of course, but when you were unobserved, you skied down Lodgepole.

"Even though the trail is extremely steep at that point, an experienced cross-country skier could handle it. However, he would have to do a number of telemark turns. As all you skiers in the room are aware"—I was sure I detected the trace of a smile—"anyone doing a telemark in deep powder is going to leave a distinctive trail. The turns are much wider."

The Bishop's tone hardened. The banker paler than before, swallowed, and kept his eyes on Regan.

"Mr. McClain died of suffocation, from a broken trachea," the Bishop said. "The official verdict was that the damage was caused by a tree limb. But I telephoned a friend in the military six hours ago and asked about the combat capabilities of a trained Ranger in the United States Army. I was told that a fully trained Ranger is capable of inflicting death without aid of any equipment in eighteen different ways. According to my friend, a karate chop to the Adam's apple will, if administered correctly, fracture the trachea, leading to death by asphyxiation. I was interested in this information, of course, since Mr. Masterson was trained as a Ranger."

He looked at Masterson for reaction, but the Prez maintained his impassive gaze. I noted that Cathy was now looking at her husband; her look revealed something akin to horror.

"Mr. McClain was wearing an outlandish, chartreuse ski outfit that day. Everyone knew that that outfit was a gift from his daughter. I think you suggested the gift to her. Perhaps actually purchased it for her." The Bishop glanced at Cathy. "I see by the look on your wife's face that such is indeed the case. I apologize, Mrs. Masterson, for exposing your husband in such unseemly fashion. I had no other way.

"Perhaps, Madam, you were aware that he had purchased a second, identical outfit? So Miss McClain could give one suit to her father for Christmas while your husband reserved the second for himself—for some unspecified purpose? No? I'm not surprised. You see, that was the element in his plan which was to provide the perfect alibi. He kept it secret from everyone. Even you."

Another stare-down between the silent antagonists. I was beginning to dislike the ice-cold glare in the banker's eyes. From that moment, I made it a point to watch his every move. I noticed the Sheriff was doing likewise.

"Yes, Mr. Masterson," the Bishop went on, "you murdered your friend in the midafternoon and left his body where it certainly would not be seen. You knew that, since you and the dead man were the only two who ever skied that run. Then you skied down to the McClain lodge. You changed into the chartreuse outfit and downhill equipment. Then you took the lift to a spot where someone who knew Mr. McClain would be likely to see you. Wearing goggles identical to his, with his trademark cigar between your teeth, you were certain to be taken for your dead friend by anyone more than twenty feet away. You had even practiced skiing in his style. And you found the perfect witness in Mr. McKay.

"Having made sure you were seen by him, and

having waved at him in appropriately McClain-like fashion, you skied back down to the Resort as fast as you could. You got rid of the incriminating chartreuse outfit, changed into après ski, and hurried into the bar to establish your alibi. From that point till the moment the body was found, you made certain you were in the company of unimpeachable witnesses at all times. Which meant that—"

Ka-boom! A huge commotion drowned out the Bishop's words. Every neck in the room swivelled, all eyes turned toward the source of the noise: Junior and his doomed chair. The latter had finally cracked under the weight of the former and deposited him onto the floor with a crash.

Every neck, I said. All eyes. The Bishop's. Mine. Sheriff Fred's. But there was an exception.

The trained Ranger, waiting and watching for such an opportunity, saw his chance and reacted instantly. He was across the room in a flash, behind the wheelchair, his right arm locked around my boss's neck. Wrenched backward by the sudden attack, Regan was lifted partly out of his chair. His hands clawed the air.

"Don't anybody move!" the murderer commanded. "I'll snap his neck!" The look in his eyes told us he meant exactly what he said.

LII

Three guesses how I felt.

A foolproof plan, right?

The big, strong Sheriff, and big, strong me. The idea was, we'd let the Bishop do all the talking. All Fred and I had to do was prevent the murderer from gaining the upper hand. And where were we when needed? Watching a beached whale and a demolished chair.

Nice job, Davey.

But I hadn't surrendered, by any means. I watched the look in Masterson's eyes as he tightened his hold on the Bishop's neck. I managed to keep my feet well under me in preparation for eventualities. Although I doubted I could be as cat-quick as that bank president, I intended to do my best if and when the opportunity arose.

My peripheral vision kept me aware of what other people were doing.

Ann was white as a sheet. Missy kept looking back and forth from Masterson to her husband.

McClain seemed none the worse for his fall. He was still struggling to extract himself from the debris of the broken chair.

Hastings still had not moved. He'd been sitting to the immediate right of the Bishop. Now he was looking up at Masterson with a mixture of revulsion and respect.

Sheriff Langston looked like I felt, and probably felt even worse. After all, he was the official nominally in charge of the proceedings. Furthermore, he'd been the one specifically assigned, in our plan, the seat next to Masterson. His face was unreadable, but his eyes, locked in on Masterson, gleamed with hatred.

And meanwhile, Cathy Masterson was moaning, "Ted, no! Don't do this! Oh God!" hands pressed to her cheeks.

Masterson studied his wife, Regan's neck lodged firmly and easily between his right elbow and his chest. The Bishop had quit struggling. Now the Bishop tried to relieve the pressure on his neck by pressing the arms of his wheelchair. His face was flushed, but he didn't appear panicked.

"I'm sorry, Cathy," Ted said calmly, his eyes flicking from Langston to me. Her moans subsided to low sobs. "There just wasn't any other way, darling." He glanced down at his current victim, then to the rest of us. "The life of this man depends on the cooperation of everyone in this room. And I mean everyone."

Regan's face was getting redder every second, but his powerful hands still supported his weight on the arms of his wheelchair. He seemed able to breathe—a little. His eyes were fixed on mine, meaningfully, though what he could have been trying to tell me, I couldn't imagine.

He was obviously trying to communicate something —and whatever it was, I'd damn well better figure it out, and quickly. Hastings was gaping in disbelief at his erstwhile friend.

"Ted, *why?* After all Bob did for you! And, my God, poor Barbara! *Why*, Ted?"

Masterson, his eyes darting everywhere at once, didn't appear to hear him. Instead, the Bishop gave the answer, in a strangled voice. "He was stealing from the bank. Weren't you, Mr. Masterson?" Regan gasped a bit, struggled for air and continued, all the time keeping his eyes on mine. He was planning something that involved me, but what?

"You couldn't abide an outside audit, could you, sir?" A labored breath. "You never took a vacation, and for good reason . . ." Gasp. "You needed to be . . . on the premises, so your defalcations would not be discovered." His voice was getting thinner as Masterson's grip tightened.

As he was speaking, he'd narrowed one eye at me and flicked two or three glances downward to his left. I looked—saw nothing but the floor. What the hell was he up to? Want to know how you spell "frustration"? Getting strange signals from a person with a 220 I.Q., when yours is in two digits.

The Bishop's face was now beet red, his eyes popping with the effort to breathe.

"Good guessing, Bishop," Masterson said in a tight, calm voice, his eyes still flicking back and forth from Langston to me. He obviously didn't expect opposition from anyone else in the room. From the looks of things, he wasn't going to get any.

"My 'friend,' " he half-snarled the word, his voice growing emotional for the first time, "that son of a bitch, would never pay me what I was worth. Want to know what he did for me the first year we made five million bucks? And had the highest return on assets of any bank in the state? Gave me a *plaque!* Yeah! Said it'd be 'demeaning' to offer me money, since we're *such good friends!*"

The Bishop still kept his gaze on me, his eyes flicking vigorously to the left. I still didn't know what he had in mind. Then I saw his left index finger, on the arm of the wheelchair, flicking; flicking and clenching. Almost as if he was trying to exercise it; trying to exercise the muscles in his finger . . .

"So, how'd you nail me, old man," Masterson demanded shrilly. "I want to know *how you did it.* Come on, how'd you figure it out?" He released his hold slightly, so the Bishop could talk. Regan took a huge gulp of air. His face showed no panic, but he was still flashing me those damn signals: eyes flicking left, left index finger flexing. I had to figure it out P.D.Q. or it was going to be, in an expression I've heard lawyers use, "mooted by circumstances."

"Your ball point pen," gasped Regan as distinctly as he could in that stranglehold, his eyes boring into mine, flicking left. "You left it at the murder site up on the slope, where Mr. Goldman found it yesterday. It reads 'Alsip Traders Bank.' "

Say what? I thought. Here came the pitch, and me without a bat in my hands. My mind was racing. My *own* pen was in my shirt pocket, but that was the only ball point pen I knew anything about.

Masterson was as puzzled as I. "What are you talking about?" He looked narrowly at me.

"Show him, David!" The Bishop's voice was harsh, strained, his eyes popping.

A glimmering of understanding began to penetrate my thick skull. I was starting to get it—

and not a second too soon. Who says I'm a slow learner?

"Yeah," I said, as calmly as I could, "here it is." I pulled my pen from my pocket. Getting slowly to my feet, I studied the side of the pen as though reading, and muttered, "Yep, 'Alsip Traders Bank.' " I took a step, but stopped abruptly as Masterson warned me away with his eyes and tightened his grip on Regan's throat.

I shrugged and sat back down, trying to mask the tension within. The next move was mine, and if I ever needed to be accurate, now was the time.

I was sure I knew what Regan was planning. For it to work, the pen had to be easy to catch, but a little low. *Too* low and the killer would just sneer at it when it plopped on the floor. Too high, and his arm would be out of reach.

"Here you go," I said in the manner of one trying to be helpful, and carefully underhanded the pen to Masterson. I lofted it toward him in a soft toss, just a little to his left, so he could reach it with his free left hand without releasing his stranglehold on the Bishop. Giving myself full credit, I think that toss was just about perfect. The results sure were.

Without letting go of Regan's neck, Masterson casually extended his left hand to catch the pen. Instinct? Training of an athlete? Overconfidence? Whatever the cause, his left hand was out there to complete the game of toss I had initiated. But the hand never touched the pen.

Because, like a bear trap, the Bishop's own left hand snapped on Masterson's wrist, hurling him toward the floor. The murderer's head whiplashed backward as the Bishop's powerful muscles hurled him face-forward. Masterson's death-hold on Regan's throat didn't loosen. Like a single tumbling meteor, the wheelchair and both men hurtled onto the floor with a crash that rivalled Junior's.

I was moving as soon as Regan's hand closed on the murderer's wrist. But before I'd reached full momentum, a six-foot-six-inch horizontal blur of khaki-covered muscle whizzed by me. A quarter of a second later, Fred Langston had Masterson locked in a spine-bending half-Nelson.

"Got him, Fred?" Stupid question. But this seemed to be a day when my stupid-quotient was high.

"No sweat," the Sheriff said calmly, forcing the banker to his feet. Masterson's face was a mask of pain.

Seeing the culprit was being well-disciplined, I turned to the Bishop who seemed little the worse for wear. With some help from Hastings I got him back into his wheelchair. I was starting to check for bruises on his neck when he irritably wheeled away. Obviously he was fine—back to his customary disposition.

Meanwhile, Langston had forced his captive away from the rest of the group toward the fireplace. He had him up on his tiptoes. The banker's right arm, firmly in the grip of an unyielding fist, stretched behind his back almost to his neck. His left arm dangled uselessly. (Later, at the hospital, they discovered that he'd broken both bones in his left forearm, undoubtedly from hitting the floor in the Bishop's grip, underneath the weight of both bodies.)

The Bishop's wheelchair was still operative, though it carried a sizeable dent on the left side where it had hit the floor. My immediate guess, which later proved accurate, was that my boss would refuse to have it fixed. He'd never give up that battle scar, his permanent badge of honor.

I was anticipating a harsh, or at least sarcastic, comment from him for the way I let Masterson get that chokehold on him, but the Bishop surprised me. His first words, after he got his voice back, made me feel like Dwight Gooden on an excellent day. Though he only spoke three words, in a very hoarse whisper, they sounded like golden trumpets in my ear:

"Superb toss, David."

Sunday. August 28

LIII

That Sunday was the kind of day the Tourist Bureau would like everyone to forget. Gusty winds, gray skies. During the day, rain conditions ranged from medium showers to drenching downpours. The games at Shea and Yankee Stadiums were both rained out. Ugly, real ugly.

The storm had been brewing the night before, when I'd made the Bishop and Ann wait in the car, on the way home, while I phoned Rozanski from a booth on the highway to give him the long-promised scoop. By the time that fifteen-minute conversation was over, the rain was coming down in buckets. I got soaked running back to the car, much to the merriment of the two passengers, who were in a mood to be easily amused. I didn't mind a bit. It was worth some damp clothes, to have Chet back in my debt again.

But, all the lousy weather in the world notwithstanding, the day couldn't have been nicer. I felt like Gene Kelly in *Singin' in the Rain.* We had *done* it. Father William was off the hook and so, in a sense, were the two thousand priests in the Archdiocese.

That was confirmed, too, when I called Joe Parker at his home, just before eleven. He assured me Homicide had no intention of keeping that Monday-morning appointment with the priest. As far as the department was concerned, the case was solved and the murderer behind bars. Oh, they were still curious about the mysterious Charles Ryder. And they would be delighted to have his statement if and when he was ever located, but they weren't wasting valuable time hunting him.

So I had the pleasure of calling my erstwhile golfing buddy, Father Willie, and giving him the good news.

Willie seemed fascinated by our encounter with the people up in the lodge, and as I told him the story, he tried to fit together the missing pieces.

"Why did Masterson kill his *friend?"* he wondered. "It doesn't make sense."

"Yeah, but remember, Willie, Bob McClain was about to sell the bank. Meaning an outside audit. Ted Masterson's years of embezzling were about to come to light in a very big way. Exposing him as a major league felon."

"I still don't understand how the Bishop *knew* Masterson was the murderer," Willie went on. "What gave it away?"

"It was those ski tracks, Willie. Tell you the truth, that's why I keep the Bishop around—to figure out things like that. The Sheriff told *me* about the tracks, and what did that mean to *me?* Nothing. I'm thick that way. But the Bishop put it together with what Masterson was doing that afternoon—and, *voila,* it all made sense. Masterson *had* been cross-country skiing, just like he said. What he didn't mention to anyone was that he'd skied down 'Lodgepole.'

He made a few telemark turns, then glided on down to where he and Bob and agreed to meet—halfway down 'Lodgepole.' He knew no one else would come that way.

'And when Stogie Bob came down, there was friend Ted waiting. 'Hi, old buddy.' And the next thing Stogie knew, Masterson was delivering a karate chop to his windpipe. Lights out."

Willie was silent a moment, absorbing this none-too-pleasant picture of a friendship ended. Then he insisted, "What doesn't make sense is why Masterson would go after Barb. I just don't get it."

"Willie, you've got to understand, Ted was walking on thin ice. As long as he had just internal audits, he could handle the bank. And Bob Jr. would never go against him. Of course, Junior was dying to sell, but that was no problem. As long as Barb refused, with her 50%, there wasn't a thing he could do. So Masterson was safe as long as she hung firm. But when she began to waver, it was nightmare time all over again. He tried to keep Barb in line, but he couldn't push too hard. And when he finally saw she'd gone over to Junior's side—"

"He jumped on the first chance he got to remove her," Willie mused.

"Leaving the highly controllable Junior to deal with. Piece of cake—or so he figured."

The ugliness and uselessness of it all overwhelmed both of us for a minute, and the phone line went pretty silent for a while. I recalled the photos I'd seen of that pretty blonde with a knife sticking out of her chest. That image would probably remain vivid with Willie for the rest of his life.

Willie finally broke the silence. "Dave," he said,

"I can never thank you enough. You've probably saved my life. But I need to tell *you* something. I called my Abbot yesterday and gave him pretty much the whole picture. And we agreed it's time for me to come home. Maybe I can complete the Ph.D. later. Right now I've got to get my life together.

"Frankly, I'm probably going to be spending the next three months or so in a center for alcoholic priests. Then we'll see where I am. I'm facing another struggle, too: the Abbot thinks I ought to tell my mother about the whole thing. That's going to be tough. I just—" He broke off.

An awkward silence followed while I tried to think of something to say. I was just on the brink of a clichè when he got his voice back and asked to speak to the Bishop. I let the clichè go, told him good-bye and buzzed the Bishop. After hanging up, I sat staring at the ceiling. Who the hell was going to listen to—much less laugh at—my latest jokes, now that he was going God knew where?

What he and the Bishop had to say to each other, I never learned, but the conversation lasted fifteen minutes. All I can tell you about it is, the Bishop looked happier after it than he had before. Hell, for all I know, they just talked about biblical manuscripts the whole time—I wouldn't put it past either one of them.

Right after that—by now it's getting along toward noon—my client stopped in, without an appointment. That's my *paying* client, namely Miss Ann Shields. Not that her coming was a total surprise. She'd warned me, the night before, that she had something she needed to discuss with me.

The Bishop, always eager to horn in whenever

police work or a pretty girl is involved, invited us to hold our meeting in his office. With him there, naturally.

"Are you sure you're all right, Bishop?" she cooed, fluffing some nonexistent raindrops out of her abundant brunette hair. "Don't you think you should see a doctor about your neck?"

I scowled. Sure, be concerned about him. What about *me?* I was in the rough and tumble, too—sort of. Of course, the Bishop loved the attention.

"Really, Miss Shields, it was nothing." I felt like throwing up.

"It was, too, something! I was sure you were going to be murdered. I thought we all would be. How did you know exactly the right moment—?"

Oh spare me. Let me switch to a more palatable portion of the conversation.

"But, Dave, that thousand dollars was only a retainer," she argued later, "and you've spent more than that just out of pocket, I'll bet. You did what I hired you to do—catch a killer, and get him behind bars. I *insist* on paying for that."

"It's a question of professional ethics," I answered, wanting to keep things on a high moral plane. "As I told you at the outset, I was working on *two* jobs: catching the murderer, for which you paid me, and keeping Charles Ryder's true identity a secret. Well, Charles Ryder was a *pro bono,* in a way . . ."

The Bishop slowly shook his head and rolled his eyes, but that was only envy. He can't stand it that he's not the only guy around here who knows some Latin. So I ignored him.

". . . which made it nice to have your thousand to cover expenses and then some. And I'm grateful. But the rest is due from Charles Ryder, not from you, and collecting from him is something I'll have to do. I know, I know, I'll probably never see a penny. But that doesn't matter. One of my guiding principles in life is, Virtue Is Its Own Reward."

Regan snorted contemptuously, but I didn't care. As for Ann, she stopped insisting after that, and we parted still friends. If you're curious about the aftermath—whether she and I ever get together socially once in a while—sorry, you'll have to draw your own conclusions. Sally Castle is still very much in the picture, and why should I give her one more reason to be mad at me?

And speaking of my favorite shrink, we had a most amicable phone conversation later on, that damp Sunday afternoon, during the course of which she thanked me again for the baseball tickets and gave me a play-by-play on the twi-nighter. The Mets split: Darling beat Hershiser but Gooden, despite twelve strikeouts, lost the rain-shortened nightcap. Following the baseball round-up, Sally and I made a date for that evening which, I am happy to tell you, I did *not* cancel out on. Things between me and my favorite shrink have been copacetic ever since.

Our final visit that day, before Regan was able to take his accustomed Sabbath rest, was from Inspector Kessler, who arrived about fifteen minutes after Ann left. He was mad as a wet hornet, though I couldn't see why. Frankly, I don't think he knew himself. He wanted to see both of us again. So the Bishop, who was in an unusually good mood—due, probably, to Ann's fawning all over him—hosted the party in his office. Kessler, in his own fussy way, did most of the talking.

"I've just finished a one-hour phone conversation

with Sheriff Langston, up in Catskill County, and what you pulled up there is an outrage, Bishop. I'll be frank. I'm thinking of taking this one to the Cardinal."

"Out of your jurisdiction, Inspector," Regan murmured complacently, leaving me uncertain whether he referred to Catskill County or the Archdiocese. Or even some higher venue. But Kessler's response indicated he knew what Regan meant, or at least thought he did.

"I know that, dammit! Uh, excuse me, Bishop. But for you and Davey to go tearing off with your information and not telling me about it, is—"

"Excuse me, Inspector," Regan interrupted mildly, "but, with all respect, we had no information that was not available to you. Mr. Goldman and I merely put our heads together, drew a few conclusions, and cruised up there to test our theories."

"Yes, and damn near—excuse me, Bishop—nearly got yourself *killed* in the process."

"I was counting on Mr. Goldman's training," the Bishop answered calmly, with just the hint of a smile. "I was certain that no sedentary bank president would be a match for my associate's guile and swiftness." Low blow that. Still, he'd already given me the compliment-of-the-year for that slow-pitch pen toss. And his calling me his "associate" gave me a semi-warm glow.

"Well," Kessler said, grumpily. "It looks as though Masterson's first trial will be up there, for killing the dad. The State's Attorney met with Langston this morning, and that seems to be the way they want to go. They think they've got a good case." Kessler looked sharply at the Bishop and me, then introduced what I believe was his real reason for coming.

"If we could find Charles Ryder, we'd have a lot better case than we have, on the murder of Barbara McClain." He glared at us again. "We're not going to go crazy looking for him, now that we've got the killer in custody. But I'd sure like to have a talk with him." The words hung in the air for several seconds. Finally the Bishop spoke.

"Mr. Kessler. I believe it's hopeless to think that 'Charles Ryder' would add anything to your case. We have to assume he slept through the entire performance. Masterson said as much last night. I don't blame you for wanting to speak with him. But let me also address your implied question: no, I have no more knowledge now of any 'Charles Ryder' than I ever had."

"Nor I," I added voluntarily. The Inspector looked angrily at the Bishop, then at me.

"Aw, go to—!" He stopped himself. The good, churchgoing Protestant was not about to tell a bishop—even a Catholic one—to go to wherever he was thinking of, no matter how mad he got. He stomped out without saying good-bye.

EPILOGUE

Nice, neat murder. Committed, investigated and solved—all in a single week. But on the off-chance that you might be interested in a couple of later developments . . .

First of all, Masterson is currently serving a life sentence for the murder of Robert McClain, Sr. His temporary insanity defense was a bust. The jury returned in less than two hours with a unanimous verdict of Murder One. At the moment it's questionable whether the State will ever try him for killing Barbara. An assistant D.A. I know told me the other day he doubts it.

"How many lives can one guy serve?" was the way he explained it. I just shrugged. When lawyers start throwing around that kind of abstruse, technical jargon, they lose me fast.

Finally, I would like to add a very personal postscript. This happened five weeks later, October 1, a Saturday. A very happy Shabbat, as it turned out, for this good (I don't say "religious") Jew.

It was a nice day, sunny, with a first hint of winter chill in the air. An item arrived in the mail. About this item there were several interesting points.

First of all, the envelope itself. Expensive stock, thick and cream colored, with a person's name—no address—embossed on the flap. And then, the way it was addressed. In precise, feminine handwriting, it read "David Goldman, Investigations, 890 W. Thirty-seventh Street, New York City." That's the address of the mansion, which I never give out to clients. In the lower left-hand corner, same handwriting, were the words, "Personal and Confidential." It was postmarked Chicago, Illinois.

But most interesting of all was what the envelope contained: a folded, blank sheet of stationery of the same stock as the envelope, carrying the same embossed name, folded around a personal check. The latter was filled out in longhand by the same hand that had addressed the envelope. Dated September 28, it was payable to Mr. David Goldman, and, under "Purpose," was written "For Professional Services Rendered." The signature—same handwriting—was that of the person whose name was embossed on both envelope and stationery: "Marguerite C. Fuller." And below the signature were the words, "Thank you and God bless you!" The check was for ten thousand dollars.

It seems virtue really is its own reward.

About the Author

WILLIAM F. LOVE was a Benedictine monk at St. Gregory's Abbey, Shawnee, Oklahoma, and was ordained as a priest in 1958. Following his resignation from the priesthood, he became a banker and banking consultant in Chicago. He holds a degree from St. John's University in Collegeville, Minnesota, and an M.B.A. from the University of Chicago. He makes his home with his family in a suburb of Chicago, where he is working on more novels in this new Bishop Regan mystery series.